Praise for R

"An intoxicating blend of wholesome sweetness and tear-off-your-clothes steam...Ruby Barrett's writing leaves me breathless."

—Rosie Danan, author of *The Roommate*, on *Hot Copy*

"A delightful office romance for the #MeToo era...
This is a winner."

—*Publishers Weekly* on *Hot Copy*

"Ruby Barrett's *Hot Copy* is filled with everything you could
want in a romance novel: main characters who are easy
to root for, a charming cast with sequel potential,
and plenty of sizzling love scenes. The genre needs
more heroes like Wesley Chambers,
a soft man who embodies non-toxic masculinity."

—Meryl Wilsner, author of *Something to Talk About*

"Ruby Barrett's *Hot Copy* is a sizzling debut—sweet,
steamy and oh so satisfying, this book stole my heart
on every blissful page. Wesley is the soft-hearted,
glasses-fogging hero we all need, and Corrine is a
powerhouse heroine who doesn't shy away from
the job she wants, or the man she deserves."

—Katie Golding, author of *Fearless*

"Barrett's work was a delight from start to finish.
Her masterful storytelling and electric prose
shined throughout."

—Charish Reid, author of *Hearts on Hold* and
The Write Escape, on *Hot Copy*

**Also available from Ruby Barrett
and Carina Press**

Hot Copy

THE ROMANCE RECIPE

RUBY BARRETT

carina
press

carina press®

Recycling programs
for this product may
not exist in your area.

ISBN-13: 978-1-335-50691-7

The Romance Recipe

Carina Press
22 Adelaide St. West, 41st Floor
Toronto, Ontario M5H 4E3, Canada
www.CarinaPress.com

Printed in U.S.A.

To Meryl and Rosie, for letting me tell you first.
To Michael, for your most unconditional love.
To my queer community, especially my Later Life Queers, especially, especially Danielle.

THE ROMANCE RECIPE

Chapter One

Amy

A restaurant has a certain indefinable quality on a good night. With every seat filled, it's loud. The bartenders sling drinks with panache. The front of house staff moves around each other like dancers, while the bussers are more like ghosts, slipping in and out so fast you never notice there was a table waiting to be flipped. Expo quality controls every single morsel so that the plates are always Instagram-worthy, and nobody has to wait more than twenty minutes.

A good night smells like the signature cocktail and the house special, perfectly paired.

A good night smells like money.

Tonight is not a good night.

"I'm done, Amy."

Chad throws his white chef's coat onto the hostess stand, sending a cup of pens flying and toppling the tablet displaying the seating chart off its stand. Maggie yelps, righting the tools of her hostess trade.

I cover the phone receiver with my palm. "Chad. What the— So sorry. Can you hold another moment?" I say into the phone. "You're done *what*?" I hiss at him.

He slaps his Sox cap onto his head. "Here. I'm done here." He rips open the front door, letting in the smell of cold and rain.

The customer on the other end of the line has hit a rhythm that seems like she did not, in fact, hold for another moment. "I don't see the problem," she says. "Give the table away," the woman says.

As if I would be having this conversation with her if there were anyone I could give the table away to. The door slams shut behind my sous-chef, and the few people who are currently in the dining room stare. Which I'm sure was his intention.

I am putty, slowly pulled apart by a line cook and absentee reservations.

"We have a twenty-four-hour cancellation policy that I reminded you of on our confirmation call," I say, my Customer Service Voice cracking under the strain of wanting to run after Chad. I sound like the Stevia version of myself, artificially sweet—and not as good as the real thing, if I do say so myself. "If you can't keep your reservation we'll have to charge you the twenty-five-dollar cancellation fee."

As if twenty-five dollars will cover the hundreds this table was probably going to spend.

The tabletop set for ten guests sits pride of place at the front of the room. Framed by the floor to ceiling window, the empty table is reflected back at me, so really it looks like twenty empty place settings. The visual equivalent of poking a finger in an open wound.

"Listen." The woman who was supposed to be here with her nine friends forty-five minutes ago drops her *oops I forgot* act. "We're not showing up. And your cancellation policy is nice and all but you never asked for my credit card and I'm not giving it to you so no, you can't charge me for the table anyway. But if you keep *harassing* me…"

I left her one message asking where she was.

"… I might be forced to leave a less than stellar review."

The worst thing restaurant owners ever did was decide that the customer is always right. Customers can be right. Sometimes. So can a broken clock twice a day. Doesn't mean I'm going to give it free food. And it certainly doesn't mean I'm going to let myself and my business, that I've spent years preparing for and countless hours building, be bullied by a no-show.

"You know what?" I turn toward the wall, hunch over the phone to spare Maggie this "do as I say, not as I do" behavior. "Leave your bad review," I hiss. "I don't give a shit. We don't need your business."

A damned lie.

She laughs like a person who wears coats made out of puppies. "Are you sure about that?" The line goes dead.

That went terribly, but the great thing about running your own restaurant is that you never have a second to stop and think about how you could have handled that better.

Or that maybe you should have listened to your head chef when she suggested taking down customer credit cards at the time of booking a reservation, for situations just like this.

Or to pee.

Or breathe through the sick feeling in your gut.

Because there's always another crisis to deal with.

I grab Chad's chef's coat and run out the door after him.

He slouches against the window of the brunch place next door, cigarette glow lighting his face. I knew he wouldn't go far. He'd want a chance to tell me his side. I dodge the crowd of umbrellas on the sidewalk, holding his coat over my head to get to him.

"What the hell." I'm breathless from that ten-foot sprint. "You're quitting in the middle of a service?"

His gaze slips away from mine and he shifts on his feet. Suspicion prickles the back of my neck.

"She's gonna be the end of this place, Ames." He waves his hand around, the ash drifting toward me. I step back. "She's all…" He throws his cigarette on the ground. "She's all show," he says in disgust.

"Why don't you come back inside and we can talk things through with Sophie?" I suggest with more artificial sweetness than I gave the no-show on the phone.

He sighs and shakes his head with a quick jerk.

Chad came with me from our old restaurant and has been with me since I first opened Amy & May's. He's been loyal and hardworking, and that's the *only* reason I gave him a second chance on our zero-tolerance harassment policy. But his second chance is burning up with the cherry at the tip of his cigarette.

I punch his coat into a ball and toss it at his chest. "You did it again, didn't you? I vouched for you, Chad," I hiss.

A passerby snorts their laughter as they walk past. This is just great. An empty dining room, a bad Yelp review, and now the owner of Amy & May's is having a conniption in the middle of the street.

"It was just a joke, Amy," Chad whines.

I step in closer to him as incentive to keep my voice down. "It's not fucking funny. I don't want to hear it," I cut him off, slashing my hand through the air as he opens his mouth, most likely to tell me how Carly, the new dishwasher, actually *likes* it when he makes comments about her body.

I've been working in restaurants since I was sixteen and I've been harassed in every single one of them. Now that I'm in charge, no one working for me is going to experience that.

Sophie "Hollywood" Brunet and I don't agree on much but on this one thing we do.

"You can come by tomorrow to clear out your locker and get your last paycheck. And fuck you for saying that Sophie is going to ruin my restaurant when it's your behavior that caused this." I spin on the heel of my über-unfashionable, ultra-comfortable black canvas slides.

"I'm not the only one who thinks so," he says to my back. I stop at the edge of the awning, the rain already soaking into the toes of my shoes. "She cries in the walk-in."

I absolutely love it when men tell me things I already know.

"She's always worried about her Instaspam."

He knows exactly what social media platform he's talking about, he just thinks he's better than anyone with a profile.

"She can't make a decision to save her life."

"She made the decision to fire your ass," I say, but only so I can hide the sinking feeling in my gut. My staff has lost confidence in their kitchen leader.

And so have I.

He shakes his head. "Whatever, Amy."

"Goodbye, Chad."

The restaurant seems even quieter since I ran out mere minutes ago. My head chef, Sophie, stands at the expo station. A lock of her auburn hair has fallen loose from the black bandanna around her head, and her face glows from the heat of the kitchen. The light makeup she wears to work has run, leaving her wide eyes with a smoky look. I nod to her and tell Maggie I'll be back in a bit. I stomp—because it feels good despite being totally unprofessional—down the hall next to our open concept kitchen and the bathrooms and push through the door with a sign that reads Staff Only. I bypass the staff locker room and throw myself into a chair in my cramped office, kicking the door closed with my foot. I flip through my problems like my mom used to look for dinner inspiration in her Rolodex turned recipe book.

There are three unanswered texts from my brother on my phone but zero returned phone calls from my father.

After a year of success my dream restaurant is inexplicably tanking. We're bleeding staff and customers.

Despite years of experience, I can't find one surefire strategy to get more butts in seats.

There's an unopened email in my inbox from the landlord and I know what it's going to say. That I have three months to make up the rent owed, or we're out.

And yet, like the losing end of a CW Network love triangle, the only thing I can think about is that lock of hair and how it stuck to Sophie's lip, the way her hazel eyes only seem to get bigger and bigger when I walk toward her.

Sophie is my biggest problem of all.

Ever since I first watched her on the final episode of *Pop-Up Kitchen*, I've wanted to kiss Sophie Brunet. The idea of kissing her hooked me but watching her hold her own against the biggest asshole TV chef of our lifetime and a kitchen full of men made me want to take a chance on her. After watching the finale, I fell down a wormhole of past episodes, watching her skill and passion turned into easily consumable reality TV fodder. I scrolled through years' worth of her Instagram grid until, stupidly, I felt like I knew her from the carefully curated snippets she gave followers, starting as a line cook at a five-star hotel in Montreal all the way to her job as a sous-chef at Table Hanover, her last job before she quit to join the cast of *Pop-Up Kitchen*.

When I sent an email to the address listed for her agent, I chalked it up to a mild crush, a strong Negroni, and the frenetic energy that comes with being wide-awake at two in the morning. When Sophie herself responded, excited, *thankful*, for the opportunity to run her own kitchen at my zero stars restaurant, I thought I could set aside the attraction and focus on putting Amy & May's on the Boston scene. It was a relief to finally have someone to do this with, to share the absolute panic that comes with fulfilling your dream before you turn thirty, and watching it light up around you. To have someone to help put out the fire.

But if anything, my attraction has grown, despite that everything Chad said is technically true.

She does spend a lot of time in the walk-in. She's always bent over her phone, worrying at her plump pink lower lip, frowning at the screen. The change was like whiplash. One minute our restaurant was thriving. Reservations months in advance, the atmosphere electric every single night. There were plenty of rubberneckers. People wanting to eat food prepared by someone who was on TV once, like the tangential proximity somehow made the food taste better.

And maybe it did. Until it didn't. Because suddenly it was like Sophie's fame ran out. And everyone just…stopped coming.

The last few months, she's been nothing like the badass woman she was on the show, quietly acquiescing to all my ideas, blindly nodding to everything I say. Even her suggestion to take credit cards at the time of reservation was more of a question. But still, I should have listened.

Now I'm back where I started, doing it all alone. Except this time with a side of an even bigger unrequited crush, on a straight girl, no less. Maybe my biggest mistake of all was thinking I should rely on anyone but myself.

The rest of dinner service goes off without a hitch. If only three tables but no more no-shows counts as not a hitch. "Where's Sophie?" I ask, after the last table has settled.

Carly jumps, dropping a pan into the sink. "Sorry, ma'am."

The restaurant is quiet. Only the closing staff still here.

"Please, no. Don't…" I shake my head. "Don't call me that."

She bends over the pan in the sink, the *shwish shwish* sound of the scouring pad grating at my shot nerves. "She's in the walk-in," Carly says.

Of course she is. I sigh. When we were eight, my twin brother, Wes, and I snuck out of bed and watched *Jurassic Park*. I was so traumatized by the scene with the raptors in the kitchen that to this day, the chill I get when I close a walk-in freezer door behind me is as much from fear as it is from cold.

Sophie doesn't turn around, writing the date on a sauce container, as the door slams shut behind me.

"Next time, can you at least warn me you're going to fire someone?" I wrap my arms around my middle in a fruitless attempt at staying warm.

She doesn't turn but bobs her head in a curt nod.

I take a few steps deeper into the freezer. "I'm not upset. I shouldn't have given him a second chance in the first place. I'm sorry that you had to deal with him."

"You don't have to apologize to me," she says. There's no accusation in her voice. None at all. I hear it nonetheless. Sophie wanted Chad gone the first time Carly came to her asking if she could be scheduled on the days he wasn't working. But we'd lost so many staff already, I panicked and fought to keep him against my better judgment.

She turns to face me, her chef's coat undone, her nipples, hard from the cold, visible through her white tank top. Sophie and I blink at each other and quickly look away. Her cheeks turn a darker shade of red.

So, great. Not only have I failed Carly, I've made Sophie uncomfortable, too.

"Sorry," I say quickly. "It won't happen again." Second chances or checking her out. "And you were right about taking credit card numbers."

I start to rearrange stacks of individually wrapped dough on the shelf beside me for something to do with my hands. I hate it when other people are right. I hate admitting it more. I'd scoffed when she'd suggested it at our last meeting. Actually scoffed. Because taking credit cards wasn't something we'd ever done at the restaurants I'd worked at before.

"I don't want our guests to feel like we don't trust them," I'd said.

Sophie sighs so audibly Carly can probably hear her. It's the only pushback I ever seem to get from her anymore, this sound she makes when she's frustrated but won't say anything. She takes the dough from my hands, putting the frozen disks back where they were. This close, I watch as her chest rises and falls with each breath. Underneath her foundation, dark purple rings her eyes. This close, she's so *warm*, even in this dark freezer. When she's close like this, I get caught up in her and forget my own frustrations with my head chef or that my restaurant is slowly crumbling around me or that I feel lonely at the end of the night and for once I don't like it.

Sophie's jaw is rigid and she is conspicuously not looking at me.

Sometimes I want to grip her shoulders, under her coat, skin to skin, and tell her—*beg her*—to fight with me. Tell me I was an asshole for giving Chad a second chance. Tell me if my ideas are bad. Or good. Anything.

Whenever I get this urge, it's time to eighty-six myself from the conversation.

"Let's talk tomorrow," I say, backing out of the freezer, too warm after being so close to her. "About the new menu. Ten?" I ask.

"Actually," she says. "There's…" She presses her lips together.

"Spit it out, Hollywood."

She narrows her eyes. She hates that nickname, she is so totally done with me.

Same, girl.

"I got an offer. From a guy I know from *Pop-Up Kitchen*?"

Mom gave me breathing exercises when I was kid. A way to manage my anger when it came up on me fast, to keep me from jumping to conclusions, lashing out at her or my brother, but mostly my dad. In the freezer, each breath is so conspicuous, so obvious. But I focus on them anyway because even though she hasn't *said* anything—even though I'm *not*, I'm absolutely not jumping to conclusions—I know exactly what she's going to say.

"He offered me a job," she says.

"Head chef?" Somehow my voice sounds totally normal even though I am screaming internally.

She shrugs, in this effortless, cool way she has. "Sous."

"Why are you telling me this?" I ask. Kitchens are cut-throat. You don't tip your hand, unless you want to get fired. Or maybe I'm about to be leveraged.

"I know things aren't going well." She stares pointedly at me. "You won't let me see the books but… I know that part of it is my fault. I want to stay here and run this kitchen, but I just needed you to know that I'm considering it."

"If you know things aren't going well then you know I probably can't match whatever they're offering you."

She shakes her head, her eyes worried. "No. I'm trying to be…helpful."

"Well, thanks," I say. "For the help." My voice sounds exactly as bitchy as I feel right now. "I got to go."

"Amy."

"It's fine." Everything is fine. My restaurant is tanking and I'm losing my chef and I'm only upset about that for professional reasons and not because I find myself periodically wondering how soft her skin is. My stomach growls. And I've forgotten to eat. Again.

Everything is really fricking great.

"I made you a take-out plate," she calls. I turn in the door-way and sitting on the expo counter is a silver take-out tin, most likely filled with what's left of tonight's under-ordered special. In moments like this, my crush for her absolutely leaps, but I know these moments aren't for me. She's always caretaking our staff in small ways that I'm completely inept at, like making meals for folks who've had a grumpy guest or who were run around all night. Or who have absolutely no idea what they're going to do next.

The plate is still warm. "Good night, Hollywood."

She looks at me only as the door starts to close. "Good night, Amy."

For once I am relieved to not be the last person out of the restaurant if it means I can get some space from the woman who turns the center of my chest into warm goo, while si-multaneously sending me into a panic.

"Carly." I lean against the wall beside her sink. "I'm really sorry about Chad. I broke my own policy when I didn't fire him the first time. It won't happen again."

Carly can't be much older than I was when I started work-ing in a restaurant. She smiles at me, so huge she reminds me of Wes. They both show you what they're feeling with their whole chest.

"That's okay, Ms. Chambers—"

"Amy. Please."

Carly smiles down at her feet. "Most kitchens don't have a policy at all. I really appreciate you standing up for me."

"Yeah, well, it was Sophie, mostly," I mumble. Carly is en-tirely too wholesome. If Wesley were here, they'd be instant best friends. But my brother and I aren't as similar as we seem. "Make sure you descale the espresso machine tonight," I say.

I say good-night and take the back door to my car. By industry standards, eleven is early. I could get a drink at Luxe and meet a nice girl, have another one of those emotionless hookups my brother accuses me of having to avoid "intimacy" and "feelings." Or see if Jeremy wants to take a breather from studying for once to hang out with someone who's not dumb-struck in love, like Wes.

But I drive in the opposite direction of my apartment, away from my favorite gay bar, and Jeremy's new place, and park my old red VW in front of a house with all the lights off except for the one over the front door. I pull the take-out plate and utensils from the paper bag. The weight of this entire day, every one of my problems, is enough to turn me off this beautiful meal but I make myself eat it, even if it's ash in my mouth. I haven't had anything since breakfast.

This is where I feel closest to Mom. Outside her old house that's filled with a new family. Wes hasn't been back since we sold it last year. He says he's ready to move forward, which is hilarious considering I had to convince him to sell in the first place.

It's fitting that I do this alone. Commune with my mother alone. Cry, into pasta with cream sauce, alone.

I do everything else alone. Why not this?

Chapter Two

Sophie

For a woman who's covered in sweat all night for her job, I should really stop putting myself in these situations.

"Again," my coach says.

My glutes and hamstrings burn. Stiffness builds in my erector muscles, fatigue setting in. A bead of sweat runs from my hairline, down my forehead, and along the bridge of my nose.

"Again."

I stifle my whine and hinge at my hips. The drop of sweat falls to the rubber-mat floor with a wet splat. I'm going to need a mop and bucket by the end of this training session. My hands scream as I wrap them around the knurled surface of the barbell. I'm loath to admit it but my grip will go before my legs do.

"Flex more with your right glute."

"I know," I grit out. I can feel the weakness in that side. No matter how hard I push I can't get the muscle to fire.

"Again," Natalie says as the plates hit the ground after another shitty lift.

I can't suppress the groan fast enough but I lead it right into my next exhale and lift again.

"Better," she says, and I can feel that it is. "Good."

"Again," I say. Good isn't good enough. Good hasn't felt like enough for a while now.

"Sophie." Natalie presses her sneakered foot on top of my bar. "You're gassed."

I grind my molars together, hinged over the barbell. "I want to go again." They say once you start to monetize your hobby you need to find a new hobby. For so long cooking was a passion, maybe not quite a hobby, but something I did because I *loved* it. Now I get paid for my passion and suddenly I'm not good at it anymore. I found something new in weightlifting, a way to feel strong, something to be passionate about again. If I can't be good at cooking anymore, then I at least want to feel good at this.

But I don't have to look up to know she's crossed her arms over her chest. She's benching me for the day. "Nope. You're done. Besides, my next client is here."

I sigh and stand slowly. Natalie shakes her head. "You're not even going to celebrate?" she asks. "That's a PR." She points at the bar and I do the mental math, counting the weight of each plate and the bar. Holy crap. She's right.

"Two hundred pounds?" I ask.

She holds up her fist and I bump mine against hers, grinning. "Whatever changes you've made," she says, stepping closer to me even though I must stink, "they seem to be the right ones, for your performance at least. You've made huge gains in the last few months."

"Thanks, Nat." I put away the weights. She lingers like she wants to say more but I keep stacking plates, knowing that eventually she'll run out of time and start her prep for her next client. Of course the moment she's gone I wish she weren't. I wish I were brave enough to say something to her.

Natalie found out that Paul and I broke up the same way everyone else did: through the statement his management team made on social media, which got picked up by some local entertainment outlets and a few reality TV bloggers. I never bothered to post anything or make any kind of statement.

One season on a cable TV reality show does not a celebrity make, even though my former agent wildly disagreed.

But those are the changes she's referring to, that my breakup with Paul has been good for me. While I'm not sure she's wrong, I'm not certain she's right, either.

Despite losing my connection to fame—and the man I was going to marry—my follower count only grew after our breakup, which made my agent, and Amy, ecstatic.

Although for vastly different reasons.

I disappointed the former, though after firing her that's not as important to me anymore. Apparently, I wasn't "leveraging my breakup" enough for another reality show appearance. And I disappointed the latter because more followers has not translated into more patrons to our restaurant. Most of my followers have used the breakup as an opportunity to speculate openly in my comments about what's wrong with me, if I was cheating, that I was too ugly or chubby or talentless to keep him anyway.

I look over my shoulder, checking to see if anyone's paying attention to me. Once I'm convinced they couldn't care less, I snap a few photos of the stacks of plates and of my sweaty self in the mirror, trying to find the balance between posing and not looking like I'm posing. I've spent hours studying influencers' and celebrity chefs' social media. Their pictures are always perfect. Gorgeous people, beautiful food. None of them look like they feel a chest-crushing sickness when they post new photos and watch the likes and the comments and the views roll in.

In the change room, I find a quiet corner and spend too long obsessing over which photos to use, which filter.

I just want to cook.

I only do this because Amy & May's needs me to. If it were up to me, the only photos I'd post would be of the dishes I cook, the only videos would be of my cat, Fifi.

The gym is supposed to be just for me. It's an hour of my time, five days a week to clear my head and my heart. Since I spent most of my career working in kitchens with cis men who thought their food tasted better by virtue of their gender, I learned early that I needed a healthy place to expel my frustration. Turns out, for me, the best way to do this is by picking up heavy objects and putting them back down again. But because, according to my agent's director of social media, there are these things called content pillars, nothing was left sacred.

My finger hovers over the screen, my heart pounding. With this post will come the likes, the comments—some complimentary, some not—and the DMs, mostly from gross men. That's just a side effect of being a woman on the internet, according to Samantha's sage advice.

This is the definition of a rock and hard place, trapped between doing the things I have to do for my job and playing Russian Roulette: The Internet Penis Edition, every time I open my DMs.

Screw it.

I send it off into the ether and distract myself by scrolling through my timeline. As my sweat dries it leaves my skin itchy and tight. At this time of the day, Natalie's studio is quiet, with only one or two coaches and clients in, the early birds having already come and gone and the lunch time crowd not on their breaks yet. So I don't feel too self-conscious sitting on a wooden bench in my sports bra, my shoes off as I stare at my phone.

I stop my scroll on a photo of a lingerie model turned reality star I met once at a charity event I attended with Paul.

She's white, blonde, built exactly like you'd imagine a lingerie model would be built. Her laugh is the thing I remember most about her, though, the sweet but husky way it melted through me as she'd pressed into my side, her warm hand wrapping around my forearm as I'd done an impression of a producer who'd worked on both of our shows. In this photo she smiles coyly at the camera, her hair in pigtails, the energy drink she's supposed to be selling secondary to the smooth expanse of skin and curves on my screen.

Natalie's voice filters down the hall and through the door, pulling me out of my social media stalking. I flick my thumb up the screen, photos flying by too quickly to register until the scroll slows on none other than Paul DeCosta's profile.

There was a time when this photo would have sent me into a spiral, seeing his arm around the shoulders of a beautiful woman. But I'm too distracted by the caption to care where his hand is:

Excited to announce your next favorite culinary reality show: Cook for Camilla. *Celebrity chef and food critic Camilla Vargas will be your host, and every episode tasks a new restaurant with the seemingly impossible: receiving the Camilla Vargas stamp of approval. The first season hits TV screens this spring. Head to the link in my bio to apply to have your restaurant featured.*

It's so strange to think that if we were still together, I'd already know about this show. I'd have been privy to all the negotiations and I'd get to hear what it's like to work with Camilla Vargas. I'm happy for him. Truly. Paul is, undoubtedly, ecstatic about it. He lives to work.

In the photo, the two of them smile at the camera, open and unposed. She's the kind of polished and classically beautiful celebrity chef he's used to working with, but my gut check yields no bitter jealousy or worry that I'd made the wrong choice.

Paul was very clear. He did not want this breakup, and he couldn't quite understand why it was happening at all.

Despite the positive impact this breakup seems to have had on my gym performance, it has tanked my professional life. I don't know if Amy has clocked the change or if she's even aware that my breakup coincides perfectly with the changes at work. It doesn't matter that I broke up with him or how right it felt the moment I'd said the words out loud. It's like my worth, my talent was tied to him, and he took it all with him when he left.

This new job offer is the potential for a clean slate. An opportunity to get my spark back. Even if it is a demotion.

Idly, I rub at the finger his ring used to sit on. If my mother had a say, Paul and I would be back together. We'd be married already.

But then, Mom doesn't know why we broke up. She wouldn't understand. She might even repeat the same things Paul said when I told him that I didn't want anything to change between us but I think I'm bisexual.

His words were so quiet, so careful, when he'd asked, "Why are you telling me this if you want nothing to change?"

And since he hadn't immediately dumped me, kicked me out of his bed, I'd thought, *this is going well*. So, I'd been honest and said:

"Because it's an important part of me and I want to own it for myself. I want you to know and love every part of me."

He'd sat up, rearranged his pillows until he was comfortable, and then he'd said, without an ounce of irony or sarcasm, that it was great that I was on this *internal* journey but he didn't see a reason to make this public. He wanted it to be our little secret.

Hearing those words was like when I slice through my hand during dinner prep. That kind of cut doesn't hurt at first. I only know I cut myself because the give on the blade is different in my own flesh than it is on the flesh of fruit or meat. But moments later I feel just how deep the blade went, through skin and into muscle.

Paul cut me in a way that bled all over, hurt for weeks after, left a scar. To hear the same sentiment from my mother would be like holding my wounded hand to the range and turning on the gas.

A notification pops up on the screen for my meeting with Amy about our new menu.

Great. Another meeting in which all my ideas will be turned down.

After sitting for so long my legs are stiff, I shuffle to the showers. I wash and get dressed quickly, stopping for one last look in the mirror. But I hardly recognize myself. Not because my cheeks are pink from the exertion or my hair is wet.

This isn't me, quiet and scared. I'm not the kind of woman who's afraid to speak her mind in her own kitchen. I couldn't have made it to the finals of *Pop-Up Kitchen* by keeping my mouth shut.

My confidence is shot.

I don't know whom I can trust anymore with these new, fragile pieces of myself. Not after I couldn't trust my soon-to-be husband with them.

Another notification from Amy pops up on my screen. An apt reminder, since it's not entirely true, that I can't trust *anyone*. More than half of the staff at Amy & May's are queer and that's not by accident. The restaurant is a safe space. If there was anyone to trust, I could probably trust Amy. I could tell her these new things about me and she'd think it was important.

But that's not why I've kept my mouth shut. If I told her, she'd *know*. She'd clock it from the other end of the dining room. There would be no way for me to hide how completely and totally infatuated I am with tall, snarky, secretly delicate Amy Chambers.

Amy is wearing my favorite shirt. This shirt has the power to incite total panic in me if the fabric so much as brushes my wrist when she reaches past me in the kitchen. It's that sweating, elevated heart rate, turned on like a teen browsing the underwear section of the Sears catalog kind of panic.

I never know where to look when she wears this shirt. Not at the shirt. I certainly cannot, under any circumstances, look at the shirt.

It's just a shirt: a basic, white button-up blouse. The fabric isn't the usual crisp kind used for an oxford, though. It's looser. Probably a polyester blend. The way it drapes over her frame draws my eyes over her broad shoulders and the way she always, *always* stands with her shoulders back, her spine straight.

Amy Chambers dares you to fuck with her, to just fucking try.

But like a total cliché, it's the neckline on the shirt that's my favorite part. Amy is tall and lean. The V-neck has a long way to go in its deep dive. On me it would probably graze my belly button but on her it's mid-chest. And at the right angle, when she moves a certain way, I can see just a glimpse of the small swell of her breasts.

So, no. I do not look at this shirt.

Amy sits down across from me at a two-top near the expo counter, the huge stack of files she slaps onto the table blocking the worst of The Shirt, which I am absolutely not looking at anyway.

To be safe.

"What?" She tucks her hair, straight today instead of her usual curls, behind her ear.

I blink into focus. I was so busy not looking at The Shirt I forgot to actually look at her. "Your hair," I say dumbly. "You…changed it."

She huffs, an amused and exasperated sound. "You sound like my brother. Yes. I changed it." She flips open the file folder on top and leafs through the papers.

I tip the legs of my chair to one side to get a better look at her. As well as taking the hair straightener to it, she's added an undercut beneath her bob.

"It looks good," I say.

She rolls her eyes like she doesn't believe me. I wish she could feel my heartbeat because between that shirt and this haircut, there'd be no question that I love it.

"It does," I say. "I like the curls, too. I like all of your hair." I cringe. *I like all of your hair?* My face heats and I busy myself with pretending to have a cough to distract her from what I can only assume was my poor attempt at flirting.

Amy's face contorts, a frown on top and a smirk on the bottom. "Thanks," she says slowly. "So. The menu."

"Right." I pull my chair in closer and open my laptop. "I know you wanted to do more seafood and I agree that it's a logical addition, but I don't think we should add so much." I point to the three new seafood dishes she's added to the mock-up menu. "We've got access to a great supply chain, but I think it's going to cost a lot of money to do something that everyone else in the city is already doing anyway. Plus we have the plating to think of. One of the things people love about Amy & May's is the domestic vibe."

I hold up the delicate porcelain dishware that's been set out for tonight's service. Amy spent months driving around the state, stopping at garage sales and antiques markets, buying up sets of fine china to give the decor a homey and vintage vibe.

"I'm thinking scallops, oysters, of course, could work with

this kind of dishware but if we start getting into…" I pause, looking for the word. I grew up in a bilingual household. My mother Anglophone and my father Francophone. I speak both languages fluently but sometimes my words get mixed up. Today its *fruit de mer*. It's the word I want to use in English that I can't, for the life of me, remember.

"Crustaceans," I blurt out instead. "Which are often paired with heavier meats, we run the risk of changing the entire vibe of the restaurant. We can't serve king crab and sirloin on these plates."

Amy tilts her head to the side. "I think that's the most I've heard you speak since we started working together."

I shrug, hiding my face behind my hair and doing a quick inventory of the number of words I could have possibly spoken, on average, in the past.

"You have a point about the *shellfish*, Hollywood," she says, smirking.

Shellfish. Obviously, I meant shellfish.

I should just tell her to fuck off. For the nickname, too. But I am desperate for Amy to think I am tough, like her. Cool in that way that only truly cool people really are, where it's effortless. She can't know that sometimes I lie awake at night, dissecting every one of her smirks, or when our eye contact lingers too long, or that her nickname might mean something more, rather than just a silly moniker for a disaster of a person. Instead, I smile, closed lipped, just in case.

"And you make a good point about the dishes. But I think it can't hurt to test it out." She slides her index finger, the nail short and blunt, down the column of a spreadsheet, the numbers decreasing in size. She closes the binder before I can get a peek at what those numbers mean but I think it might be our restaurant's revenue.

I sigh, pushing the sinking feeling in my chest further

down. "Yes. A test couldn't hurt. Maybe we could choose one or two dishes and invite the front of house staff to try it on a Monday."

"I was thinking we add them to the menu starting on Tuesday and offer them for the next two weeks to see how they perform."

"You want my kitchen to learn…" I scan her menu mockup again. "Three new seafood dishes in less than a week?" I ask.

"I have faith in them." She nods. "And you." But she says that much quieter.

Do you? I want to ask. But I don't. Because I'm too scared to hear the answer. If there's one thing I trust Amy to do, it's be too honest.

I let out a slow breath, planning the logistics of sourcing and ordering the new ingredients last minute. "What menu items should we get rid of then?" I scroll the menu.

"None," she says dismissively. She studies her spreadsheet, completely unaware she's messing up my life with that one word and looking goddamn beautiful doing it. Miniature alpine skiers could jump off her eyelashes and land safely on the plump pink cushion of her lower lip.

She's a beautiful witch.

One of the best things about Amy & May's is the small menu. Since before I started cooking here, Amy adopted the smart strategy of choosing a few menu options and perfecting them. A restaurant doesn't need pages and pages of offerings to succeed. In fact, that's usually a hindrance to success.

"Amy," I say slowly, testing and throwing out a few different approaches to yet another new conflict. "I don't think this is the right way to go."

She cocks her head to the side, crossing her arms over her chest. "And what would you do differently?"

I pull up the recipes I'd been brainstorming on my phone. "There's really cool stuff happening in vegetarian and vegan cooking. This chef in Ottawa—that's in Canada," I add, to which she rolls her eyes, "creates high-quality, high-priced tasting menus with vegetable and fermentation-focused foods. I'd love to be able to try stuff like that, and the best part is we could use the fermentation process as part of our brand."

Amy peers at the photo I've pulled up, rows of jars of different fermented foods, backlit by a soft golden light. The layout is similar to something you'd see in a steakhouse but with carrots in mason jars rather than the vast wine selection on display.

"This kind of food-decor combo in the Amy & May's space lends itself to the overall domestic vibe," I say, leaving my phone in front of her, a strategic move.

Amy sits forward, leaning on her elbows. She peers at my phone screen like she doesn't quite trust it, her lower lip caught delicately in her teeth.

Holy crap. It's working.

I'm not going to have to come up with three new recipes in the next few days.

She blinks away from the screen. She gives me her profile, her jawline elegant, her neck long, accentuated by her short hair. "No. I want to go with shellfish. Maybe we can try this in the spring."

I huff out a breath through my nose, so frustrated with this imperious, "Amy knows best" attitude, it's better to say nothing at all. But she hears my sigh for what it is.

Annoyance. Resistance. Fatigue.

"What else can we do?" she asks, her tone sharper than I've ever heard it. She sits back in her chair, like she's just as surprised as I am at her outburst. Quieter, she says, "I pay my staff a fair wage. I don't ask them to rely on tips for their livelihood. I'm trying to bring in health insurance this year. I can't do any of that if people don't come to the restaurant." She shakes her hand at the empty dining room. "No one comes here. People are depending on me."

"I know that," I say slowly, trying to control my tone and my temper. "Maybe if you explained why you think shellfish is better than easily sourced, inexpensive vegetables that we can do all the prep for ourselves, it will help me understand…"

"Because I said so," Amy snaps.

I rock back in my chair. Amy and I have argued before. We've sent out warning shots, sniped at each other. Well, she's sniped. I've rolled my eyes and sighed. But we communicated that way, at least, without getting out of hand.

This is out of hand.

Her jaw is set but there's panic in her eyes and they shine bright like she could cry. I've seen this wild look before. It comes when an owner will do anything, even the wrong thing, to save their restaurant, and seeing this panic on cool, aloof Amy, I second-guess myself. Not for the first time since I've worked here, since Paul and I broke up.

I've disappointed so many people already, and Amy has been doing this since she was sixteen. The same age I was when I got my first job as a dishwasher in Le Plateau back home in Montreal. So what makes my expertise better than hers?

I close my laptop.

Since having more spare time, after Paul, I've had the opportunity to source local farms and research how to forage for edible mushrooms. A flicker of resentment for Amy burns in me as my dream of expanding our non-animal proteins goes up in flames.

"Fine," I mutter. "We'll do it your way, then." We might not have a restaurant to try it my way with, come spring, but there's no point in making things worse.

The thing is, I feel for her. Amy pays everyone above minimum wage; the prices of our dishes are higher than our neighbors' because we don't expect our guests to tip. Health insurance and benefits in the service industry is practically unheard of. But it's like Amy had a vision for what she wanted her restaurant to be and she's never let anyone in on the secret. She steers this ship alone and expects us all to blindly follow, even me, her head chef. I used to trust her enough to do that. But now...

"Do you have a better suggestion?" she asks.

How about letting me run my own kitchen? Before I can muster up the courage to say so, a notification pulls our attention to my phone lying on the table between us.

Amy's jaw ticks. "More followers?" she asks and there's an edge to her voice I've never heard before. Some days, when I'm feeling really low about myself, I wonder if the only reason she offered me a job was because of my perceived fame. When I first started, people would ask for photos. I could feel their eyes on me while I worked, the pressure to perform exceedingly high knowing there were fans out there waiting. I wonder if she even believes I have talent.

I flip the phone around and open the notification. A new DM. Super.

"Ew," she says.

"Sorry." I delete the message, a blush creeping up my cheeks. They're obviously not my fault. I'm not asking for them. But it's embarrassing nonetheless, for a strong woman like Amy to see the creeps who follow her head chef.

"Does that happen a lot?" she asks. "Those kinds of messages."

"A side effect of being a woman on the internet." I shrug, repeating the line my agent used to convince me not to delete my accounts.

Amy says nothing, but her gaze travels over my face, heating my skin.

"What?"

"What does your fiancé think?" she asks after a quiet moment.

"My ex-fiancé didn't like it any more than I did. But what could he do about it?"

"Sorry." She cringes. "Did I already know that? That he was your ex?"

"I haven't talked about it much, so maybe not."

After another beat of silence she says, "Do you...want to talk about it?" Amy's face is contorted into a mask of discomfort.

"Talking about it looks like the very last thing you want to do."

Her laugh is stilted. "I'm not great with advice. But if you ever want to grab a drink and unload..."

"Thanks," I say quietly. The sound of her frustration, the feeling of my own, is far too fresh to want to take her up on that offer. But much like I know if I told her I'm queer, she'd be supportive and happy for me, I believe her when she says she'd let me talk at her about all the weird shit that's been going on in my head since.

She nods at the phone. "So what's Paul up to now?" she asks. "Now that he's not marrying girls off of *Pop-Up Kitchen*?"

I open the app, ignoring her dig about our whirlwind romance and fast engagement. The screen fills with Paul's and Camilla's faces again. "See for yourself." I turn the phone toward her. "Have you eaten at a Camilla Vargas restaurant before?" I ask. "She's championed the shift toward non-animal proteins in the last few years." I add a little dig of my own.

Amy narrows her eyes. I stare back. I said what I said.

She smirks, sending a thrill through me, before dropping her gaze to the phone.

"What's this?" She frowns, pulling the phone from my fingers. Her light brown eyes travel over the screen. She huffs. "Sophie, what is this?" She flips the phone back at me.

"It's what Paul's up to. He's producing a new show." I gesture at Camilla in her sexy white sheath dress, her dark hair cascading in loose curls over one shoulder. Paul next to her, he's let the gray grow in around his temples and he's clearly been hitting the gym since we broke up. We used to go to Natalie's together, but he's found a new trainer who's clearly got him on a bulking regimen. He's beefed up.

With space and time from when I first saw the announcement, I can admit Paul looks handsome. He looks hot, actually. So does Camilla.

When I finally confronted the truth, that straight girls don't think about kissing other girls, they don't get crushes, and they certainly don't get themselves off to the idea of getting another woman off with their mouths, I considered I might be gay. Then promptly spiraled into panic since I had recently accepted a marriage proposal from a man.

I spent weeks staring at Paul, at our male friends, complete strangers, trying to understand the attraction I felt. The scientific conclusions I came up with were:

Women's asses: hot.

Men's asses: also hot.

That's when I knew I needed to accept I wasn't as straight as I thought I was.

"Your fiancé is producing a new show with Camilla freaking Vargas?"

"Ex-fiancé. But yes. I found out this morning."

If Paul and I were still together, our friends would be messaging me to scream about the new show. But my phone has been silent. It seems our friendships only extended as long as our relationship did.

Now I'm left in this confusing liminal space where I'm angry with him but I care for him but I don't want to be with him but I don't know *how* to be with a woman or if I want to be with a woman and if I did I wouldn't even know where to start.

"Hollywood. We have to do this."

I look up from the hole I've been burning into the table with my stare. "Do what?"

She shakes my phone at me. "This. This show. Paul's show. Why didn't you mention this before?" She sounds aghast, betrayed.

I laugh awkwardly as I try to grab my phone from her. She drops it back into my hand, warm from her palm. She doesn't break eye contact, wiggling her eyebrows. "We should apply to be on the show."

I laugh again, real, warmer this time because that's silly, ludicrous. But my laughter slowly fades as she takes longer and longer to join me over here, on the just kidding side of the table. "Amy," I say.

"Think of the publicity if we won."

That's exactly what I'm thinking about. The new followers, the rubberneckers who aren't here for the food, just to say they ate at the same restaurant, maybe sat in the same seat as Camilla. The way they don't really care if we win or lose, succeed or fail, we're just entertainment ready for their consumption.

"N-n-no. We couldn't. We can't."

"Why not?" And she sounds genuinely curious, like she can't think of a hundred different reasons why we should absolutely not apply to *Cook for Camilla.*

I splutter. "I can't go on my fiancé's new TV show. That would be…favoritism. Nepotism." I throw my hands out. "Whatever."

"Ex-fiancé," she corrects.

"Even more reason *not* to," I hiss. "He'd think I was trying to get him back or something."

"Are you kidding?" She's practically standing out of her seat. "Now that you're broken up, I bet the producers and the audiences will eat up the drama. They'd be stupid to say no to you. You mean ratings."

I shake my head. My stomach sinks, sours, not just at the idea that I'd be ratings fodder, but at the inevitable attention, the speculation. People tagging me in conversations about what this facial expression meant, what I did wrong on the previous episode. It would be *Pop-Up Kitchen* all over again.

I learned so much on that show. New skills and techniques, and that I'm far more capable than I thought I was. And that stardom isn't for me. The other contestants had a fire in their eyes when the cameras came on. They showed up ready to perform, I showed up just to cook. I woke up every day ready to create good food. But I was the one consumed, my spirit, my confidence. The only thing that got me through was Paul. And now he's gone, too.

This time it would be worse. It would be *Pop-Up Kitchen* but with a secret, of my identity, of this silly little crush I have on this infuriating restaurant owner.

And forget any attempt at privacy, for me or her. To be back in the limelight, not as a chef presenting quality food made from scratch but as a sideshow, the desperate, loser ex of a high-powered producer.

"No," I whisper. "God no."

"Hollywood, please." Amy sounds desperate but I can't look at her. Or maybe I can't see her at all. "Think of what it would be like if we won…" she says again.

That's the worst part. I am. If we won, maybe Amy would trust me with my own kitchen. If we won, the revenue we'd generate would not only give me the freedom I'm craving to create the menus I want. It would mean I could stay here at Amy & May's, as head chef, instead of having to work for some other chef in some other kitchen.

"I think we should apply," I hear Amy say. "The worst that could happen is we get rejected."

Finally, I focus on her.

Amy's smiles are like the slow, warm burn of a habanero pepper, the spice of ginger. That smile is almost enough to convince me, just like the first time I met her.

She'd shown me around this place. I'd followed in the wake of her peach scented shampoo, my heart pounding, barely able to form words. I'd met plenty of pretty girls before, been attracted to them in ways I hadn't fully understood—or maybe in ways I didn't want to understand.

But Amy. She's fierce and a bit loud and she commands the attention of every room she's in. At least, she commanded my attention. The last time Amy looked at me like this I took this job and broke up with my fiancé.

I want to save this restaurant. But I can't keep doing things just to impress this pretty girl. Not when what she's asking me to do has the power to break me.

"No." I stand up. The chair screeches against the hardwood floor. "Don't ask me again. I'll do your stupid shellfish dishes. I know what you think of me," I say and she has the audacity to look confused. "That I've lost my talent, that I'm some loser who can't cook anymore."

Her eyes widen and the echo of my words in the empty dining room make me wince. "But going on TV won't fix any of that. If you want to go on this show, you can officially find yourself a new head chef."

Chapter Three

Amy

If there is any place in the world capable of giving me an existential crisis it is my brother's girlfriend's guest bathroom. There's no other room in the world that makes me feel like I do not have my shit together.

First of all, I don't have a guest bathroom. My one-bedroom/living room/kitchen, one-bath apartment has a century-old porcelain sink with a crack in it that will one day be my landlord's problem. On any given day there are up to five plants bathing in my tub.

By contrast, Corrine's bathroom is so bright and white it's almost blinding. The only plant that lives here is a succulent that she should really move to a room with a window. The towels are folded so crisply they look like they're overstarched but they're actually so soft I rub one against my cheek as I dry my hands. A subtly scented candle burns on the countertop.

This bathroom has a 401(k) and a timeshare on Cape Hatteras. Meanwhile, last week I hit up my head chef to get us on a reality show so I can make sure we pay rent this month.

My father's booming voice cuts through the peace of this bathroom turned meditation space. Perhaps its only flaw: not soundproof. I follow the sound back out to Corrine's dining room. Corrine and Wes's dining room, rather. My brother moved in with his former boss turned girlfriend last month.

Though when she suggested that they host our dad for dinner, I think he thought about moving out for a split second.

It's Corrine's desire to impress the one parent we have left that keeps her smiling in my father's direction as he goes off on some tirade about who knows what. Wes sits rigid in his seat next to her, his ears red and fists clenched. My brother isn't like me. He gives the benefit of the doubt. He turns the other cheek. He waits and waits and waits for people to show him their goodness, while I excise them from my life if it takes longer than five minutes to appear.

Except when it comes to our dad.

At some point, I'm not quite sure when, after Mom died maybe, our roles reversed. Wes has no patience for the man anymore while I keep coming back for more, like an abused puppy who's never known any better. It would almost be easier if he were outwardly cruel. Then maybe the bitch I've always known myself to be would appear. Maybe she's just not being given the right stimulus, what with his casual disregard for most of my existence.

Operation Bill Chambers, You Are My Father (So Act Like It) may have launched too soon for my brother. But if I didn't launch now, it might never happen. It's not like Dad would take it upon himself to fill this mom-sized hole in my chest. For some stupid reason, I assumed he would know that with our mother gone we'd need this. But he's clueless.

As usual.

I put my hand on his shoulder. "Maybe we should get going, Dad."

Wes stands, the chair scraping against the floor. "I'll call him a cab."

"I can drive him," I say.

My brother clenches his jaw, his glasses skewed from rubbing his eyes. He's had a habit since we were kids, he fidgets.

Plays with his sleeves or scratches at this spot above his ear. Since he met his girlfriend, he's become more sure of himself. Only in the most stressful situations does he revert to these old tics.

Corrine comes up behind him, her hand on his forearm. He looks down at her and she smiles. He shrugs, the tension leaking from his body, but he's not deflated.

Just peaceful.

"All right. Let me know you get home safe?"

I turn away before I answer him. Wes would accuse me of jealousy, probably. As twins we've always been the creepy kind of close that freaks out our friends. There was a time, a short time, when Wes would have been right. I was jealous of the closeness that he and his now girlfriend share. I thought his gain meant my loss. But that's not what makes me turn away from them now. Their relationship hasn't taken something away from ours.

It's highlighted exactly what's missing in my own life.

I'm a lesbian who started her first restaurant before she turned thirty because after watching my mother's life slowly fade, I knew I couldn't wait one more second to do the scary things in life. I wasn't going to distract myself with a relationship while attempting to fulfill my lifelong dream. My life could start once Amy & May's was off the ground.

Now Amy & May's is off the ground. Kind of. It's chugging along the runway, hurtling as fast as it can, nose up but unable to convert RPMs to flight, and running out of runway.

So, yeah. I would kill for a distraction.

That's probably what my attraction to Sophie is. I'm desperate for a distraction, for someone to slide her hand along my forearm and take my mind off things, to remind me I'm not alone.

"I will," I say. "Let's go, Dad."

We hug while Dad gives a brusque goodbye from the front door. "Thanks for dinner," I whisper to Corrine.

She squeezes me tight. "Thank the grocery store for pre-cooked meals."

Their front door closes behind us, leaving my father and I alone in the bright lights and oppressive silence of her building's hallway. Without waiting for me, Dad strolls to the elevator.

"How's...work?" I ask, following after him. Normally it's Wes who can't stand a silence. Thanks for that, bro.

Dad's cheeks are red from the three scotches he had tonight. He condescended to drink from Corrine's apparently abysmal collection, muttering about the "swill" the whole time.

He's tall, like Wes and I, and shares the same shoulder hunch as my brother, from a lifetime spent trying to fit into spaces made just a little too short for them. "Fine," he grunts.

"That's great," I say, with false brightness. When he doesn't respond in kind I say, "The restaurant is..." I pause. If he were Mom, I'd tell him everything about how the restaurant is doing.

If he were Mom, he'd already know. But he's not Mom.

"Doing great. We're testing a new menu."

He grunts again. A quick *uh-huh*.

"I think it's really going to help with, you know, numbers." Even that small admission leaves me raw and vulnerable.

But that's the great thing about Dad. He's not paying enough attention to bother noticing, what I said or how I feel about it.

He steps onto the elevator with the sort of leisurely pace of a man who's used to people and machines waiting for him.

"My chef is really excited about it." That's a bold-faced lie. My chef has barely spoken to me for the past week. I thought her silence was bad before I asked her to sacrifice her emotional well-being for the sake of my restaurant's bottom line.

I texted my apology that night, after our dinner service, after hours of silence and quietly simmering anger. I had no idea it was that bad for her, or that she felt so strongly about a return to reality television. She never responded. Our conversations have been in-person, courteous, professional, and distant ever since. I miss her quiet huffs of annoyance and the bite in her tone when she pushes back.

Dad scrolls his phone. He does one of those finance jobs, with bonds or mutual funds or what the fuck ever. The kind of job where he has to take clients out for fancy dinners—never to my restaurant though—and where he gets to expense things like Wagyu beef and gentlemen's clubs.

"If this menu is successful we're going to open another location. On the moon."

Dad whistles through his teeth.

Cool. It's nice to know that at the very least my father's primary parenting technique remains disassociation.

"You should come sometime," I say. "To the restaurant."

He grunts. "You still driving this thing?" he asks as I lead him to my car, the one he bought for Wes and I when we got our driver's licenses. Well, I got my driver's license. It took Wes a couple more tries.

"I am," I say, careful to regulate my tone so as not to seem prematurely defensive.

"Why don't you buy a new one?" he barks, as he slides into the passenger seat.

Because they cost money, Dad.

Money I don't have because every last cent goes to the restaurant. The light from his phone screen turns his face a ghostly shade of blue in the darkness of the condo's parking garage.

I shrug and pat the dashboard. "A new car doesn't have these memories."

I had my first kiss in this car. I've filled the hatchback from countless trips to the garden center in this car. I've shared a joint with my brother in our mom's driveway on the hood of this car more times than I can count.

"Well, it's a shit box," Dad says.

It's strange, the small ways he can still hurt me. My father's opinion of this car shouldn't matter at all. It's just a car. But hearing his disdain is like taking a bullet.

"I like it," I say quietly.

Dad says nothing and this time I let it stand.

As kids, my mother always said I was most like our father. At the time—since none of us knew he was a philandering liar—I took it as a compliment. Dad was successful. He worked too much but he gave us such a beautiful life. He was strong, stoic, and people looked up to him. I looked up to him.

But now I wonder if she saw our dark sides, too. All the ways that my quiet, sullen, grumpy ass resembled his. Unable to make connections the way she and Wes could, a leader, but also, always, alone.

For the rest of the car ride, I try to think of a way to break the silence. If only because silence would be my father's baseline and so now, to prove I'm nothing like him, I must speak.

But god, talking to him sucks. I have to actively remind myself of why I'm pursuing this relationship with him: because he's the only family we have left, because he needs us even if he would never admit it.

Despite the awkward silence in the car on my way to my dad's condo on the other side of town in the Seaport District, the quiet after dropping him off breaks me. Normally, I'd go park outside Mom's house. Maybe listen to some really loud music and scream into the quiet of her old street on a Monday night. Maybe cry. Maybe both. But Mom's is for when I'm sad. I'm not sad. I'm agitated.

My parking brake makes an unfortunate screech as I crank it in my usual spot behind the restaurant. The wind cuts down the alley, and with the parking lot empty with the restaurant closed today there's nothing to block the freezing cold that slices through my clothes. I jog to the door, not bothering with my coat in the cool February air. I jam my key in the lock but I'm met with none of the resistance I usually get from the old metal. The lights are on as I step inside.

Holy shit.

"Who the fuck closed last night," I mutter. Whoever it was is about to get fired. They left the door unlocked, the lights on, and…music playing?

I walk slowly through the back hallway, past my office and the staff locker room, and poke my head out the door to the front of the restaurant. "Hello?" I say quietly.

The dining room lights are low, but the overheads from the kitchen spill into the dark hallway. The music is louder out here, something electric with the kind of bass that reverberates through your chest. As I stand in the doorway between the front and the back of the house, a sliver of fear trickles down my spine. What am I doing walking in here when the door is unlocked, after hours? It could be anyone, a burglar, maybe. Someone with an axe to grind. Chad's pissed off face flashes behind my eyes.

Slowly, I close the door. I'll go back to my car, drive around to the front of the restaurant, park down the street, and try to figure out what's happening. Then decide what to do. Before the door can close, a quiet humming comes from down the hallway and I stop. It's not a fan or a fridge motor kicking on.

The voice is feminine, following along to the beat, adding in snippets of words here and there over the instrumentals.

"Sophie?" I say, more to myself than to the person in the restaurant with me, but there's no answer. Fuck it.

On the table in the staff room there's an old, dirty fork. I grab it, holding it over my head. If it's not Sophie—the only other person with a key—I'll throw this crusty old fork at them and run like hell.

"Sophie?" I call again, as I creep down the hall. Something sizzles in a pan, utensils clank. More humming. Smoke sits in a haze along the ceiling. The hood fans aren't on. A clear safety violation. My heart pounds in my throat but there's no fear. Maybe that makes me stupid. I'm just so sure, more sure with every step, that I'll see Sophie when I turn this corner, and I am excited. After an evening spent with my father's stagnant apathy, Sophie's sighs, heavy through her nose, rolling her eyes when she thinks I don't see, her small retaliations, thrill me. Here, one on one, I can apologize and listen and find out why she's so against the show, what happened to make it so unbearable.

I round the corner. Sophie faces the oven range, her back to me. Her hips sway to the music, the denim clinging to the firm globes of her ass. Her hair is piled on top of her head. There's so much of it and for a moment, a flash in the pan, I imagine it fanned out on my pillowcase. The way the sun would turn it a thousand different hues, dark brown to burned copper.

I tuck the thought away. It's not for me.

"Sophie. Hollywood," I say, finally loud enough for her to hear me over the music.

She jumps, spins, screams, all at the same time. Her long-sleeved black T-shirt clings to her curves in ways her standard white chef's jacket never could.

"You scared the shit out of me," she screeches. Her eyes jump from my face to the fork that I'm holding like a knife over my head. I drop my arm.

"I thought you were Chad," I say dumbly.

"Chad?"

"I thought you were disgruntled." I toss the fork onto the counter, the clatter on the metal counter muted by her loud music.

She shrugs, a slotted spoon in her hand. "I'm normal. I'm gruntled."

My rib cage feels like it's filled with hummingbirds. "Good," I say. "I'm glad. That you're gruntled."

"Where's your car?" I ask, pointing toward the back of the restaurant, where my car sits alone. This whole mortifying ordeal could have been avoided if she'd parked her boat with four-wheel drive in her designated parking spot.

"I parked out front," she says. "It's..." She frowns down at the food. "Scary back there at night."

Great. Now she's hot and a great cook and smart and also *fucking adorable.* "Do you want me to put more lights up back there?"

"No. No, it's fine."

"Clearly, it's not fine. I can fix it."

She shakes her head, frowning. "No, I just mean..." She shakes her hands at the pots and pans bubbling around her. "I'm cooking, I mean."

She's defensive, and she rests her hand on her hip, like she's self-conscious but trying to bluster her way through it. But she shouldn't be worried. She's charming. My chef is charming. Me, specifically.

I step into the kitchen. "What are you cooking?" It smells divine. Smoky and nutty. My mouth waters.

Sophie turns back to the stove. Her shoulders rise and fall. "Mushroom gravy," she says. "I'm testing recipes." She looks at me over her shoulder, a challenge in her eyes. "Vegan recipes."

She's not even embarrassed to be caught cooking the opposite of what I've asked her to prepare for our menu. But do I care at this point? The longer I stand here the more mentally exhausted I feel after that dinner with Dad. And she's talking to me at least. She's not hiding in the walk-in again. She ignores me, chopping, sautéing, tasting defiantly. Watching her takes me back to binge-watching her show.

She was daring, rebellious. She took risks. The show, and having her here now, it reminds me of why I wanted to open this restaurant in the first place.

Food is family and tradition and new friends and experimentation. Food is a biological necessity, it's breathing, but within that basic human need is art. Unlike paintings and sculptures, literature or music, we get to consume this art. And Sophie's art melts on my tongue. I get to tear it with my teeth.

Food is visceral and pleasurable and I'm not bragging when I say I am a good cook. But that's like saying I can draw well when Sophie painted the Sistine Chapel.

Food makes me feel good and I think, after her reaction last week, that maybe Sophie has lost some of the joy she gets from food.

"Can I try some?" I ask.

"I guess." She shrugs. "If you want. There's no shellfish," she says, smug.

We need to clear the air. Or I do, at least. "I know I can be a bit pushy sometimes," I say.

She pauses in her stirring and laughs, making it sound far more sarcastic than I ever could.

"I'm...overbearing, okay? I get it. I know. Sometimes I think I know what's best and I have a hard time hearing other people. I did that to you last week and I'm sorry."

Sophie plates the food. It takes me a moment to figure out what it is. Potatoes, cut into thick fries, mushroom gravy, and... "I thought you said this was vegan."

"It is."

"Those are cheese curds." I point at the white semi-solid

blob. "This is poutine." I can barely keep the contempt out of my voice.

She spoons excess gravy along the edge of the plate, breaks sprigs of parsley off the stems in a mason jar to garnish the dish. "It's vegan cheese. Here," she says, sliding the dish toward me. "Get that look off your face and try some."

She drags her finger through the gravy in the pan, sucks it off her skin. There's nothing inherently sexual about a chef tasting their food, except when that chef's cheeks are pink from the heat and the neckline of her plain black cotton tee reveals just the top of her cleavage, an inch, nothing more.

And I've suppressed a mild attraction to this chef since before I met her. She's turned something innocuous into me wondering what that sauce might taste like complemented by her skin.

Sophie takes a pinch of salt from a ceramic jar and sprinkles it over the dish. "Try it now."

I pull out two roll ups from under the counter and pass one to her. She smiles a tight-lipped thanks and I don't think she's let me off easy about my past behavior. "I do it to my brother, too," I say, unfolding the cloth napkin and leaning my hip against the counter. "My managerial experience started in the womb." She laughs, once, a quiet *ha*, that I see more than hear but it feels like a win.

I hold my fork over the food, but I can't bring myself to break up the perfection of her plating. Even if it is poutine.

"You should take a picture of this," I say. "For your Instagram."

She huffs, annoyed, but says, "Good idea."

She pulls her phone out of her back pocket and I step out of frame while she takes a few photos from different angles, some videos, and tinkers with filters.

"Thanks." She smiles at me over her shoulder, her mouth

wide, her cheeks round. I've never seen a smile like this on her before, the uninhibited kind. I didn't know she even had this kind of smile in her, but that's my own fault.

She steps aside, nudging the plate toward me again.

"In high school I made my brother take weightlifting with me." I laugh at the memory of my then-gangly brother on the bench next to guys on our high school's football team. He'd already had plenty of experience in the weight room because he was on the baseball team, but he was never going to be able to compete against the guys in that class. "I was worried that he wasn't confident enough and I thought getting stronger would help."

She piles dishes into the sink. "Did it?" she asks. I didn't think she was paying attention.

Finally, I stab some fries onto my fork, making sure to snag some of this alleged cheese. I've never been a huge fan of animal-based poutine so I'm not sure what she thinks she's going to do with this.

Sophie stops what she's doing to watch me.

"Not really. I ended up benching more than him and he tried not to let it get to him, but I think it did. He can definitely bench more than me now though, so that's a win. For his masculinity at least." I shrug and take a bite. *"Oh my god."*

The gravy is so creamy, rich, with just a hint of acidity. The potatoes are crisp and the cheese... I'd never say this out loud, but I might like it better than the real thing.

"Hollywood," I say with my hand over my mouth. "This is..." I close my eyes; chewing and tasting and swallowing sometimes needs to be done without the distraction of sight. "Divine." I pile my fork higher. "How'd you do this without real cheese?"

She pulls her own fork out of the roll up and sets her elbow against the counter, taking a delicate bite. Sophie closes her eyes, too. She hums as she chews, her mouth turned up at the corners. She presses her lips together, sighing as she opens her eyes. "Cashews," she says.

"Magic," I counter. She meets my gaze. I've been staring at her for too long. I take another bite of food. Food is the best distraction.

"I weightlift," she says after a few quiet moments of chewing.

"I can tell." Fuck. That was stupid. "You're just…" I gesture to my own arms, my hips. Double fuck. This is stupider. "You're very fit."

"I know." Her shoulders shake and her voice bubbles with laughter.

I nod. Take another bite. Triple fuck. I shouldn't be this flustered around my head chef. My straight, heartbroken head chef.

"Why are you telling me about your brother?" she asks. She doesn't know she's saving me from this conversation but I'm thankful anyway.

I savor my last bite before swallowing. It practically melts in my mouth. "I'm trying to say I'm sorry. In a very roundabout, convoluted way. I pushed you to apply for that show without thinking about how you might feel about returning to it, and I'm sorry. It's not an excuse for my behavior, but I know I can be a bit of a bull sometimes. I'm trying to find a way to make this place great, like I know it can be. I get overprotective sometimes and it clouds my judgment."

Sophie's eyes look dark green in the bright overhead lights of the kitchen. "So wait. In this analogy am I your brother that needs to be protected or is the restaurant your brother who needs protecting from me?"

"Neither. You're merely a victim of my stubbornness."

"I wouldn't say I'm a victim. I should have explained how

I was feeling instead of yelling at you. But yeah, I guess, to be fair, I didn't think you were that interested in listening to what I had to say about it."

I wince. "Can we be honest with each other?" I ask. "I feel like we haven't been fully ourselves since this arrangement started and maybe that's one of the reasons why we're having trouble working together."

Sophie looks down, pokes at the food. That wasn't the reaction I was expecting or hoping for when I asked if we could be honest. "Yeah, I mean, what do you want to know?"

"Are you happy here?" I gesture to the quiet, dark dining room. "Do you like cooking here?"

"Yes," she says slowly. My stomach sinks. "It's different from what I expected."

"Different how?"

"I thought I'd have more say over the menu. I thought I'd be planning my own menu, honestly."

That's actually pretty reasonable. "I could probably give you more control. I'm not saying I didn't have a hand in keeping you at arm's length from…"

"Creative control?"

"Right. That. You probably deserve…"

She arches an eyebrow.

I sigh. "You should have more control over the menu," I say. "But sometimes it seems like…"

"What?" She straightens. "You said we should be honest with each other."

We should. But how do I tell someone they've lost their spark. "Sometimes it seems like you want to say something to me, and you don't. You could have asked for more freedom, you know? You can tell me things. I want to hear them, and I promise you I'll listen."

Sophie sighs. "Okay." She doesn't sound like she believes me.

"Tell me," I say. "What do you want?"

She straightens and points at the dish. "I want this dish on the menu."

I nod. "Done." That's easy. This dish is delicious.

She smiles again, huge.

"What else?" I ask, because I want to know what my head chef needs to be successful, not because I might be addicted to making her smile like that.

Her lips falter and she looks away again. "Can I ask you a personal question?"

"Sure."

"You're gay."

My heart stutters, for no good reason. "Yeah," I say slowly. "That's not a question."

"Sorry." She shakes her head. "Can I ask how, or I guess when, you knew? That you liked girls?"

Sophie takes our empty plate to the sink, adding it to the pile of dishes already soaking. I've been asked this question before. But usually when someone asks it in this non sequitur kind of way they're not asking about me. They're asking about themselves. My brain takes a few moments to fire off some random neurons as I consider the possibility that Sophie Brunet might be asking me about my queerness to understand her own.

"I always noticed girls. I was obsessed with Disney princesses, and no one really thought anything of it because of course a girl would like Disney princesses, but it probably had more to do with the fact that I *liked* them and not that I liked them, you know?"

Sophie perches on the edge of one of the chairs beside the chef's table. She pulls her leg up and rests her chin on her knee.

"Around middle school all my friends had crushes on boys, but I didn't." I shrugged. "I had crushes on my friends. I knew then but I didn't have the language for it. It wasn't something I'd seen or been exposed to. I didn't know any other queer kids, let alone adults. When I was fifteen, I kissed my brother's best friend, Jeremy. I needed to see what the fuss was about. My brother doesn't know about that and hopefully he never will." I laugh. Jeremy Chen was probably the worst person I could have experimented on. It was basically like kissing my brother. "It was…not for me." I grimace.

Sophie laughs.

Normally, if someone asks "when did you know" it makes me feel like a zoo animal they want to study. But the way she fidgets makes me think she's nervous, not nosy. "How about you?" I ask awkwardly. "Did you…always know you were…?" I gesture at her, so she can fill in the blanks.

She winces. "I'm sorry. I wasn't trying to put you on the spot. The reason I asked is because if we apply and we get on the show, your sexuality will probably come up. You have to know that being on TV even if it's just for one twenty-two-minute episode brings people out of the woodwork. Producers might try to exploit your sexuality as a way to show that they're *so* progressive for token queer representation or turn your *struggles* as a queer woman into trauma porn. You stop being in charge of your own narrative."

She's saying important things. I know that I should focus on them, like what exactly happened to her on that show. And yet, I'm stuck on "if we apply."

"Wait. Back up. What are you saying?"

She rubs the back of her neck. "I appreciate your apology and your commitment to honesty. And I agree the restaurant could benefit from getting on the show. But I need you to be fully aware of what's going to happen. It's a lot of work, and it can be seductive, the cameras, the attention, the illusion of fame."

"Hollywood, seriously?" I rush forward, grab her hands, and pull her up from the chair. "Are you serious? You want to apply?"

She rolls her eyes.

I bounce on the balls of my feet, squeeze her hands. My chest fizzes like a pop can. "Well?"

"Yes. I want to apply."

Before I take another breath, I wrap my arms around her and squeal and squeeze. "Sophie. Thank you." She's forced to join me in my bouncing—it's the only way we'll stay standing, I hold her so tight. "Thank you." I say it over and over again. "I know we might not get on the show but if we do…"

If we do, it means a fully booked reso on any given night. Enough Yelp reviews to bury that woman's from the other day. My dream gets to keep being a reality.

I pull back just enough to look her in the eyes when I say thank you again. But now I'm aware of the press of breasts, round and full against mine. Her fingers grip my biceps. More of her hair has fallen out of its bun and it frames her face, short hairs sticking up from the heat, longer ones curling around her ears. Her exhales feather over my collarbone, warm and far more intimate than I should let them be.

"Thank you," I whisper, anything louder might shatter the control I have over my hands. I don't want to plunge my fingers into her hair without her permission.

Sophie's tummy shakes against mine, her breaths coming in small, short gusts. She closes her eyes and steps away. "You're welcome."

She tugs at her shirt, pulling it down, then back up when it reveals more of her chest. "I'll work on the application tonight and send it to you before I submit it." She grabs a rag and rubs at a spot on the stainless steel counter.

"Great." I plaster a smile on my face. The stoves are off but

I'm on fire. I'd even consider standing in the walk-in, velociraptor fears be damned. "Do you..." I take a deep breath. My mouth is dry. "Want me to clean up?"

She shakes her head. "I've got it," she says and without another word, slips into the walk-in.

She stole my hideout. "Okay. Bye."

I turn on my heel, my heart pounding partly from excitement but mostly from confusion. The back hallway blurs in my vision as I rush out the door. I throw myself in the car. "What the fuck was that?" I say to the dark alley outside my windshield.

I need to get a hold of this silly crush, or it'll be the only thing the cameras will pick up when we get our chance on the show.

Chapter Four

Sophie

Once I get a seat in the coffee shop near Paul's office, I peel my layers off. He's perpetually late but I arrived early enough to give myself the perception of having some control over this situation. I shove my hat and mittens into the sleeve of my coat and unwind my infinity scarf from around my neck, but that is not enough to combat the intense humidity in this corner of the shop. Even the window beside me has fogged up.

I snap a quick photo of the steam curling out of my hot drink and slap it up on social media, with some emojis instead of words for a caption. I pull my sweater over my head and when my hair and I emerge in a cloud of frizz from the green fleece, Paul stands there, across the table from me.

"Hi, Soph," he says, one hand in his pocket, the other holding a steaming mug.

"You're early," I say dumbly.

He arches one eyebrow. "You said ten."

"Yeah. It's ten. That's early for you."

He laughs quietly at my familiar ribbing, sitting in the empty chair. As he too divests himself of layers, I study him for more changes to add to the ones I clocked in his photos on social media since last week. But he moves the same way he always did, fluid, confident. Despite everything we've said to each other, he's familiar, a warm blanket, my favorite green fleece sweater.

Paul takes a small sip of his drink and nods at my own mug. "I would have bought you a cup of coffee."

"I know." I wrap my hands around the mug. Every part of me sweats except for my fingers, which are ice cold. "I asked you here. Technically, I should buy you the coffee."

"Why did you ask me here?" He always gets straight to the point and I was prepared for that until right now. Why did I ask him here?

Sweaty, nervous, forgetful. I've been like this all week. Every spare moment my mind wanders back to stand in our kitchen, chest to chest with Amy. It's why I've kept myself so busy, perfecting my plant-based poutine, preparing our audition for *Cook for Camilla*. I've even booked extra sessions with Natalie; there's not a single muscle in my body that isn't sore right now.

The casting call for Paul's new show was a relatively simple form, not unlike the one I filled out two years ago for *Pop-Up Kitchen*, still buzzing at midnight from a busy dinner service. Straightforward questions like name of business, location, type of cuisine, number of seats. The call asked for photos, video, and a link to our website, so I spent an early afternoon playing with lighting and angles, trying to find the best ways to make Amy & May's shine from my phone's camera. Most importantly the call asked for an explanation of why we wanted to be on the show and it's not like I can say, *because we think it will help us make more money*. At least not in such a direct way. But at least it was a great distraction from Amy's peachy shampoo.

Every night for the past week, I've fallen asleep dissecting that smell, the exhaustion in my body and brain never heavy enough to pull me under in peace.

I can't decide if I want to buy a bottle for myself or press my face into her collarbone again, if the smell is only that good because it's attached to her.

"Right. You see…"

"I'm sorry." He grimaces at the interruption. He slides his hand across the table but stops short of touching me. "Soph, are you okay? You seem a little…"

"A little what?"

"Not yourself."

I laugh, flex my fingers around my mug. There are inches between us, but the gulf is insurmountable. Paul's eyes are unreadable. My stomach sinks low into my yoga leggings. What if he thinks I'm here to…for…reconciliation?

"You have a new show," I say.

He tips his head to the side. From one blink to the next, his face changes, his eyes shuttered.

I think I'm going to be sick. *Oh god.* He did think I was here to reconcile. I take a deep breath, staring at a fake knot in the fake wood table.

"Maybe the producers haven't told you yet, but when Amy found out… She owns—"

He nods. "Your restaurant. I remember."

Paul counseled me through the decision to accept her offer. Ultimately it was him who got me to sign on. He'd talked up how exciting it would be to be able to build my own menu, to start from scratch. How after *Pop-Up Kitchen* it would be my opportunity to spread my wings and show the culinary community my range.

Paul wanted me to counter Amy's job offer with a proposal that included a cut of the restaurant. That's how he got his start: he bought a small percentage of a viable business, then more and more until he was majority owner. I couldn't afford it then, and he'd offered to help, but I wanted the first stakes I had in a business to be mine. Completely mine, but before this, before we started to tank, before I started to suck, it was a little pipe dream of mine, to own my own restaurant one day.

I guess out of everything, I owe him that much. He made me believe it was possible.

I burn my tongue on my fast sip of coffee. "Right." I wince. "The restaurant isn't doing great." My voice lowers to a whisper; admitting this to Paul feels like a betrayal. The type of thing Amy will twist her mouth at when she finds out, a crease forming between her eyes as she tries to remain cool and calm but fails. My chest clenches, but it's too late to shove the words back inside my mouth.

Paul moves straight into business mode. "When you first signed on you said that things were going well."

Paul frowns as he leans forward, his "thinking" position. His seriousness was one of the things I fell hard and fast for. Who am I kidding? Falling hard and fast is about the only thing I do.

Technically, relationships between the cast and crew were prohibited on the show. But everyone did it. And after meeting other reality TV cast members from other shows, I realized our show was the rule, not the exception. At least I wasn't on a dating show, where I was supposed to be falling in love with someone else when I fell in love with Paul. But between clandestine meetings and the weighted stares on set when we thought no one was looking, we were a sure thing before the first episode aired. I didn't want to trust it at first, convinced he struck up a relationship with a new cast member every season. But after some furious googling and after seeing his own sweet nervousness, I felt assured that our relationship was as extraordinary to him as it was to me.

He produced and consulted for *Pop-Up Kitchen*, having successfully started restaurants throughout New England over the past decade. His presence and tightly held control intimidated me at first, but in the long hours on set between filming, setting up lights, touching up makeup, and waiting for the asshole host to finish whatever hissy fit he was having that day, Paul was surprisingly funny, making corny jokes that only I ever seemed to laugh at. He made a point to be kind to everyone on set. I thought my crush was unrequited until we walked back to the hotel together after a late night of filming. I'd almost been kicked off that night. Paul had admitted, his voice shaking, that he wasn't supposed to have favorites, but he was so glad I was staying. He'd kissed me at my hotel room door.

I'd invited him in.

He'd said no. Our relationship had always been like that: me pushing the pace, him reining us in. Part of it was the show. He was a constant, steady and kind, and it felt like he was the only person who didn't have it out for me. But part of it is just me. I fall headfirst, eyes closed. I practically leap into love with arms wide.

He'd treated everything about us with such caution, with so much care. To say that something like my sexuality, so new that it was still fragile and paper-skinned, was a secret?

It was devastating.

"Things haven't been going so well," I say, glossing over the details. "Amy and I found out about the show, your new one, the other day and she—well, we—thought maybe we should apply. I mean, who doesn't want Camilla Vargas to eat their food, right?"

Technically, I shouldn't be starstruck at the idea, not after cooking on *Pop-Up Kitchen*, and considering all the famous people Paul has introduced me to, but even if I'm feeling a little sick about the prospect of being in front of a camera again, the idea of being in the same room as Camilla Vargas is enough to push the nerves down, for right now at least.

"I sent in our application and I wanted to give you a heads-up. I didn't know if our history completely precludes my involvement in the show. Honestly, I worry some of the producers might like the..." I gesture between us. "Tension."

I laugh because really, it's ludicrous to think that anyone would be invested in my relationship history. But then Paul sits back in his chair. He smiles awkwardly down at his hand, now curled in a fist on the lacquered wood. My stomach bypasses my yoga pants completely to sit in my boots with my sweaty feet.

"Why are you making that face?"

He sighs. "I already knew about your application."

"You knew?" My blood sours with embarrassment. "Why'd you let me blabber on?"

"I didn't know that's why you were here," he says slowly, still not looking at me.

"Why else would I be here?"

He looks out the window, sips his coffee.

Right. I'm a terrible person.

"Listen, Paul, I'm—"

This time he makes the connection between us, covering my hand with his. "It's fine," he says quietly. "You don't owe me anything, Soph. I still owe you so many apologies. I'll never forgive myself for how I handled things that night."

The espresso machine screeches and a barista calls, "Abdul, flat white." Life goes on all around us as we do one more impromptu postmortem on our relationship.

I swallow the sudden lump in my throat. There was a time I wouldn't have hesitated to cry in front of him. Paul handled crying like a pro. But I don't even know why I want to cry right now, if it's because he hurt me or because I think I've hurt him.

For a long time I thought that if he'd reacted differently that night, we'd still be together. But as I search his familiar face, the scar on his chin and the nervous tic in his right eye, I'm not sure that's true. We fell hard and fast, but maybe we burned out. Maybe we were always going to end up here, on opposite sides of the table. For months I've blamed him, but what if this is how it was meant to be?

"You're here because you want to be on the show," he states, flatly.

"I'm here because I don't want you to think I expect you to get us on the show."

He nods. "Noted. Thank you."

A man with brown skin and white-framed glasses sits at the table beside us. His outerwear spills over the booth toward me. As a unit, Paul and I turn our knees away, leaning closer to keep the rest of the world out.

"What's Camilla like?" I trace the rim of my mug with my index finger. My hands have lost a lot of fights with knives and they look like it, but the good thing about surrounding myself with people like Amy and Paul is they see it as a sign of success, of lessons learned and skills earned.

He frowns. "She's...well, she's...a great chef." A blush rises under his short beard. "Very professional."

The urge to tease him about that blush and his close proximity to culinary royalty tickles the back of my throat but I swallow it down. "She's a hero of mine. She's done so much."

"Mine too."

"You said you already knew about my application..."

Paul hums noncommittally.

"The producers are considering it?"

He sighs, smiling. "You know I can't tell you that."

"I know. I'm assuming they're going to play up the connection between us."

He laughs. "Are you already strategizing?"

"No, of course not."

"You've always been so good on camera. I was hoping that maybe you'd given thought to returning to television more permanently." Paul speaks slowly, quietly, choosing his words carefully and not quite meeting my eyes.

I can't keep the cringe off my face. "This will be a onetime thing." I'm not sure what he's talking about. I never watched my episodes of *Pop-Up Kitchen* once it aired. It was too much for my anxious heart to relive the high stress, the intrusive questions during the one-on-one interviews, and I can barely remember it anyway, the actual *cooking*. It was like once the cameras were rolling my brain turned off and all I could do was cook.

"There's a project I've got in the works. I think you'd be perfect for it," he says.

I shake my head, trying to inject my words with as much sincerity as possible. "I'm only doing this for the restaurant. Not for some foot in the door for a television career."

"We'll put a pin in it," he says.

"I'm serious, Paul. I'm no good for TV. I'm focusing on improving the kitchen."

He shakes his head, smiling ruefully. "I don't know where you've gotten it in your head that you were terrible on TV."

Oh, I don't know. Maybe it was the terrible things people said about me on *Pop-Up Kitchen* fan message boards and in my DMs. Or maybe it was the sick feeling I'd get in my stomach right before the director called *action,* or how the stress caused me to disassociate to the point that I couldn't remember what I'd done or said.

"I'm a chef. Not an actor."

His chest heaves on the kind of beleaguered sigh that reminds me we've had this conversation too many times.

"I hope this doesn't cause problems for you," I say. "If you're dating someone else or something…"

"I'm not," he says quickly. The man beside us pauses the clacking on his keyboard to peer over at us. "I'm not dating right now," he says, just for me.

We stare at each other across the small table. This is the part where I say I'm not dating anyone, either. Because I'm not. But I *am* quietly obsessed with the woman I work with and I'm afraid if I open my mouth while remembering the press of her breasts against mine, the memory will make the words sound like a lie and I'm not ready to talk to Paul about anything even remotely related to women. Especially women named Amy.

"Thanks for meeting with me," I say, my voice garbled and strained. "I know you're really busy."

Paul is quiet for so long, like he's waiting for me to look at him before he speaks again. When I finally do his smile is understanding, kind.

Paul stands, chugging the rest of his coffee in three long gulps. I follow him, untangling the sleeves of my coat from my sweater, spending far too long examining the piling on my mittens. I leave my coffee, cold and full. Paul steps into me, one hand on my hip, kissing my cheek, in the most routine way that for a second I am flashed back to eight months ago when it was exactly that. He smells like this coffee shop and the warm undercurrent of his cologne.

All I crave is a lighter, fruity scent.

"There will probably be scouts coming into Amy & May's this week," he murmurs quietly into my ear.

I pull back. "I thought you weren't allowed to say anything."

He shrugs, winks. "I didn't say a word. But one of the restaurants we'd already chosen had to pull out—some issue between the owners—and we have an empty spot so..."

If location scouts are coming to the restaurant that means we're almost assuredly going to be chosen. I squeeze his hand, smiling up at him while nerves grip me.

"Thanks, Paul."

Chapter Five

Amy

I hear her before I see her. Sophie's bubbly giggle winds its way down the hall before she pops her head around the doorway. "Do you have a sex?" she asks.

I cock my head as Sophie's face slowly morphs from friendly to shocked to horrified. Her eyes widen, her face turning a deep shade of red.

I've had plenty of crushes on women I work with, but this one is bad. Even her extreme embarrassment isn't enough to deter my overactive imagination from wondering how far down that blush goes.

"A sec? A second? Do you have a second? To speak with me. And not…no, no sex. Just seconds. Probably more than one. Do you have a few seconds?"

I close the laptop with a quiet click. "Yes. A few."

Sophie closes the door behind her, sitting in the chair tucked against the wall. She unbuttons her coat and dusts flakes of wet snow off her beanie. She keeps her eyes firmly on her knees. She could be avoiding me because of the sex-sec mishap or because my eyes still feel so hungry for her. We've been orbiting around each other for the past few days, satellites that absolutely must communicate but can under no circumstances intersect.

She's flushed. Frenetic energy rolls off her in waves. I resist the urge to feel her forehead for a temperature. After rearranging herself in the chair, feet down, then one leg up, then cross-legged, she finally stills.

"Are you done?" I ask.

She nods.

She looks like she might crack open with the lightest tap. I want to wrap her up, protect her from sharp edges and hard surfaces.

"What's up?"

"There's a good chance we're going to be chosen for *Cook for Camilla*," she says.

The fireworks and whizz-bangs going off in my brain are muted by her tepid reaction. Her mouth smiles but her voice shakes.

Holy crap. We're doing this. It's happening.

"That's great. Right?"

"Yeah." She nods fast, like she's trying to convince us both.

"Are you sure?" I'm excited. I want to jump around, pull her up with me, and scream.

She looks like she might laugh or throw up.

She breathes deeply and finally meets my eyes. "Yes. I'm sure. Just…preparing."

My brother was supposed to work for a family friend the summer after we graduated. But then Mom got sick—sicker than she already was—and he decided to stay home to take care of her. Sometimes I wonder if when we were floating around in all that amniotic fluid as fetuses, his umbilical cord got the entire supply of compassion and I got none. It's not that I'm not compassionate, that I don't care. I feel things strongly, especially for the people I love. But I also don't know how to tap into it. When people cry, I pat them on the shoulder and get the fuck out. When they're scared or sad or nervous, I fight the thing that's troubling them, and I've been informed that sometimes that's not what they need in that moment. They need compassion, a soft place to fall, not an angry girl with brass knuckles for emotions.

Wes gave his whole life over to our Mom. I think he thought if he scrubbed her puke hard enough, if he scheduled her appointments efficiently enough, if he loved her with everything, he'd keep her alive.

I couldn't do what my brother did. But I took care of all the bills. I swear Wes thought the lights stayed on because the electricity company took pity on us. I made the calls to insurance companies and had groceries delivered. In other words, I take my instinct to fight and make it easier for other people to do their jobs. To be compassionate.

I stand but she looks up at me, her eyes deep green pools big enough to fall into, and I sit my ass back down. I roll my chair toward her, stopping short of touching her.

"You're worried," I say. "About being in the spotlight again."

She rolls her eyes. "I'm certainly not under the impression that there's any kind of spotlight aimed in my direction." She gestures at herself. "Look at me."

That's the problem. I am. Sometimes she's all I can look at. Even when I close my eyes, I can see her. I shake my head to dislodge the shape of her imprinted on my eyelids.

Focus, Amy. You're a businesswoman, not a clit with a compass for hot women.

"I'm a nobody. I'm a footnote in an old season of a professional cooking show."

The back of my neck tingles, an actual bristle, at the word *nobody*.

First of all, I don't hire nobodies to run my kitchen. Second, Sophie is a talented chef. Perhaps her only fault, if it could be called that, is her lack of confidence, which seems like a recent development.

I've seen the numbers she pulls on social media. Despite Wes's assurance that likes are a vanity metric, tens of thousands of people think of Sophie as more than a footnote.

"It's just...a lot."

"All you need to focus on is the menu we're going to serve to Camilla. I'll take care of everything else."

She arches a skeptical brow. "What does 'take care of everything' entail?"

"Social media, honing skills training for our servers, general restaurant admin. I'll take care of it all."

"You mean the stuff you already take care of."

"Hollywood," I growl. "You know what I mean. Do you trust me?" I want—need—to hear her say it.

"I guess."

Womp.

"That's okay, Brunet." *Shake it off, Chambers.* "You will."

I wink and flounce out of the office. It's probably just my imagination. But I think she checks out my ass as I leave.

Chapter Six

Sophie

Attn: Amy Chambers and Sophie Brunet,

Please prepare for locations manager and team at Amy & May's, between 10am and 1pm on Sunday, February 3. Can you confirm the address and your contact information below?

Best,
Dorothea Glenn
Production Assistant—The Edible Network, North America

A plate of congealed mushroom risotto lands in front of me.

"What is this?"

"I took it to table 8. You said table 8, right?" Toby, our new expo, whispers. His dark eyes are frantic.

"Yes." I pull the chit off the receipt spike. "Mushroom risotto, table 8. Why isn't this at table 8, Toby?"

His eyes widen and a deep blush covers his face. He tucks a strand of hair that's fallen from his ponytail behind his ear. "They said they didn't order the risotto." His whispers come more and more frantically.

"Again?"

"Again. They said they ordered the special, the…the…" He looks up like the guests' order will be written on the ceiling. "Crab cakes and prime rib." He grins, pleased with himself, except the risotto—one of my additions to this menu—still sits here, quickly cooling on my expo counter. I was considering it as a potential dish to serve Camilla—*if* we get on the show—but how am I possibly supposed to test this recipe if I can't get it out to guests on time and at temperature?

"Crab cakes are here, chef." Jameela, my new sous-chef, slides the plate to me and I wipe a cloth around the edge of the hot dish, squeezing chipotle-mango puree in an arc around the side. Table 8's prime rib has already been sitting under a lamp for half a minute.

"Here. Take these to 8. I'll figure this out."

I need to be on the range. Jameela is a fantastic replacement for Chad, skilled and capable with zero harassment, but she's only been here a week. It's unfair of me to ask her to run this kitchen without its leader, but today is Toby's first day and there was no one to train him. Amy is slammed at the hostess stand with Maggie. Which is good. We're not busy, per se, but we're busier. Busier than we have been. Busier is good. Busier means money. Except busier is only going to last for so long if we can't get our food out to the right tables. I scan the seating chart for the third time tonight because thrice Toby has brought food back. Once I was willing to chalk it up to first day jitters, but now I feel like I'm being punked.

"What the…" I scrunch my eyes closed and try again, glancing between the chart and tables in the dining room. Real patrons and two-dimensional tables and food swim behind my closed eyes but when I open them again, I finally see the issue.

I rip the seating chart off the counter and hold it up in front of my kitchen staff. "Who did this?" I hiss.

I am not a yeller. I hate head chefs who can't keep their cool in the kitchen. Dinner service is tough enough without an emotionally stunted anger management dropout stomping around, spraying spittle everywhere.

The open concept kitchen keeps everyone's behavior in check. Kitchens in general can be loud and aggressive places. We don't need our guests to witness back of the house dirty laundry. But this is my kitchen, goddamnit. And no one messes with my kitchen's ability to produce good food on time.

"Who did what, chef?" Carly asks. The whole team is looking at me like I've lost my damn mind.

I take a deep breath, the kind Natalie would tell me to take before I'm about to lift something that weighs more than me. "Jameela. Can you please make another mushroom risotto on the fly?"

"Yes, chef." Bless all sous-chefs not named Chad.

"Thank you, Jameela." I turn back to Carly. "Who's been messing with our seating chart?"

Carly looks at the floor. Three prep chefs avoid my eyes.

"Someone answer me," I say slowly.

"Amy," Carly says quietly. "Amy said she told you this morning that she was adding three new two-tops."

My scalp prickles, hot with embarrassment.

"And she asked you to make sure the chart reflected the change." The poor girl winces. I would too if I had to correct my fool of a boss.

I close my eyes and let my head drop back. More than anything I want to take my hair out of this bonnet and rip the buttons open on this jacket. I'm hot and tired and frustrated. I just want this night to be over.

But it's only 8pm. We have at least two more hours of service left. Chastened, I go out to what was formerly table 8 and let them know their risotto is on its way. I comp the plate when I get back to the kitchen.

After a quick inventory of the rest of the team, everyone seems to have pulled themselves out of the weeds. It's me, just me, dragging this team down. I slip into the freezer. The cold prickles at the sweat at the base of my neck. I fight the urge to pull my hands into the sleeves of my coat and walk deeper into the freezer, all the way to the back. It's not even that much colder back here. It just seems that way. The cool air makes its way into my lungs, burns at the tip of my nose and lips.

The walk-in is my safe haven. The perfect place to collect my thoughts, hit reset. I need a reset tonight.

Carly is right. Amy did tell me about the changes to the seating chart. She told me that the servers have been upselling the crab cakes and our second most expensive bottle of red wine all week. And she told me about her new social media schedule: daily photos and videos that require her to walk into my kitchen and hover over me while I work. She's giving me *Pop-Up Kitchen* flashbacks when the cameras would get in close during a stressful cook. It's what she was doing this morning when she told me about the new two-tops, taking photos, styling the photo and *me*, yammering excitedly about the email we found in our inbox this morning, informing rather than asking about location scouting.

That was enough to make me feel sick to my stomach. Until she'd tucked some of my hair behind my ear.

"So we can see your face," she'd said, and my heart had exploded; one touch from her and suddenly I couldn't control my beats per minute. Her fingertip slid along the length of my hairline, over my temple, and I felt it *everywhere*. Along my jaw, against the pulse point in my throat. My nipples, between my legs.

Forget emails, forget dinner services.

"You're a mess," I say, my breath a cloud in front of me.

"Hollywood."

I whip around. Amy stands in the doorway.

"What are you doing?"

"We need to talk," I say.

She steps farther into the freezer but keeps the door open, her arm stretched out behind her. The sounds of the kitchen filter into my quiet, cold hiding place. I wish she'd let the door close behind her. If we were alone in here together, I could unleash on her. All this frustration with her changes, not a single one that she's run by me. She only tells me about them after the fact. But my biggest frustration is with myself, not her; she's just the trigger. I'm frustrated that I'm a mess of hormones and panic around her. I'm a little scared, too. If I unleashed on her would I yell? Or would I do something else?

Something I can't take back?

The thought, a flash of her skin, slick and sweaty against mine, erases the freezer-therapy. I'm so goddamned hot. I pull at my chef's jacket again.

"Talk about what?" she asks.

I close my eyes. "After," I say. "We'll talk after." I brush past her, trying my best not to touch her but, still, somehow, I'm wrapped up in her heat.

The first thing I do is change the seating chart. Then I open my email app.

Address and contact info confirmed. We'll see you tomorrow.

I guess we're doing this. I tighten the black bonnet around my hair, straighten my jacket, and get back to work.

My body is tired after dinner service, but my mind is like one of those online recipes with a rambling introduction and too many ads and pop-ups. I splash cold water on my face, trying to get my arguments straight. In high school, my guidance counselor told me that using *I feel* statements were an efficient way of communicating during conflict.

When you make changes to the restaurant without consulting me, I feel like you don't care about my contributions.

When you make these changes while I'm busy trying to do things like train new staff, I feel like I can't give our new sous-chef the attention she deserves.

When you wear that blouse, I feel sexually frustrated.

My arguments need work.

The restaurant is almost empty when I walk out of the staff room. Amy is going over the receipts with Maggie, so I pour myself two fingers of whiskey at the bar. I don't even like whiskey that much. The burn is all I crave.

"Good night, Sophie," Maggie calls, pulling her coat on.

"Thanks, Maggie. Good night."

Amy locks the door behind her, turns off the dining room lights, and pulls the shades down in the front window. The restaurant fills with the *whoosh-whoosh* sound of the blacked-out fabric covering the windows.

She follows me back into the kitchen without another word. I perch against the chef's table. If we ever used it, our guests would sit on the other side, technically outside of the kitchen but looking in on everything that happens. But we've never had someone reserve the table and I can't help but think maybe it's me. Maybe no one wants to watch *me* cook.

Amy stands on the other side of the counter, her back straight and feet planted. It always seems to come down to this, the two of us facing off in this kitchen.

Her hair, curled tonight, falls in her eyes. She's wearing that shirt. My favorite shirt. It drapes perfectly, as if it was made specifically for her.

Maybe she got it tailored. Maybe she just has the perfect

sample body. Maybe Amy would look good in an oversize T-shirt or a parka. Maybe it's not the shirt at all.

Maybe it's Amy.

"What are we talking about?" she asks.

The problem with confronting my attraction to women at thirty-one years old is I've had no opportunities to experiment with it. There's been no flirtation, not with any kind of intent. There's been no chance to kiss, to touch. There was some testing the waters in my twenties, the kind that I'd think about for hours after. Those nights were often lubricated by vodka and the excuse of performing for some male friend's gaze and satisfaction. But really, they were always, secretly, for me.

Now Amy stands here, and even though she isn't mine—she's my boss, my business partner for lack of a better term, whom I kind of want to strangle sometimes—it feels like she's all for me, too. She meets my gaze without hesitation, with pride. Her chin tipped up, ready to fight. A tremor rolls through me, and I know with sudden clarity that as much as I want to fight with her, I want to burn my tongue on this woman, too.

"These changes," I say, my voice catching in my dry throat. "I can't keep up."

Maybe that's what I need. To burn out on Amy. To step fully into these feelings, into myself. Maybe that's what will help me to take back some control of my life and my kitchen.

She frowns. "I told you that I'd do this. I said you need to worry about the menu we serve to Camilla Vargas. I'll take care of the rest."

"Amy, we don't even know if we're going to make it onto the show. Why do all this if nothing comes of it?"

"The location scouts are coming in tomorrow," she says, like that means something.

I close my eyes. My lids are sandpaper. "Scouts are not enough of a guarantee for you to be fucking with my kitchen."

She narrows her eyes. "I'm fucking with *your* kitchen?"

I stand straighter. "Yes. My kitchen. You made a last-minute change to our seating chart. We didn't have enough time to prepare."

"I told you about it this morning." She looks like she might want to strangle me, and I don't know what it says about me that I'd be okay with the feel of her fingers against my throat, pressing into my pulse, my jaw.

"I'm saying that this morning isn't enough time. I had to comp a meal tonight."

"What I'm really hearing is *you're* fucked. Not the kitchen." She folds her arms over her chest.

Instead of answering her, I take another sip of whiskey. The amber liquid is an almost perfect match for the color of her eyes. Traitorous alcohol.

"This isn't working," I say quietly, the fight deflating me. My list of frustrations burning off my tongue with the eighty-proof.

She releases a frustrated breath; it sounds so bitchy I could scream. "It could work if you just—"

Apparently, the only thing my fight needed was another dose of Amy's attitude. "No 'if I just'! There is no 'if I just'!"

Despite having known Amy for less than a year, fighting with her feels like something I've done before. It's not particularly enjoyable but it's been like this with her from the beginning, this layer of comfort that we share with each other. I could say just about anything to her and she could say anything to me.

I lied when I said I didn't trust her. You can only fight like this with someone you trust. Which is the only explanation for why I say, "If *you* would just listen to me when I tell you how I want to run my kitchen, and if you just stopped *distracting* me—" My growl fades between us.

She blinks, rearing her head back like I've slapped her. As if she isn't acutely aware of how I turn into a disaster around her.

"With your..." I point wildly at her, my hand still clutching the tumbler glass. "Peach body spray. Yeah. I know it's from Victoria's Secret. I looked it up."

Amy uncrosses her arms, a dimple peeking out of her cheek, and I forget to be embarrassed. I forget everything except how overwhelming her presence is.

"What else?"

"Pardon me?"

Kitchens are not supposed to be this hot when the stoves are cold, and the dinner rush is long over. So why is my skin on fire? I pop the last two buttons on my chef's jacket. Amy's eyes bounce from my face, down. I untie the bonnet, pulling it off my head and letting it fall to the table. I yank the elastic band out of my ponytail and scrunch my fingers into my hair. I bite my lip to stop the moan from escaping as my scalp screams in relief from the heavy weight of my updo.

"Well? What else?" she asks.

"What else what?"

"What else am I doing to distract you?"

Amy is long and lean. She towers over me as she flicks a curl out of her eyes with the cool twist of her head.

What am I doing? God, what the fuck am I doing?

"You know what you're doing."

When Amy laughs she always sounds a little caustic. She throws her head back, her jaw sharp like that laugh. "I really fucking don't, Hollywood."

I've always hated lobster, cooking them specifically. To throw a live animal in a pot, boil it alive, it knows it's drowning in a pool of fire and it can't do anything to save itself. That's where I am right now, drowning in a pool of fire, flinging the blame at her to try to save myself. It's time to face the music and let myself burn.

"I'm sorry." I set my whiskey down. "This isn't your fault. It's mine. I lied."

A look of shock passes over her features before she shutters them completely. "You don't want to do the show anymore," she says, like she was expecting this.

"No. Not at all. I'll still do the show, *if* they want us." I look down at my black Converse. "I told you that I would tell you things. When I'm feeling… I told you I would be honest. And I'm not being honest."

"You can tell me anything, Sophie." I've never heard Amy sound so pillow soft before. It's her tenderness that gives me the courage to confront it.

I like women. I'm attracted to women. I'm attracted to you. Four words. Simple, true words. But I've never said them to a woman before. They're a truth that hasn't existed outside of myself and it doesn't matter how true they are, they're terrifying.

The words can't get past my throat, where my heart beats harder than ever. I close the distance between us with two short steps. Touch her the same close way she touched me the last time we were facing off in the kitchen, my hands on her forearms, my breasts brushing hers.

Amy holds herself so still. She'd be a statue if it weren't for her fast breaths and her pulse thrumming below her jaw. Her lips part, I tip my chin up. All she'd have to do is bend, an inch and I'd be kissing Amy Chambers.

"You've been drinking," she says, barely a whisper. Of all the possible objections she could have, she's chosen my sobriety.

I shake my head, a lock of hair sticks to my lip. "Only two sips. I'm not drunk. I promise."

Slowly, like she's afraid she'll scare me, she lifts her hand, brushes my hair off my mouth with the pad of her finger.

"You're queer." She doesn't ask.

"I'm…" My heart beats so hard I could choke on it. "I want you." And maybe if we do this I can get it out of my head. I can't keep blaming her for my infatuation.

"Did you ever think about if I want you?" she asks in a flash of teeth, sharp.

An immediate blush crawls up my face. "Oh god." I step back. "I'm sorry. I'm so sorry. Last week." I recalibrate that moment between us, the seconds that felt like forever when I was so close to her, I was holding her exhales in my mouth. Just like in my youth, I obsessed over that moment when in truth it probably meant nothing to her. "I thought…maybe you…"

She grins, her mouth morphing from something I could cut myself on to something I want to fall into. "Come here. Of course, I want you."

She plunges her hand into my hair, closing the gap between us, and she kisses me. Just like that, like kissing me is the natural conclusion to this, a fight about seating charts. She kisses me like she has no idea that this kiss feels like my first one because in a way it is. My first kiss when I know who I am, better than I ever have before.

Her lips are warm and soft. Her fingers sift through my hair, her nails scratch softly over my scalp.

I'm an implosion. A series of powder kegs igniting inside me, until I'm nothing but blood and heat and heart.

A moan cuts through the thumping in my ears. Me. I'm moaning against Amy's mouth, and she smiles into her next kiss. Opens my lips wider with her own. Her tongue brushes mine.

"Holy fuck." I barely recognize the sound of my own voice.

"You're shaking," she says. My fingers tremble against her jaw.

"I…" I'm dizzy. The room spins with my lust but as long as I'm holding on to her, I know I'll be okay. "I really like kissing you."

I pull her mouth back to mine, not giving her a chance to respond. But my legs really are shaking, lust or not, so I walk backward until my ass hits the chef's table again, spreading my legs so her hips fit between my thighs. My pulse throbs in the tips of my fingers, in my breasts. If she brushed the knuckle of her index finger along the seam of my panties a few times, I'm sure she could get me off. That's all it would take.

Suddenly, it is absolutely necessary that she do that. Now that I've felt what it's like to kiss her, I can't go another day without knowing what it's like to come for her.

"Is this okay?" I ask, my fingers brushing her collarbone, down the soft plane of her sternum.

Amy looks down at me like she's seeing me for the first time. "Shouldn't I be asking you that?"

I shake my head. "I want this. I've wanted this for too long."

"Sometimes I think you hate me," she whispers.

"God, no. I want to scream into a pillow because of you sometimes, but…"

She laughs and the husky sound vibrates against my hands, reminding me of where we are. "Is this okay?" I ask again.

She nods, her hands never stop moving, through my hair, against my temple, my jaw.

The blouse is held together by a set of small snap buttons, discreetly sewn into the hem. Gently, I pop each one to reveal the delicate white lace of her bralette. Amy's breasts are small, her rosy nipples just visible through the webbing of the fabric. It's so much, too much. I'm a deer in headlights. Now that I have what I want in front of me, I have no clue what to do.

I trace the loose triangle of the fabric and goose bumps follow my path like contrails in the sky.

"Wait." She gathers my hand in hers. "Have you done this before?"

"Yes," I say, too fast to be believable. "I've…fooled around with women."

She arches an eyebrow.

"I'm bi," I say. "But I've never been with a woman like *this* before. On purpose. For me." I glance up at her. "As if that makes any sense to you."

Amy does everything on purpose.

"It makes sense." She rests her hand on my chest, her finger hooked over my collarbone. "But if this is your first time, I think I should get to direct the play."

A girlish giggle escapes me. "We can do whatever you want. But." I can't meet her eyes. "I don't know how good I'll be at making you feel…good."

She tips up my chin. "This makes me feel good," she says into another kiss. Amy presses in closer, cupping my jaw, trailing her fingers down my throat. "Making you feel good makes me feel good."

I shudder as she pushes my chef's jacket off my shoulders. She peppers kisses over my bare shoulder, pulling the thin straps of my tank and bra down slowly. For years I've toyed with the idea of touching women I meet, kissing the smiley barista in the alley behind my favorite coffee shop or pushing the nerdy tour guide against the wall down a quiet museum hallway on vacation. But for the last few months, lying in bed at night or daydreaming on the way to work, my head has been filled with Amy. I've mapped out this woman's body. Decided, step by step, what I'd want to do, in what order.

Like a recipe.

It was a natural instinct, how I make sense of the world.

Start my base with kisses, gentle touches. Take it slow, experiment to see what works and what doesn't. Taste. Always, always taste. Her lips, her skin, whatever she'll let me put my mouth on. Create balance, pleasure with a sharp bite of pain. Excess with the need of wanting more.

In my mind, I've lost myself in her. I've imagined her gasps and her screams and felt her fingernails dig into my skin. I've heard her beg me.

But in reality, I sit on our chef's table and let Amy undress me, totally overwhelmed that I am here, that this is happening. It's happening. To me, only for me; for me and her. Not for the gaze of someone else, not under the guise of a wild night. For the first time in my life I'm doing something I never thought I'd be able to do.

Amy's holds my breasts in her hands, staring at me like I am something beautiful. I press against the table, my head falling back. An invitation for her to go further. If this doesn't work, I'll skip straight to begging.

"I'm going to take this off," she says. She doesn't ask, but she's not bossy, either. Her voice is reverential.

"Yes." I reach back to unfasten my bra and meet her hands. She smiles, wolfish. "I've got it."

Each new step, every piece of clothing removed, every act ticked off a list I made a long time ago, takes my breath away. Amps up my excitement. I'm so wet it's embarrassing.

She draws my bra straps down my arms. My bra left red marks over my skin. She rubs them with her thumb, kisses them, avoiding my nipples until they're peaked and tight. I'm panting, my shoulders thrown back. I whine for her.

She brushes her thumb over my nipple and I grunt with frustration and want.

I gasp. "Please."

"Please what?" she murmurs into my neck.

"Kiss me."

She places a slow, open-mouthed kiss to my pulse point. I growl because that's *not* what I meant, and she laughs. Lifting my breasts up, together, she doesn't look away as she wraps her lips around my nipple, sucking the bud into her mouth. I cry out, anchor my hand in her hair. She moves back and forth between my breasts, licking and sucking until I'm shaking. She pushes my legs apart, the seams of my pants straining. She could rip them open, rip me open, and I'd thank her.

Her hand lands on my belly, just above the waist of my stretchy work slacks. A perfect match for my underwear underneath made for comfort and not the seduction of my business partner.

She kisses between my breasts. "Why are we doing this?" she asks.

I frown, trying to understand the question.

We're doing this because it feels good. We're doing this because it feels right, doesn't it feel right? The inevitable conclusion to months of frustration and infrequent moments of alliance.

"Because...because..." I close my eyes. In the dark, her hands ground me. Just feeling, not seeing, I can think. My heart steadies. I open my eyes. "Because I want you. And I think you want me, too. And whatever happens after this, we'll be okay. We're still partners, Amy. We'll always be partners first."

I hold her jaw gently, press my palm gently to her throat. She closes her eyes, sighing.

And just like that she pops the button on my pants.

Without thought, I giggle. This is happening. It's *been* happening but I keep forgetting it's real and now, I think, Amy Chambers is going to fuck me.

"Are you going to fuck me now?"

Spoilers. I need to know what's next.

"If you want me to."

I nod. "I do."

She tugs at my pants and I lift my hips. "I do too."

She drops them in a ball of fabric on the floor between us. I prepare a speech for how dowdy my underwear is. The faded black cotton. The high-waist, high-leg cut doesn't look as sexy on me as it does on the model. I'm about to have my first sapphic experience in granny panties.

But the words die on my tongue as she holds my legs open further with her knees. She trails her knuckle, just like I imagined, down the fabric between my thighs. Lightly, just enough to feel the pressure against my clit and to feel how wet I am.

"Is this for me?" she whispers. She slips her hand into my underwear, rubbing two fingers over my lips.

I nod. "Yes." I gasp.

Torturously slow, she slips one finger between my folds and stops with the pad of her finger on my clit. I cry out, even this light pressure pushes me to the edge. I'm wanton, hyperventilating from the lightest touch.

"Breathe," she whispers, moving her hand from between my legs to flatten her palm against my lower abdomen.

"I'm sorry." I laugh softly. "Everything feels like the first time again. I'm a mess."

"It's kind of flattering," she assures me. "But how about we focus on just one thing."

"What's that?" I rest my hand low on her hip, my fingers toying with the back pocket of her slacks. She's still completely clothed, only her blouse gapes open, teasing me with her lace bralette, the soft swell of her breasts.

She drops her hand again between my legs, slipping under my panties, and slides one finger inside me, slow and all the way to the knuckle. My eyes fall closed.

"You coming," she says.

I nod. "Yes. Yes, let's focus on that."

She moves her finger inside me, over me, painting my lips with my own wetness. The pleasure has simmered below the surface of my skin for so long that her cursory touches are magnified. I grab at her, pulling her closer to me, covering her mouth with mine, feeding her my every moan and gasp. I slip my hand into the gap in her blouse. Her nipple pebbles through the lace, the softness of the fabric at total odds with the sure way she touches me. My hips move, matching the rhythm of the slow, fierce way she fucks me. The kitchen fills with the sounds of my whimpers but Amy is surprisingly quiet for a woman who has always been able to come up with a ready response to an out of line client.

"Amy." I think I'm begging. Her thumb moves over my clit again and again, her finger in me, but now that I'm putty in her hands I can't do it. I can't come. "Amy, please."

I slip my hand beneath her bra. Her skin is hot beneath my palm. I kiss her sternum. "Please," I whisper into her skin. "Oh god, please."

She pulls her hands away so suddenly it takes me long seconds to realize it, to stop kissing her. "What are you doing? Why'd you stop?"

She tugs at her hair. "Stand up." She pulls me up by my hips. "Wh-what?"

"I really do distract you." She sounds smug.

"I… It's just…this is my first time," I mutter as she turns me around and places my hands flat on the table.

"Whatever you say, Hollywood." And then, in my ear, "Don't move."

Amy palms one of my breasts. Her soft pink nail polish looks obscene gripping me, the dusky rose of my nipples peeking through her fingers. She draws her other hand between my breasts, over the swell of my stomach, beneath my underwear. The vision of the black cotton stretched over her hand might be burned into the tender skin behind my eyelids for the rest of my life.

In this position I can't touch her, can't see. I can only feel where every part of her is pushed up against me. And hear her quiet encouragements, bordering on commands, in my ear.

"You're so wet for me, Hollywood."

"I bet you taste like honey."

"You come like a dream, I just know it."

"You can do it, Sophie. You're going to come so hard on my hand, Sophie. I can feel it."

Her petting becomes faster, tighter. "I want to," I promise. "I want to so bad."

A tear falls down my cheek.

"Do it, beautiful girl." Teeth press into my skin, the tender spot where it meets the shoulder. The wave of pleasure finally crests. I shout something unintelligible. Barely words. My fingernails scratch against the wood, searching for purchase as my legs shake and I come. I gush over her hand, the insides of my thighs painted with all of this pleasure that belongs to her.

"You did good." She kisses my temple. Vaguely, I acknowledge I might be hurting her with how tightly I grip her wrist, but I can't make my muscles release.

"You did so good, Sophie."

From anyone else that would sound like a condescending line. But from Amy, I only want to hear her say it again and again.

The chef's table looks fine. Completely normal, really. No one would know that I just had *sex* here. In my *professional* kitchen.

"We're going to get shut down," I mutter, buttoning up

my jacket because sure, that will save this tableau of health code violations.

Amy walks out of the back hallway, her face flushed but her blouse also rebuttoned.

"We should…" I make a wiping motion.

She nods. "I'll take care of it." She stops out of my reach and closing the distance between us feels too vulnerable. It says too much.

"How do you feel?" she asks.

I take stock. "Amazing, actually. But…" I gesture at her. At her extreme lack of orgasm.

"I'm fine."

"Oh." Fine. Fine. What a terrible word fine is, to leave a lover feeling *fine*.

"Amy, I…"

She shakes her head, smiles. "We're partners, right? And it's not like two industry workers haven't hooked up before."

I touch my palm to where my pulse beats hard against my throat. "Right. Partners. You're the owner and I'm the chef. We run a restaurant together." I've hooked up with plenty of front and back house staff in my younger days. I want to say that now, as if to prove that I'm okay. I can handle this.

"And now you won't feel distracted," she says, matter-of-fact.

I can't believe I called her a distraction. "What about you?" I ask.

She shrugs. Her face is remote. Pleasant, friendly, but miles away. I don't know what I thought the aftermath of all this would be. But it wasn't this. Finally having the chance to kiss her, touch her, felt like validation. The look on her face, though, that feels wrong.

"Me?" She takes a deep breath, tucking a curl behind her ear and looking away. "I wasn't distracted at all."

Chapter Seven

Amy

I need as much darkness as possible when I sleep. After busy nights, when emotions run high, I'm too amped to rest any other way. But last night I forgot to draw my blackout blinds, too distracted by Sophie's taste still lingering on my tongue, and once I was in bed it helped to watch the moon move across the sky. Sort of like when I've had too much to drink and have to stick one leg out of bed to ground myself to the floor while the world spins. I needed grounding after last night.

Now the morning sun bakes my forearm and the side of my face as I lounge in bed, and despite getting UV radiation directly into my retinas I'm the sleepiest I've been all night. Sleep was restless and unsatisfying even after I got myself off, biting my pillow and hearing Sophie's short, surprised gasps as she came.

My grumbling stomach is the only thing that can pull me out of this sunbeam and into the kitchen. When my brother and I moved out of our mom's house after she died, the most important feature I looked for in my new home was a good kitchen. I ended up with a bachelor apartment with almost half of the floorplan devoted to cooking space. I need to air out my linens a lot but it's worth it to be able to make big breakfasts in the morning.

Soon my seven hundred and fifty square feet are filled with the sound of sizzling bacon as I chop vegetables and grate cheese for my omelet. The day doesn't feel like it's ready to start until my stomach is full and satisfied. I could eat breakfast food for every meal. Ironic since my own restaurant doesn't serve breakfast or brunch. That would require me to get up too early for work and I'd miss the opportunity to make this myself.

Cooking breakfast is a meditation. A chance to review the past day and to prepare for what's to come. But this morning my only mantra is Sophie, the smell of her, her taste. The hopeful way she smiled at me when I came out of the bathroom last night, and how it seemed completely normal to want to rip my heart out of my chest and put it in her hands for safekeeping as long as it meant she'd always smile at me like that. The sickness in my stomach as she left, looking as confused as I felt, though likely for a wildly different reason.

I eat, not letting myself ruminate on the hurt on her face when I acted as if she doesn't distract me at all.

The location scouts come today.

I have no clue what they're scouting for, but I want the restaurant to look its best. I'm not as excited as I thought I'd be, though. Sophie's warning rings loudly in my head. How my privacy won't be my own and the producers might exploit something like my identity for the sake of the show. It tarnishes the shine.

I clean up and wash the dishes, then fill my watering can.

"What do I do?" I ask Hazel, my string of pearls succulent, and I don't know if I'm asking about the knot in my stomach, about the show or Sophie. I move to my next plant, a little morning glory working its way up a trellis I fashioned out of skewers. This ritual is like the moon last night, grounding me against this dizzy, nauseated feeling, filling me fuller than breakfast did.

"The thing is, Fern." I trim dead leaves from the sword fern that was my mother's. "Sophie is a new baby queer." My plants have never responded to me—thank god—but they've grown bigger, thrived because of these conversations. It's a mutually beneficial arrangement. I get to barf my feelings all over an impartial third party who can't tell anyone, and they get great care.

"And from the way she was looking at me, last night was not enough of a distraction. But she should spread her wings. There's a whole world of people out there," I say quietly. I would know. I've slept with a lot of the queer ones.

"Would I have loved to bring her back here and lay her out on the bed and take my time with her? Obviously," I tell the snake plant Wes gave me as a moving gift. My stomach drops again, that sick feeling returning. "It's better that I bow out," I say. "She deserves someone who can spend all their time on her. I've got distractions of my own."

The plants don't respond. Which is still good. But this is the first time that I kind of wish someone had heard me. More than anything, I wish my mom—the eternal optimist—would remind me gently that if anyone could understand my distractions, the crazy hours, the way I absolutely saturate myself in work, it would be Sophie.

"It's not normal to feel sick about someone," I mutter. If talking about her feels this way that's a sign that this should be just a onetime thing.

No one has ever made me feel sick before.

My standard work uniform consists of dark slacks and a white blouse, while the servers get to wear whatever they like as long as it's black or mostly black. But today I find myself lingering in front of my closet. I want to wear something nice for the scouts. But it wouldn't be for them. That's just what I'd tell myself. It would be for her, and I'm not supposed to be doing anything special for Sophie other than giving her the chance to explore what it means to be queer.

I shove my feet through the legs of my blackest pants and angrily tie the neck bow on a silk blouse I hardly ever wear. It's easily my most femme piece of clothing. Part of me is tempted to wear that blouse Sophie hates to love, but it still smells like her and the combination of that plus the way her nose crinkles when she's mad (and she'll undoubtedly be mad if I wear it) might do me in before the scouts even arrive.

I listen to an audiobook on the drive into work, but I'll have to rewind on the way home. I don't hear a word. It's just a churning stomach and an endless loop of worry about will we get chosen and what it will mean if we are chosen and will being chosen be enough for us to dig out of this hole and always the tug, low in my belly, reminding me that when it comes to my head chef I can't think clearly.

I turn off the security alarm and flick on the lights, my footsteps echoing through the empty restaurant. I cleaned the table last night, wiped it down with cleaner, and even rummaged through our broom closet for wood polish. But in the harsh light of mid-morning it needs another wipe down. Are those fingerprints glinting in the high polished reflection? Better not risk it. I spray our house-made cleaner all over the table, wiping it down in long, slow sweeps.

Once I kissed another server after hours in the back booth at my first job. As assistant manager at my next restaurant, I had an extensive "friends with benefits" relationship with a bartender with a tongue ring. The furthest we went in the restaurant was a make-out session in the staff room. I have never had sex in a restaurant, in a kitchen no less.

That was stupid. But then, Sophie makes me feel kind of stupid. I never should have lied. Of course she distracts me.

Hiring her was stupid of me. She's talented, she could have hitched herself to a bigger kitchen, a better one with more money, but she chose to partner with me. Amy & May's holds her back, even if it's worked out better for me than I could have imagined.

That's how Sophie finds me, wiping furiously at the place where I made her come last night.

"I thought you said you were going to clean up."

"I did." I'm breathless from all the physical exertion of destroying evidence. "I am."

Her hair is still a bit wet, hanging loose around her shoulders.

"Were you at the gym?"

The strength in her arms and legs as she braced herself against the table last night, the quivering in her thighs and stomach. She was beautiful.

"Yes," she says slowly. "Why do you ask?"

I shake my head. "No reason." That sick feeling is back and as she frowns at me, then launches into an explanation of what to expect from the location scouts, the feeling morphs. Like oil spilling, slick and warm through my limbs.

"They'll be checking out the general aesthetic of the space, logistics for shooting like lighting and parking crew trucks, that kind of stuff." She drops her bag on the table and passes me to pour herself a glass of water.

The simple act of Sophie walking toward me sends my heart pounding. And as that irrepressible warmth reaches the ends of my fingers and the tips of my toes, I know this isn't sickness. This isn't nausea. It's butterflies.

I have butterflies for Sophie Brunet.

"Oh shit."

"Are you feeling all right?" she asks. Water glistens on her lower lip. I can't decide what I'd rather do: lick it off or *be* that drop of water.

Ohhhhhh shit. "I am a truly useless lesbian."

"What?"

"Nothing," I say quickly. "I feel fine. Thanks."

She looks like she doesn't believe me. "Listen," she says after a moment. "I think we should talk..."

That's the last thing we should do. I need to go sit in front of Mom's house. I need to talk to my brother. I need to go back to bed. I do not need to talk to Sophie about last night and the feelings that may or may not be forming because of it.

God, I'm worse than my brother. He went and fell head over heels for his boss. Now my chest feels all mushy for my head chef. The Chambers kids really need to expand their dating pools.

"What's there to talk about?" My voice goes shrill. I can't look her in the eye. I'm sweating.

She folds her arms over her chest and absolutely glowers at me. If this were over our kitchen, some fight about who to hire or if we need to stay open an hour later, I'd set my hands on my hips and prepare to face off. But I'm not a talker. I'm a fixer. A doer. Talking is how I ruin things. Talking and, apparently, fucking.

"I don't know. How about this?" She points at the table. We should just get rid of the damn thing. Whose terrible idea was a chef's table anyway?

Probably mine.

"We should be preparing for the scouts to come." I leave the kitchen, her eyes boring holes into the back of my head, and pull up the blinds. On the other side of the window, a handsome white guy with laugh lines around his eyes and a trendy scarf and jacket combo stands on the sidewalk. He jumps back, having been caught trying to peek through the window. He smiles and waves as more people join him on the sidewalk.

Sophie rushes past me and unlocks the front door. "You're here, too." She sounds as nervous as I did moments ago.

"I thought I'd join the crew. I realized I'd never seen Amy & May's in person."

His voice, of all things, triggers the memory. He's called before, during a dinner service, but that was months ago, well before he and Sophie broke up.

"This is Amy. Amy, this is my…" Sophie stutters over her introduction, her cheeks turning red. I'm sure she meant to finish that sentence with *fiancé*. "He's…"

"The producer," I offer. "Nice to meet you."

Paul laughs amiably, and if Sophie keeps looking at me like I'm made of sunshine for that save I'm going to have to kiss her in front of her ex-fiancé-producer and I'd prefer not to give the straights a show today.

I shrug. "Now what?"

She narrows her eyes, the look reminding me that we were in the middle of a conversation. Rather, she wanted to be in the middle of a conversation.

Sophie spins on her heel. "I'm Sophie Brunet." She introduces herself to everyone in the crew, shaking hands and smiling like she hadn't just emotionally backed me into a corner. "Shall we?"

The crew, three guys with cameras and what look like meters for measuring EMF readings in an episode of *Ghost Hunters*, follow her like obedient baby ducklings. Sophie stands in the middle of the dining room, describing the layout and how many guests we expect on our busy days, Thursday to Sunday. She transforms into the head chef that can wrangle a kitchen of misfits into a team excelling at their craft.

"She's got something special, doesn't she?"

I jump, not realizing that Paul has been standing beside me this whole time.

"Yup."

"She's made for this," he says. Maybe the reason I never noticed him is because, like me, he hasn't taken his eyes off her.

"A chef?" I ask.

His smile flattens and he hums. The sick feeling I get this time is real. He didn't mean chef. If not chef, what else could Sophie be made for? I look back at her where she peers over the shoulder of a photographer, studying something on his camera's screen.

This? *This.* Television? Does Paul mean she should be a producer? Paul hasn't stopped staring at Sophie.

He's still in love with her. He consumes her with his eyes, and a slick surge of jealousy unfurls in my belly. As if I have any right to her. And yet, I want to scream at him, *she was coming on my hand last night.*

Stupid.

"I'll just…" I point at Sophie, but he barely acknowledges me, looking at her like she saves birds and woodland creatures. *I'm just going to get away from your Disney prince energy, sir.*

"Hey." These are my only pair of dress pants with pockets, and I slide my hands into them now so I won't bite my fingernails.

Sophie ignores me, watching the crew move around the kitchen. From their conversation it seems this space will be the hardest to light for television. I reach for a container that's been shoved aside by some of the crew's equipment. My arm brushes against the side of her breast and Sophie freezes, halfway through a breath. Her eyes widen but she doesn't say a word. Touching her is like putting my tongue to a live wire, thrilling and dangerous.

"They seem eager," I say.

She shrugs, folding her arms.

"You have a…" Slowly, I press my pinky finger into the delicate skin beneath her eye. "Eyelash." I hold up my finger. "Make a wish."

My heart thunders from this small contact, muscle memory of what touching her last night meant. In the little bit of space between us it's a wonder she can't hear it. Sophie narrows her eyes.

"You want to throttle me, don't you?" I whisper.

Her own pulse thrums under her jaw and it's a relief to know I'm not the only one.

"You," she says, her voice tight and controlled. "Are an asshole." The last word devolves into a growl. Nothing like the breathless whisper I was going for.

With that she walks away, seamlessly transitioning back to a professional chef answering a crewmember's question. My face burns with embarrassment. This is the opposite of bowing out. Still standing sentinel in the dining room, Paul meets my eyes. There's something unreadable on his face. Confusion, maybe anger. But there's no doubt in my mind that he saw the interaction between Sophie and me. What would it have looked like to someone on the outside? Business partners turned quasi-friends sharing a quiet moment? Or one selfish lover intentionally provoking the other? I turn my back on him.

By the time the crew prepares to leave, hours later, I need to be alone. They're all so loud and pushy and in my space. Their crap is all over the place and it's going to take forever to prep the kitchen after they've tramped through it. I want to pull my hair out, meanwhile Sophie smiles and laughs while she debriefs with Paul. They stand on the other side of the kitchen counter, so I'm stuck on the periphery of the conversation. Paul, Mr. Perfect that he is, attempts to include me, looking to me every few words.

"Everything looks great. I can't make any promises, of course." He smiles at me.

Ugh. It's actually genuine. I hate him.

"The kitchen isn't ideal."

I bristle at the idea that my kitchen isn't ideal. Only Sophie or I get to say shit about our kitchen that is sometimes too small of a workspace and never gives the back of house team any privacy from screwups. I know he means in the context of filming television, but still. Back off, buddy.

"Most of the filming would be done in the dining room anyway, though."

"That's great," Sophie says. "That's great, right, Amy?" She widens her eyes at me in the universal signal for *say something*.

"Great," I echo.

"It was nice to meet you, Amy." He shakes my hand.

I say something similar back, though I'm sure it sounds like a lie. There's nothing wrong with him at all other than he and Sophie used to be a thing, a very serious, making vows kind of thing, and I—very stupidly—fucked her last night. Oh, and he looks at her like he still very much wants to be the one fucking her.

While Sophie walks him and the rest of the crew out, I slink back to the walk-in freezer. Somehow the room of my childhood nightmares has become a sanctuary against the masculine energy outside. Hopefully it will cool my nerves, as well. I lean against the shelves and breathe deep, letting the cold burn my lungs.

I should go home and take a nap. If I didn't have to work tonight, I'd grab a drink at Venus and chat up a willing woman, call a friend, one who's as sure a thing as me, like Katie or Gabby.

The door screeches open and slams shut behind me. "What the fuck do you think you're doing?" Sophie hisses, stalking toward me.

Before I can answer, she's on me, pulling me down to her mouth by my neck bow. She's a completely different woman than she was last night, when she seemed timid and sweet and just happy to be here. She growls into my mouth, bites my lip. Her tongue brushes over the tender spot and her nails make a path through the buzzed hair at the back of my head. The sensation almost drops me to my knees.

"Hollywood."

Her nickname sounds desperate in my mouth. She tugs the silk bow loose and sucks her way down my neck to my collarbone. Cold air hits the exposed skin of my chest and stomach. "Sophie." I laugh as her fingertips brush low on my belly. "Stop. We have to stop."

Her eyes are wild, her hair blown out around her face. "I want to make you feel as good as you made me feel."

I hold her wrists lightly. "I don't need that. I was happy with what we did yesterday."

She closes her eyes. "I know I'm inexperienced with women." Her breath puffs out in short angry bursts.

I brush my thumb over her cheek, burrow my hand into her hair. "I'm not worried about that."

"I know I'm not..." She looks down. "Queer enough."

"What?" I tip her chin up while sudden anger surges through my chest. "Look at me. Who told you that? Who said that to you?" I growl.

"No one." She shrugs. "The internet."

"Sophie." I wait until she finally meets my eyes. "You don't need to have known you were queer since you were a kid. You can go your whole life never touching a woman and you'll still be queer. It's not about performing your sexuality or your gender for everyone else. Being queer is about what you know to be true about yourself, in here." I hold my hand over her heart. Even her chest is cold to the touch now.

Sophie guides my head down to her again, but I pull away, button up my blouse. "And that's exactly why we shouldn't do this."

"What?" She shakes her head. "Why?"

Her footsteps follow me out of the walk-in. Room temperature has never felt so balmy.

I grab my coat, slinging it over my shoulder, and start flicking off lights. We won't have to be back here for a few hours and it's best if I get out, get some space. I stop in the doorway and Sophie stands off with me at the other end of the hall.

"I'm bowing out, for lack of a better term."

"Bowing out? I'm sorry, is this…" She gestures to her body. "A sports tournament?"

"I don't want you to burn yourself out on one experience with one woman."

"What? Like I'll fuck you so many times, I won't have any queerness left for anyone else?" She scoffs. "And who says that I am? Do you know all the queer women in Boston? Is there a group chat I don't know about?"

I blink, stunned into silence. I guess she never technically said she *only* wanted to have sex with me. "You're right. Maybe you have plans to fuck a lot of women, but you deserve to have fun, have someone who can pay attention to you—"

"You're doing it again. You're bulldozing through *my* choices, things that affect me. You don't get to make that decision for me." She bites the inside of her cheek and she looks so pretty but so sad. "If you don't want to fuck *me* again, just say so."

I want to go to her, show her exactly how badly I want to sleep with her. I'm so hot for her, despite still thawing out. But it's exactly how badly I want her that makes me say, "That's not it. It's not because of you at all, okay. We just shouldn't."

She opens her mouth but seems to think better of it and pushes back through the door behind her.

Fuck.

I stand in the hallway for so long the motion sensor light turns off. I don't trust myself to go to her, no matter how badly I want to. If we spend the next few weeks fooling around I'll never be able to keep my wanting for her off my face once we're in front of cameras, and that would just lead to more disaster. The exploitation she warned me about. Or—far worse—outing her before she's ready. As much as I want this opportunity to help save this business, I'm heeding her warnings. There's nothing more precious than my privacy or hers.

The alley behind the restaurant is always quiet, but especially so at mid-morning on a weekday. My car sits tucked between the wall and Sophie's SUV. I throw my coat in the back and settle in the driver's seat, resting my head on the steering wheel. "Stupid," I mutter. "Stupid, stupid, stupid."

All of this is stupid. I'm stupid for thinking only about how much I wanted her last night and how that might affect her today, and for walking away from her just now.

A sharp rap on the passenger window makes me jump. "Open the door." She glares at me through the dirty glass.

Put the key in the ignition and drive away, Amy.

Don't be stupid.

But I'm just not smart, I guess. I open the door. She throws herself into the car. "Let's go."

Chapter Eight

Amy

The car fills with the sharp scent of her shampoo. She's bare-faced, the blush on her cheeks from the cold or maybe rage.

"Go where?"

"Your place? Mine? I don't care. Let's go fuck."

I laugh, more at the casual way she throws out the words than the concept itself. "You're funny, Hollywood. I'll give you that."

"See, I don't believe you. I think you don't want to say I was a bad lay because you're worried it will affect our professional relationship." She leans toward me, her eyes huge and crazed. "Tell the truth, you coward."

She wants to call my bluff. Fine. I'll call hers.

Between the brick wall of another building on one side and her unnecessarily off-roading vehicle on the other, we're cocooned. Even her voice sounds muted in my car. I pull the lever and send my seat back. "Heck, why not right here, Hollywood?" I hold my arms open, like *have at it, girl.*

She accuses me of being a bulldozer and pushing through all my own ideas, but Sophie's been the one bulldozing this conversation, until now. She looks like she's hit a wall.

"Here?" She peers out the hatchback window. "It's…it's daytime."

I nod. "Guess what? It'd be daytime if I took you back to my place, too."

She huffs. "You know what I mean."

I reach for the lever to bring my seat back up.

"Wait." She reaches around me, her hand on my wrist, squeezing softly. "I didn't say no."

She crawls onto her knees on the passenger seat, plants her hand on the seat beside my thigh. "Are you saying no?"

"No." I shake my head. "I mean, I'm not saying no. To you."

"Say it, Amy," she whispers. "Ask me to fuck you."

I catch her mouth in a kiss, but she pulls away, leaving me with only a taste. "Say. It."

Her hand lands on my thigh and all the blood in my body pumps toward her. I want to feel her palm on my skin like I want my next breath. She throws her leg over the gearshift. The horn blasts from the pressure of her butt and we both jump. She collapses on top of me in a fit of giggles. Her body is warm and soft pressed to mine, and I hold her, let her shake with uncontrollable laughter, her hair falling over my face. As she pushes back, I let go.

"Get up," I say. She can't hide the disappointment on her face as she moves back into her seat. I pop my seat back up. "Get in the back."

She grins, looking from the back seat of my hatchback to her SUV. "Why don't we use my car? The windows are tinted."

I follow her gaze to the big blacked out truck. "It is stupidly big."

She rolls her eyes but pulls her keys from her coat. The locks beep and we jump from my car to hers. I slide into the back seat, a king-sized bed compared to my tiny old car. Sophie closes the door behind us. Between the tint and the overcast sky it's like nighttime in here. That time of night when we can whisper whatever we want to each other. It's easier, here, to believe my own lies when I tell myself that this is for her, and to take her face in my hands and say against her mouth, "I want you to fuck me."

She smiles slowly. Her hand slides up my leg but bypasses where I want her to stop to press against my chest. She pushes me down onto the bench seat, wedging herself between my legs. I have to bend one knee; the other leg dangles off the seat to make room for her and my long legs.

"Do you want something for your head?"

I bump it against the door handle. "I'll live."

She tugs at the neck bow again. The silk swishes against my skin and I close my eyes at the sensation and the sight of her above me. Since the first time I watched her on my old laptop screen, I've thought about exactly this. Just snippets of it. What it would be like to kiss her, to touch her between her legs and feel how wet she is, to see her lips wet from me. Now it's happening and my brain is still catching up to the idea that any of this is real. That an email I sent in the dead of night to a talent agent resulted in this eager fire sign becoming my head chef. And how my own mismanagement has pulled out this beast in her, this woman willing to fight me or anyone else if she has to.

Sophie pulls my blouse open and trails kisses between my breasts. She follows my ribs and I squirm and bite my knuckle to keep from laughing. She hitches my leg up on the seat, spreading me further. Her hands never stop moving, her fingers trace the outline of my nipple through the cotton of my bra. Her thumb makes slow circles over my inner thighs. She hasn't touched me or even put her mouth on anything with an excess of nerve endings, but she's already driving me wild.

"You're lucky I can't flip you over back here."

My voice has gone growly and there is laughter in her answering tone. "Why?"

Finally, she slips her hand under the elastic band of my bra to brush her fingers over me. I close my eyes and press my head hard into the door. "Because you're killing me, Hollywood. You're all talk. I thought you were going to fuck me."

"I'm not letting you top me," she says in a singsong voice. "Not right now, at least."

I open my eyes. She's pulled my bra straps down and her eyes are too big in her face.

"Take your shirt off at least?" I ask.

She grins but sits back on her heels. With a quick check out the windows, she pulls the ruby knit over her head. Her full hair and the lace embellishments on her bra make her look like a retro pinup girl.

"Come here." But I don't wait for her to comply. I bring her down to me and lick into her mouth. Sophie moans; the sound travels through me. I feel it like a pulse in my pussy; it curls my toes. Over my pants, she pets me. Like we're in some kind of high school fantasy, where we have to hit every step along the way: under the bra, over the underwear.

After I opened the restaurant, I stopped going out so much, stopped bringing home women, stopped responding to dating app messages. I lacked the time and the energy, but mostly the motivation. Not when I had my professional dreams in my hands and this beautiful dream of a woman nearby.

Now, she runs her tongue along my lips like she might run her tongue between my legs, and I ache for her there.

"Hollywood, please." I gasp as she presses her knuckle to my clit through too many layers of clothing. Without waiting for her response, I pop the button on my pants and push them down. Her hands tangle with mine and together we get them past my ass, but with her between my legs, they can't go any further.

"This is fine," she says, tugging a bit more. "We can do this. I've got this."

"Yeah. You do," I assure her. I arch toward her, begging for contact, throbbing in anticipation.

She bends over me while her knuckle trails over my stomach and tugs at the waistband of my underwear. "Do you like this?" she asks as the pad of her finger skims over my lips. She bites the inside of her cheek before burying her face in my neck.

"Don't get shy on me now, Hollywood," I whisper.

Her finger moves in slow circles over me. The movement is too tortuously slow to get me off but I'm so revved up it's close anyway. My legs shake with each pass of her hand; I grasp for something to do other than grab her ass or rub her breasts, but I can't bring myself to break contact. Like the second I stop touching her I'll wake up from this dream, wrapped in sweaty bedsheets and very much alone.

The windows have fogged up. Even if someone came through this dead-end alley and peeked into this car, they wouldn't be able to make out more than just shapes. But she's still more exposed than I am. "Let me suck you?" I ask, my hands on her breasts.

She nods and I pull her bra down. Her nipples are wide and the softest pink and as I take one in my mouth her rhythm between my legs falters.

"Amy," she says, like someone else might swear. "Teeth? Please?" she asks. "Bite me." She asks so quietly, as if this request should somehow embarrass her, but it just makes me more wild for her, so that I have to be careful in my eagerness to do as she wishes.

"You like that?" I ask, leaving gentle teeth marks around

her nipple. For long minutes, we're slow. She rubs my wetness over my clit; her fingers explore my pussy. I coax soft cries from her with my teeth and tongue. But every time I try to move my hands between her legs, she moves away.

"Stop it," she says, and drags her tongue between my breasts. I arch into her.

She pulls at my underwear until I lift my hips.

"Stop what?"

"Trying to fuck me. It's my turn now." She scoots back on the seat but there isn't much room for her. Her body curls over me and I realize almost too late what she's trying to do.

"What the hell do you think you're doing?" I ask, pushing her back with one hand and uselessly grabbing at the foggy window for purchase to pull myself up.

"I'm…sorry." She sits back. "I'm eating you out. Do you not like that?"

I cover my mouth to hide my smile. Cool, my baby bisexual head chef casually eats pussy in her car on a weekday morning. That's not blowing my mind or anything.

"No, I do. I very much do."

"Then what's the problem?"

I throw my arm over my face. That flash of Sophie's hair fanned out on my pillow is all I see when I close my eyes.

"If you're going to eat pussy it will be after I've spread you out on my bed to see how many times I can make you come on my tongue. And not a second sooner."

She cocks her head to the side, a sly tilt to her brow. "That doesn't sound like bowing out to me, Amy."

My face flames, more from sexual frustration than her obvious callout, and I lift my hips once more. "Can we talk about it later? Weren't you doing something?"

Sophie pulls me back down the seat. "Tell me what you like

though?" she asks, one hand slipping into my underwear. I cover her hand with mine and guide two fingers to my pussy.

"I like this," I whisper, closing my eyes as she follows my gentle prompts, finding a rhythm between her fingers inside me and her thumb.

The window is cold against my palms. I splay my hands out, trying to touch as much glass as possible to cool off. The SUV fills with the sounds of my harsh breathing and the explicit, wet sounds of her fingers in my body.

She licks up my stomach, over my nipples.

I want to scream. Everything is soaked, her hand, my panties. Oh god, she'll have to clean this car. But the shame does nothing to my arousal. It just makes me want this more. I want to show Sophie how hot this is. I rise up on my elbow to reach her mouth.

"Yes," I say into her mouth. "Exactly like this."

I cup her hand again, pushing another of her fingers inside me. The stretch is painful and delicious and exactly what I need to come. "You fuck me so good, Sophie. So fucking good."

I cry out, the sound muted by her mouth and her skin, but if someone were outside they'd hear it and I'd want them to. In this moment, I want everyone to know how wild I am for her. I fall back onto the seat as I shudder. Sophie doesn't stop until I squeeze her wrist.

I gasp. "No more."

I'm the one who just came all over this back seat, but she is the one who blooms. A bright flush crawls up her chest into her cheeks. She's a fucking goddess, with her shirt off and her tits out and her hair wild in the back of her car.

Outside, everything is quiet, the only sound cars passing on the road at the mouth of the alley. Slowly, we get dressed again. Now that I'm not on the verge of coming, my cramped position in this back seat catches up with me. My neck is sore and my feet have pins and needles.

"What time is it?" I ask.

"Noon." She shows me her phone screen. There's also a text from Paul she doesn't open, instead throwing her phone into the front seat.

I tip my head against the headrest, my energy sapped. "What are your plans for the rest of the day?"

She brushes my hair off my face. "Testing that risotto recipe."

I nod. "How are you feeling about it?"

She shrugs. "It's good, but it's missing something."

I press my lips together. The last thing I want to do is shake her confidence, but mushroom risotto has to do some heavy lifting to elicit a reaction from a celebrity chef of Camilla's caliber.

"I'm sure you'll come up with something," I say. "I have faith in you."

She smiles, shy. As if she didn't just have her hand down my pants. "You?" she asks.

"Nap, probably."

She turns, her hand on the car door handle. That's my cue to get out of her car, I think.

"Hey," I say, because I'm not ready yet.

She pauses.

"How'd you feel today?" I ask. "With the crew here and everything."

She trails her fingers through the fog on the windows. "It actually…" She peeks at me, a grin lighting up her eyes. "Wasn't as bad as I thought it would be."

I smile, my chest feels warm. "Did it feel different? Compared to *Pop-Up Kitchen*?"

She turns back to me, reaching up to sift her fingers through my hair again. I close my eyes at her touch. "I don't really know. Maybe it felt more like a team effort this time? Like, *Cooking for Camilla* isn't a direct competition. It might not be as cutthroat. And they all seemed to want to find ways to make things work rather than creating more obstacles for us."

"That's good, Hollywood. I'm glad."

"See you tonight?" she asks, as if I won't be back here earlier than that.

I open my eyes. "Tonight."

Sophie searches my face then leans forward. She kisses me softly, a good-night type kiss. "Amy?"

"Yeah."

"How about you stop making decisions for the both of us, okay?" Her voice is teasing but her point is clear.

I open her palm, kiss its center. "Fine. From now on, I'll let you make me come whenever you ask."

It's not what she wants. But it's all I'm able to give.

Chapter Nine

Sophie

The patterns and images in the gym ceiling panels all look like Amy. As I lie on the bench between sets there's the curve of a woman's hip over my head, an areola and nipple, the curl of hair between two lean legs.

"You ready?" Natalie slides into my field of vision, her hands on the bar above my head.

"Yes." I grab the bar again and set up for my next set of bench presses.

"You sure?" She keeps her hand on the bar.

"Promise." But my voice shakes, ruining any credibility I might have had.

The entire concept of sleeping with Amy to rid me of the distraction was bullshit. I'm more distracted than ever.

I set up for my lift and pull the bar off the rack. Natalie's hands hover between mine, ready to catch the bar in case I falter, but I know I won't need her. I have never felt stronger, more powerful.

If I told Amy this she'd say it was thanks to her magic pussy. I giggle as I rack the bar.

"What's so funny?"

I blink up at Natalie. "Nothing," I say. "Just…happy."

Turns out Amy is the best distraction ever.

"You should be. That's another PR."

I look back at the bar as I sit up. Huh. She's right. Again.

"You sure I can't convince you to do a powerlifting comp this spring?" Natalie asks, spraying down the bar and weights with the cleaner.

"No way. I do this to reduce my stress. If I started competing it would feel too stressful."

"That's fair." She leans against the rack. "There's something different about you. Did you..." She pauses, doing a full body scan of me. "Cut your hair or...something?"

"Nope." I laugh again. I know what she means, though. I am different. Turns out, there's something incredibly freeing about being your true self.

She shrugs. "Whatever it is. It looks good on you." She checks the big red digital clock installed over the door. "Can you stay for a bit more accessory work?"

My stomach sinks. "No. Sorry." My mom has probably already blown up my phone. "I've got to meet someone for breakfast."

Twenty minutes later, I walk out the gym a little taller. My muscles are sore in the most satisfying way. My new mascara makes my eyelashes look epically long. And despite having to endure this visit from my mother, I'll get to see Amy tonight. There have been no more panty shenanigans since I got Amy off in the back seat of my car last week, but I'm not the only one who's different since then.

Amy has been as close to an ideal restaurant owner as I could hope for. She communicates like a pro. I'm desperate to believe that we can do this without the help of reality television, but the way Amy pores over her spreadsheets late into the night after dinner service makes me think we're not even close to being able to save the restaurant ourselves.

"Sophie," my mother calls my name from across the restaurant as soon as I walk in. "*Yoohoo!* Here!" She points to the booth beside her for emphasis.

Guests and servers stop to turn and stare at me. Simply by being in my mother's presence I am once again an awkward middle schooler.

"Hi, Mom." We double kiss in greeting and I slide into the booth. "Good to see you."

She sets the napkin in her lap as she sits opposite from me. "I'd barely call this seeing each other," she huffs.

So this is going to go well.

"I'm sorry I couldn't take any time off for your visit," I say. Between my regular shifts and the extra time in the kitchen testing recipe after recipe, perfecting risotto, comparing other dishes to find the best one to serve to Camilla, I have no time to spare. "But I'll see you tonight when you come for dinner. And we can check out some museums and do some shopping this week before I have to go in to work."

She reaches over the table to take my hands in hers. "You work too much, Sophie. Like your father."

In Audrey Brunet's language, that's an insult. Dad was always working too much when I was a kid. Now that he's retired, he golfs too much. When I was little I agreed with my mother; now I don't know how to gently tell her that Dad might just have new strategies for avoiding his wife.

It would be a pleasure to work a little bit less, but rest is for head chefs who haven't driven their restaurants into the ground.

"Where is Dad?" I open the menu even though I know what I'm going to get. The only breakfast food I see much point in is eggs Benedict. You can learn a lot about a kitchen by their hollandaise sauce. "I thought he wanted to come."

She waves my question away with her water glass in her hand, the ice jangling violently and water sloshing over the side onto the white tablecloth. "He wanted to drive because you know your father."

I nod. He hates to fly.

"But I'm not spending *five hours* in a car."

I keep nodding. The horror.

"Maybe in the summer you can entice him down if you promise to go golfing with him."

More nods.

"Well, thanks for making the trip, Mom." These are the kinds of compliments my mother needs to be fed to survive. More than just an acknowledgment of gratitude, she needs you to recognize the sacrifice inherent in her actions. "I really appreciate it and I can't wait to show you around Boston."

She smiles, squeezing my hands. "It's my pleasure, dear. It would be easier if you lived closer, of course." She shakes her head with a sigh, but a server interrupts us before she can say anything more about my poor choice of residence or work schedule.

The server is an Asian woman with a short black bob and red lipstick. Her mouth is the only pop of color in this high-end hotel restaurant, with its white tablecloths and the deep mahogany stain on the furniture. I smile at her and when she smiles back, holding my eye for a breath longer than socially acceptable, I blush and take a sip of water.

Before I came out to myself I would have spent hours wondering if she was flirting with me. Now I'm excited that I was flirting with her. I think that was flirting, at least.

"I'm Beth. Let me know if you need anything," she says, directly to me.

Definitely flirting. I think. Probably definitely.

"Well," Mom says. She sounds scandalized, and I freeze. How could my mother have possibly picked up on that if I wasn't even sure it was happening? "Your cousin, Julie, got married. Eloped. Can you believe it?"

"That's great." I wrap my hands around the coffee mug Beth filled. "Tell ma tante congratulations."

She glares at me. "No, Sophie. Francine is beside herself."

"Why?" I shrug. "Clearly, Julie is in love."

"You'll understand one day when you have children. We deserve to be a part of these special days, too."

I stare into my coffee mug so I don't have to address the fact that I don't know where I stand on the whole kids thing, and so I don't blurt out, *it's not about you, Mom.*

"Anyway, you're right that Julie is in love. Her wife is a lawyer."

I snap my eyes back to Mom. "Julie is gay?" I ask.

She frowns at the interruption. "Yes. She told Francine and Gui last year. As I was saying, Julie's wife is a lawyer…"

My brain is too busy screaming to hear the rest of that sentence. Growing up, we never spoke about what being queer meant. For her to mention a queer cousin so casually… I study Mom's face as she chatters away about how Julie is going to a fertility clinic to find a sperm donor.

Never had I planned to tell my mom about being bi, at least, not in the near future. I was going to wait until I felt stable in my sexuality before sharing it with her and Dad. I'm not afraid they'll disown me, but then, I was sure that Paul would react only with love and acceptance. It's terrifying to ask someone you've known your whole life to completely restructure everything they thought they knew about you.

Because what if they say no? What if they can't?

"I only wish you could have that, Sophie," Mom says.

The leather booth squeaks as I sit back. "A wife?"

Immediately, I think of Amy, but take that thought and hold it under water until it stops kicking. Amy is not wife material. Not when what she wants is for me to spread my sapphic wings.

"I wish you could have that kind of stability in a partner, Sophie. That's why your father and I were so surprised to hear about you and Paul."

Paul. Of course. It's always about Paul.

"He makes good money and he loved you so much. What could have happened to make you want to leave him?" She leans in closer, dropping her voice low. "Was he unfaithful, dear? Because sometimes men feel like they need to go elsewhere if they're not getting what they need at home."

"Mom, *no*." My horrified shout stops Beth short as she starts to place our dishes down. I glance between her and my mother. "Sorry."

"Let me know if you need anything." She hurries off and I'm left alone again with my mother, who apparently has some shockingly archaic views on straight relationships.

"Paul wasn't unfaithful, Mom." I poke at the egg, covered in a thick layer of creamy, rich, and golden yellow hollandaise.

"I was just wondering," she says, clearly offended.

When I get home, I'm going to send Julie a congratulatory email. I'll never admit this to my mother, but I am a little disappointed she eloped. I would have loved to watch her marry the woman she loves.

Mom cuts into her waffles with enough force to scratch her plate. I pull out my phone and snap a few photos, slapping a filter on one and writing a caption about what makes the best hollandaise, making sure to tag the restaurant and hotel, and the chef, who I know tangentially through the industry.

"We broke up because I felt like I wasn't getting what I needed," I say, picking up my knife and fork. It's easier to explain it that way than to tell her he hurt me and wait for her inevitable questions of *why* and *how*.

Mom stops with her fork halfway to her mouth. "Sophie. *You* were unfaithful?" I don't think I've ever seen my mother look more disappointed, which is confusing since she just told me that it's totally acceptable if men cheat.

"No, I..." I slice my fork through the egg and warm, gooey yolk oozes out. This is a good poach.

Julie told her parents she was gay. She, undoubtedly, had the same fears I do, but she was brave and she did it anyway. I channel a bit of my cousin Julie, of Amy, who lives like she dares you to question her existence. She stands so sure in her authentic self.

"I like women, too." I keep my eyes on my plate where the egg and hollandaise meet and mix. The words have barely passed my lips before I say my next ones. "I'm bi, Mom."

I didn't know I was so terrified to say the words until I said them. My blood pumps slowly. I feel a little like this egg, my insides oozing out onto the table. But I said it. And the world hasn't ended. I'm still here. That alone gives me the courage to meet her eyes.

She chews quickly at her waffle. How she can chew so fast without choking is some kind of superpower.

"That's wonderful, dear." She shoves another bite into her mouth. "So, you're dating a woman, then?"

I blink quickly. As if blinking will somehow help me hear better. "N-no."

She *tsks*. "But you like women?"

"Y-yes."

"And men?"

"All genders, really," I clarify.

She cocks her head to the side, her eyes wide with the kind of scandalized excitement she usually reserves for gossip about the folks from the church she barely attends. "You're dating a man *and* a woman?" she whispers.

"No. I'm not dating anyone." I shake my head for emphasis. "Sorry, no. I'm interested in dating women. And men. I'd like to date. Anyone."

A look of true concern passes over her face. The panic grips me tighter.

"You broke up with Paul to date women—or anyone," she says quickly. "But now you're not dating? Anyone?"

The leather booth squeaks as I sit back. "I..."

That image of Amy resurrects itself in my brain. I could never tell my mom I'm dating the owner of the restaurant I work at, but a film reel of dates with Amy plays on a loop nonetheless: Bruins games, hikes on our days off, making dinner at home and eating on the couch by candlelight. A thousand little moments, the wanting of them deep in my chest. All of them proof that Amy was right to keep me at arm's length, to bow out, because once again my heart jumps in ahead of my brain. "I'm still figuring things out, Mom."

The restaurant is busy but I'm in a silent, surreal vacuum where I talk to my mother about dating women.

She bites her lip as she hacks at another square of waffle. "Have you met anyone? Are you on that...that..." She points her fork, the waffle dangling loosely from the tines. "Grind? The dating app for..." She lowers her voice. "Gay folks."

"Mom." God. "No, I'm not on—"

"I'm just saying you broke up with Paul presumably to date a woman."

"Not one specific woman."

She squints at me. "Sometimes we need to go through an experimental phase before we can settle down. Are you sure it's not a phase?"

The blood rushing in my ears is so loud I must have misheard her. "A phase? Mom, this isn't middle school. I'm not a goth. I'm bisexual. I'm attracted to more than one gender and Paul wasn't…great about it so we broke up."

She puts her fork down and sighs, shaking her head. "I'm so sorry, Sophie-belle. I didn't expect Paul to be a homophobe."

I pull my hand out from under hers. "It's…well, he's not technically…it's complicated." This whole conversation is complicated.

Mom nods.

"Mom, are you okay…? I want to be clear here. You're not upset at all about hearing that I'm bi?"

"Do you want me to be?" She laughs.

"No, not at all."

The sharp sting of tears comes so suddenly I can't stop them with a deep breath, or even look away. They spill onto my cheeks with alarming volume.

"Honey, what's wrong?"

Nothing is wrong except I'm not sure if I'm awake or dreaming. "Nothing," I croak and take a large sip of coffee. "Nothing is wrong. I was worried, that's all."

"Your father and I don't care who you love, dear."

The relief is like the heat that warms my chest from a hot cup of tea.

"But, sweetheart, you need to start dating."

"I… I do?"

"You have double the population in your dating pool, but you still haven't found anyone to marry?"

I blink. "I'm not looking for anyone to marry."

She harrumphs. "Maybe your cousin can set you up with someone. She probably knows lots of available women."

"She lives in Montreal."

Mom waves this away as unimportant before launching into a detailed account of her last vacation with Aunt Francine. I don't know why I'm so surprised. It's completely on brand that my mother's biggest concern is not whom I will one day marry, but only that I am married at all.

If I were a normal person, I'd probably be annoyed by this, but today I'm choosing to bask in the acceptance. *Your father and I don't care who you love.* I hold the words in my heart, like precious uncut diamonds. It wasn't the best conversation, but it has potential and it certainly went better than the first discussion I ever had on this topic.

As Mom chatters, I let my mind wander to what being out to my parents might look like. To bringing women home to Montreal to meet them, bringing Amy home specifically. Excited butterflies fill my stomach at the vision of her walking the cobblestones of Old Montreal, taking her on a tour of every Montreal smoked meat sandwich in the city, climbing Mount Royal on a busy Saturday—

"Sophie," Mom exclaims. "You're not even paying attention to me."

I press my lips together to suppress my smile. "Merci, Maman."

Her eyes widen and she shimmies in her seat. "I bet your cousin can find you a nice girl to settle down with."

I sigh and take another sip of coffee. She's doing her best with what she has. And today that's enough.

Chapter Ten

Amy

Jeremy Chen answers the door like he does everything. With far more enthusiasm than the action deserves.

"Chamberses!" His voice echoes down the third-floor hallway of his new (to him) apartment building. The building itself tries to pass for new, but the layers of peeling paint and what looks like mold blooming from the carpet's corners have ruined any chance of that.

He plasters himself against the wall to let us pass. My brother has to duck to get in. Jeremy's hair has always had the habit of growing in whatever direction he doesn't want it to, which means right now he wants it to grow down. I'd bet my Volkswagen that his hair brushes the top of his door, as well. This is an apartment for babies.

"Sick pad, bro." Wesley takes in the one room with wide eyes and a big smile like the good friend he is. He meets my gaze, grimacing, as Jeremy struggles to close the door.

"It needs a little work." Jeremy shrugs, like he heard our silent sibling dialogue. "But it's not the apartment over my parents' garage."

"Does the apartment over your parents' garage have mo—" Wes covers my mouth with his hand.

"What are we doing today?" he asks, instead.

I lick his palm, but he anticipated this and wipes it on my face.

"Gross," I hiss, scrubbing at my cheek with the sleeve of my sweater.

"How about this?" Jeremy opens a cupboard next to his wall-mounted TV. With a strong enough wind, that TV could bring the whole wall down on our heads. He holds a worn DVD case over his head.

"No." I groan.

"Yes." Wes pumps his fist.

"I'd watch the actual 2004 World Series rather than watch this movie again."

"Sorry, Amy." Jeremy shakes his head as if he is truly sorry. "Two to one."

The tray of his DVD player opens with a mechanical whirr, and he gingerly places his well-loved copy of *Fever Pitch* inside.

I stomp my foot, only half faking my level of annoyance. For a woman with only a platonic love of baseball and a distinct dislike for heterom-coms, I have seen this film way too many times.

Wes throws himself onto the folded-up futon, the only seat in Jeremy's small space.

"Come on, Amy." He presses his hands together like he's begging. "I took PTO so we could all spend time together today."

"Fine." I roll my eyes. Wes has unlimited PTO and one of those millennial bosses who encourages their employees to use it. Today wasn't a hardship for him. But I appreciate it, nonetheless.

I poke at a questionable lump on the backrest of the futon. "Is that...his bed?" I whisper once the sound of popcorn popping comes from the galley kitchen.

Wes nods. There's only one other door in this room and it must lead to a bathroom. I peek inside. There's a stand-up shower that Jeremy most definitely has to crouch in to get his hair wet.

"We have to get him out of here," I whisper, flopping onto the couch beside Wes. "This place is so small and so...so..."

"Jeremy likes it." Wes shrugs, his eyes only on the TV screen as previews for movies almost two decades old start to play.

"Yeah, but..." I gesture to the yellow-stained walls.

"Amy." Wes turns on the couch to face me. "You don't have to save everyone. You know that, right?"

"I know." I pull my hands into my sleeves. It's not cold, it just feels necessary to protect myself from this blatant *attack*.

"Do you?" he asks, his attention back to his precious previews.

Jeremy pokes his head out from behind the kitchen wall. "You want Coke or fruit punch?"

What I want is water but I'm worried about the concentration of lead in these pipes. "I'm good."

"Punch me, Jer," Wes says.

"I do know that," I say once he's gone again. "I'm not trying to save anyone. Especially straight men."

He sighs, smashing the remote to pause a preview for a straight-to-DVD rom-com. "You love your people, Amy. Fiercely. But sometimes your love..." He pauses, glancing over my shoulder like he'll find the word he's looking for there. The acrid smell of burned popcorn floats in from the kitchen. "Manifests in ways that are a little..."

"Right?"

"Strong." He grins at me, his signature brother grin, with only one side of his mouth. "If Jeremy wants to move, he'll move. If he needs help, he'll ask."

I burrow deeper into the surprisingly comfortable futon. "You sound like Sophie."

I don't look at him but he's rolling his eyes.

"I burned the popcorn," Jeremy calls.

"We know," we say in unison.

"What'd you do to Sophie?" Wes asks. The movie's opening credits start and he presses pause again, waiting for Jer.

"Nothing," I say, my voice high. "I didn't do anything to her." Except for things that could get our restaurant shut down for at least two weeks.

He stares at me from the corner of his eyes. "Weirdo."

"She…" I clear my throat. That sick feeling is back, butterflies. She's not even here and I'm officially a mess. "She said I tend to get a little pushy about my ideas for the restaurant."

Wes is quiet for so long I have to look over at him. "What?"

"What else did you do?"

Last year, Wes told me about how he was falling for his now girlfriend, then boss. My stomach still churns over the way I handled it. It's not that I thought she wasn't good enough for him, or that she was even taking advantage of him.

No one is good enough for my brother. To me, he'll always be the kid who waited for me outside the bathroom because I couldn't stand to let anyone see me cry about Dad missing another dance recital. Until we were teenagers, Mom would find us curled up in each other's beds after thunderstorms and loud fights between our parents.

It's never occurred to me that he might feel the same way about any of the women I've dated, but what if he does? What if I tell him about her and he doesn't love her immediately? Until I remember: whatever Sophie and I are, it's not serious. We're not dating.

What my brother thinks doesn't matter.

"I didn't *do* anything. We…" I shrug and look anywhere but at my brother's face. "We…"

Wes whips off his glasses, digging the heels of his hands into eyes. "Yup. Yup. Nope. I got it. I get it. Let's not…"

I laugh, high and shrill, and he stops his fidgeting to stare at me. He smiles, slow and wide and far too self-assured. If he was a cat, he'd be picking canary feathers out from between his teeth. "You *like* her."

Alarm bells. "No." My reaction is knee jerk.

"Yes," he says with the assuredness that comes from knowing a person like the back of your own hand.

"It's complicated."

"Sleeping with your boss always is." He puts his socked feet up on Jeremy's worn coffee table.

Defensiveness surges in me at the idea that Sophie's role in our restaurant might be misrepresented. "Excuse you? She's not my boss. At most we're both bosses. She's the boss of the kitchen. I'm the boss of...everything."

"You say tomato. I say you like her."

"I don't like her," I say again, mostly for myself. "I mean, of course I *like* her. She's talented and kind and beautiful and for a while there I thought she might not work out but she's really turning things around. But I don't *like* like her. We've... fooled around a little bit."

"There you go, burying the lede."

"I didn't even know she was queer until a few weeks ago. And she wasn't fully on board with this reality show idea. And now I'm trying to figure out if she likes me or if she just doesn't know any other queer women, you know? And is now really the time to start something? When I'm trying to save this restaurant and we're inviting cameras into our space. She's not even out. I don't think she's told many people." I grab his sleeve. "You can't tell anyone I told you."

He covers my hand with his. "I won't," he says, and I know it's gone in his vault along with the password to my laptop and exactly how many times I've watched *Dirty Dancing.*

"Fine. Yes. I like her." I pout, mad that he's been able to pull it out of me without saying much at all. How am I supposed to have a modicum of privacy with a twin? "But she's in no place to have a relationship right now. She needs to spread her wings and do it out of the view of a bunch of cameras. With someone who's got the time for her."

I worry at my lower lip, staring at the paused screen. "I don't think she took to her first reality show fame as well as it seemed."

"Have you talked to Sophie about any of this?"

I shake my head. Jeremy comes in with a bowl of unburned popcorn and a charcuterie board that looks like it belongs in my restaurant. "Voila," he says with a flourish.

"This looks amazing." Wes doesn't wait to start building a tiny cracker sandwich as Jeremy runs back into the kitchen.

"You should talk to her first, Amy," he says around his mouthful of food. "You don't know how she feels. Follow your heart." Like it's that easy. Wes has never had to worry about where following his heart could lead to because it's always led him in the right direction. It led him to baseball, to his career. His heart led him to Corrine.

But when you're the gay girl in what was supposed to be the Million Dollar Family, following your heart means alienating people who were already stingy with theirs, with their affection and time. When you're a woman trying to make it in the service industry, following your heart means doing it alone, and now here I am bringing Sophie into all of that.

Jeremy flops down between us, throwing his arms around our shoulders. "Ready, Chamberses?"

"Ready," Wes says.

I drop my head back on Jer's arm and close my eyes. "Ready," I mutter. Except I'm not ready at all.

Always by the climax of *Fever Pitch* I've fallen asleep. There's something about the beats of the movie or Drew Barrymore's adorable smile that feels comforting. I pretend to hate it but

I don't at all. Watching rom-coms with my brother and best friend feels like home again, sitting on Mom's couch draped in the afghan made by our great-aunt, eating an endless rotation of snacks.

Jer and Wes are riveted, the snacks long forgotten, and I'm drifting in that in between place, asleep but aware. All it takes to pull me out of this is my phone, vibrating against my thigh. With the first buzz, I'm conscious. The second and my eyes are open. Then it doesn't stop vibrating. "Ew," I say, groggy. "Someone is calling me."

Jer and Wes turn to stare down at it with me. "What is happening right now?" Wes asks.

"I don't know." I poke at the phone, ready to decline the call, when the phone number registers in my sleep addled brain. "Shit. It's the restaurant's landlord." I jump up, clutching it like it's a precious gem. "I need to take this."

Jeremy jumps up too and holds open the door to his bathroom like it is his own private office. A window over the bathtub lets weak winter light in. If I stand sideways, there's just enough room to fit between the sink and the toilet. He closes the door behind me, slamming it once, twice before the latch finally clicks.

"Greg," I say into the phone. "Hi."

"Hey," he says. Greg always sounds tired, no matter what time of day, weekend or holiday, or even the nature of his phone call. He could be calling to tell me he's retiring and still sound like the weight of the world is on his shoulders.

"How's it going?" I ask, my nerves making my voice too high. Greg never calls. He emails, and his emails sound tired, too. But if he's calling, if it can't go in an email, or wait for him to have a chance to stop by the restaurant, it's not good news.

He sighs. "You know. It's going."

"Great," I say. "That's just great. It's going here, too."

There have been a few times in my life when I knew what was going to happen next. When Mom told us she had cancer, I knew. Not her diagnosis, but I knew she was sick. When the cancer came back, I wasn't surprised when Dad left. As if my brain knew to prepare me before my heart even caught up to what was happening.

There are nights at the restaurant when I know, this customer will be a jerk before they've placed their drink order or that server will call in sick before they even pick up the phone. I wait for that feeling now, that knowing, to tell me what to expect, but there's nothing.

"I would have stopped by the restaurant," he says. He's a straight-to-business kind of guy, which usually I appreciate. But right now, my heart pounds in my throat. Right now, business might mean he's calling the rent due early.

"But you couldn't because we're closed today. Dang Mondays." I make a gagging face at myself in Jeremy's toothpaste splattered mirror. My god, this place is the living definition of a bachelor pad.

"Right," Greg says slowly. "Anyways. I know I said you don't have to worry about the bulk of the rent until end of April but…"

"How much do you need?" I ask. Better to be brave, to rip off the Band-Aid.

He sighs again. "Ten thousand."

My stomach sinks. It goes beyond sinking. It disappears. If we pay that we won't have enough to pay our vendors next month. Tears bite at the corners of my eyes and I half sit, half fall onto the edge of Jeremy's tub. "Right. Okay. Um." My voice is hoarse. "When do you need it by?"

"End of the week." The one nice thing about Greg is that he sounds like the last thing he wants to do is have this conversation. Maybe he's so tired because he actually hates being a landlord.

"Cool. Cool," I say, even though there's nothing cool about this at all. "I'll transfer the money over by Friday."

"Thanks, Amy." Greg doesn't waste time with pleasantries or questions. The line goes dead and I slump, staring blindly at the now black screen.

Someone else's TV murmurs through the thin walls of Jeremy's apartment, mixing with the rom-com coming through his bathroom door. I'm supposed to galaxy brain this problem. I know that's what I'm supposed to do. Rig up a solution with some duct tape and tenacity, the same way I'd fix a keg in the middle of a rush or get every bill settled with the power out. There has to be money somewhere, a proverbial couch cushion left unturned. But all I can think about is what Sophie's face will look like when I have to tell her to take that other job. That all this prep she's doing for Camilla, staying long past close to perfect an aioli or coming in early to brine meat, will be for nothing. There's no way we'll be in business by the time they're ready to start filming.

If we even get chosen.

The worst part is I know exactly what her face will look like. She'll be understanding, compassionate. There won't be an ounce of pity, even though it's exactly what I deserve. I've let her down, my whole team.

It's the thought of them, my team, that gets me. The tears start to trickle down my face, fat and fast, at the thought of them, mostly queer and young, having to work somewhere else. I'd tried to give them something different. An opportunity to make a fair wage in the service industry.

I failed.

The door opens, catching on Jeremy's bathmat. Wes takes a spot beside me on the edge of the tub and Jeremy sits on the closed toilet seat. Our legs tangle around each other in the cramped space. From the living room, I recognize the sounds of the movie's finale, when the heroine runs across the field at Fenway to get to the hero. The knowledge that they're missing the best part of the movie to sit in this tiny bathroom only makes me cry harder.

The only sounds are my sniffles and the movie and a quiet conversation coming from the hallway or a neighbor. I take a deep breath. "I'm okay," I say.

"Didn't make the show?" Wes asks.

"Huh? Oh. Right. The show." The show is suddenly the last thing on my mind. "No. Well, I don't know. It wasn't about the show."

They watch me, waiting for me to say more. I'm not going to weigh them down with this. Jeremy has law school to focus on. And moving into a new home that doesn't have asbestos. Wes would give me every one of his last dollars, if he knew. Which is exactly why I can't tell him. Just like I wanted to run this restaurant myself, he deserves to start his new life with Corrine without a burden.

"I think... I think I need to go for a drive."

"Yeah. I'll give Wes a ride home. You go," Jeremy says. He passes me some tissues and a water bottle.

"Thanks," I mumble.

Wes squeezes my shoulder and I avoid his eyes until I'm out of the apartment. My car's engine squeals in the cold. I don't let it warm up as I drive, with single-minded focus, across town. In the light of day, my mom's old house looks different. Lived in. Loved.

I'm thankful for the cold weather because no one is out here to see me sit and cry.

Chapter Eleven

Sophie

The way that I know cooking was the best career choice for me is how even after a day of following Mom around Boston, listening to her unsolicited advice about getting on dating apps "for the lesbians," I'm still energized when I park my SUV behind the restaurant.

Amy's car is already here and the way my heart flip-flops in my chest when I see the cherry red hatchback is dangerous. We're not a Thing. We've just gotten each other off a couple times.

But ever since Mom brought up Julie's marriage, and re-affirmed her strong desire for me to get married, I can't stop thinking about Amy. If Amy ever got married, she'd probably wear a pantsuit. Something off-white, cream colored. A satiny camisole underneath a blazer with lace trim. She'd leave her hair to its natural waves. She'd keep her face mostly bare. She'd be beautiful.

I laugh to myself, putting my fingers to my lips, buzzy and warm. Thoughts and prayers to the person who tried to plan a wedding with Amy Chambers. They'd never get to make a single choice. She wouldn't be a Bridezilla, she'd just know what she wanted and what her partner wanted, too.

I hated planning my wedding to Paul. The details were so

tedious. Who cares what color the linens are or if a DJ was preferable to a live band. All I wanted was good food, the best food for our closest friends and family.

Paul wanted to get married in a hotel conference room. Not knocking hotel conference rooms, but they're not known for their menus. But I bet Amy would let me cater our own wedding.

I drop my hand to my thigh, pinching myself through the fabric. That kind of thought isn't necessary, not for whatever it is we are.

My phone buzzes on my palm, the screen lighting up with a notification from an app I haven't checked in days, an app I haven't felt the need to punish myself with at all recently. Between giddy, silly thoughts about the owner of my restaurant and how to save said restaurant, I've been too distracted to chase the too-small dopamine hit. It's glorious. Freeing.

The back door to the restaurant hits the brick wall with a clang and I snap my gaze up. Amy stands in the doorway. She holds up her wrist, pointing to a watch that isn't there. "We just got a reso for twelve people tonight. We're full. Let's start prep."

Shit. How did she even know I was here?

They are few and far between, but some days Amy brings a gray cloud with her to work. Mostly, she's exceptional at keeping her personal problems at home. She doesn't snap at the servers, she doesn't slam doors or throw dishes. But through the windshield she looks like a live wire ready to spark.

She jabs at her wrist again before closing the door behind her with a thud. Serves me right for daydreaming. I reach behind my seat for my bag, dropping my phone inside. Every time I look back there I see her again, laid out in front of me, flushed and beautiful and slick. Vulnerable, as much as Amy will let herself be.

Slowly, I smile, feeling like the cat who caught the canary. If she's feeling a little frustrated tonight, maybe there's something I can do—besides fast prep—to help ease some of her tension.

By the time I've stuffed my bag into my locker and pulled my clean chef's whites on, Amy has a pile of chopped onions beside her. Her knife moves fast, with precision, leaving behind rows of identical onion-y cubes.

"What?" she asks, never taking her eyes off her work or breaking rhythm.

"Do you think maybe that's enough onions?"

She stops, taking stock of the pile. There's got to be at least four onions' worth in there.

"How about you just let me be in charge of food prep?" I cover her hand with mine over the knife. This close she smells like her signature peaches with something woodsy and spicy underneath.

"What?" I sniff again, trying to identify the scent. "Where were you today? You smell like…is that patchouli?"

Amy slowly turns to look at me, her hand slipping out from beneath mine. The contact was totally harmless but the loss of it leaves a burn behind, like when I've stood over a boiling pot for too long. The kind of warmth that hurts but I want to feel it again, regardless.

"My *smell* is different?"

I shrug, scraping the onion into a container and avoiding her eyes. "You have a very distinct smell."

"I was at a friend's house." But she doesn't say anything more.

"Is everything okay?" I turn back to her, my blushing under control.

"Why wouldn't it be?" She tucks her hair behind her ear, where a golden stud shines. For this one breath, I can taste the metal if I were to suck her earlobe into my mouth. I step in close, pressing my hand into her lower back.

"You seem tense. I thought maybe…"

She looks down at me, wary. "You thought what?"

I rub my hand along her back, slow, soothing circles. Seemingly despite herself, Amy smiles. It starts off shy; she doesn't smile and look at me at the same time. But slowly it changes. This smile, just like everything about Amy, is a challenge. But I've never been one to back down. I run my hand up the back of her neck, the short, shaved hair there sending a shiver through me. She might smell different, but she tastes exactly the same.

"I thought maybe I could help you relax," I say against her lips.

The security system beeps, the signal that someone has opened the back door. Amy steps away from me. "Maybe… later?"

"Sure."

"There's actually something I wanted to talk to you about so…"

She smiles awkwardly at her feet.

"Great," I say. "I love to talk." But the hair rises on the back of my neck as she still won't meet my eyes. I have a sneaking suspicion that I won't love talking about whatever has made her so awkward.

"Hey, y'all." Jameela walks in, followed by Toby. Amy puts more space between us. Like my hand on hers earlier, every movement and word from her is harmless but they burn nonetheless, this time not in that excruciating way that makes me want to go back for more. It's a cold kind of burn.

I turn back to the prep work while Amy leaves the kitchen for the host stand. Jameela takes her place beside me and we fall into the easy rhythm we've cultivated since she started.

She's a great chef and team player and it's easy to push Amy to the back of my mind with Jameela's building excitement for tonight's service.

Jameela even helps me stage a few shots for my Instagram. Tonight we're testing new specials out on our guests to whittle down our choices in preparation for cooking for Camilla Vargas. The bustle of the night takes over and the kitchen gets warm, then hot. I burn my fingers on a cast-iron pan but barely feel it because even though this full house feels more like a fluke than good fortune, tonight is a good night.

You can see the cracks in a team's performance early on. There will be a small mistake at first: meat that's been over-cooked, a custard that breaks again and again, no matter how many times you remake it. Each tiny disaster will snowball until, by the end of the night, the team is at each other's throats and nothing is coming out of the kitchen fast enough.

Tonight though, we're seamless. The term *well-oiled machine* is a cliché for a reason. Because that's what we are, anticipating each other's needs, moving in and out of each other's space like liquid. Every dish is on time and done well. It's the kind of service that doesn't leave me feeling sweaty and out of breath, even though in this heat, I am those things. This is the kind of service that reminds me how very much I love to cook, to put food together like art and reap the reward of watching people eat it, happy and satiated.

By the time our last guest leaves, I've cut everyone but Jameela and we go through the cleanup together like we did prep, with her happy energy, though a bit more tired and subdued now.

I wipe down the counter. "You can probably head out. Thanks for your great work today."

She smiles. "Thanks. See you tomorrow, chef."

I close the locker room door, leaning against it to catch a

moment of rest, and my mind wanders back to Amy. Thoughts of her have been standing on the edge of my consciousness all night. One of the best things about her is how hardworking she is. Even if she's not always making the same decisions I'd make, or when she's making my decisions for me, Amy is a pro at putting her head down and getting the job done. She can wear any hat in the restaurant, filling in for servers, mixing drinks with flair. She can change a keg and spatchcock a chicken. Tonight, it felt like she did all those things and more. I hardly saw her.

Just caught glimpses of her hands as she pulled dishes out for expo, heard the low hum of her laugh—the professional version—as she spoke to a guest sitting near the kitchen. Otherwise my head was down, too, making this restaurant work. We're a team, Amy and I. Somehow, through miscommunication and frustration, we're finding a way to collaborate that works. It takes a moment to recognize the swelling in my chest.

I'm proud.

A few weeks ago, I wasn't sure of my future here. I wasn't sure of anything, my talent and sexuality included. But we're making it work and it's unconventional, and yet, I think I kind of love it. The locker room is dull and Spartan: a set of old blue lockers Amy bought from a superstore that was closing, an old Formica table with only two chairs, a two-piece bathroom with a mirror on the door. Maybe someday, when we've pulled this place back from the brink, we can do something nice for the staff. Like get couches or redo the washroom. I want people to love coming to work here as much as I do.

I'm ready to celebrate and after tonight, I think Amy will be, too, awkward vibes be damned.

The leggings and cropped sweater I chose for tonight are casual enough that they look unplanned, but they show off my muscular legs and the soft curve of my belly while hugging my breasts. If there was a uniform to seduce Amy with, it would be this.

"How'd we do?" I ask, having changed, standing in the doorway to her tiny office.

Amy taps away at her keyboard, frowning at her computer screen. "Good," she says, absently. "Okay," she amends.

"Good." I'm choosing to focus on the positive right now. I walk around the desk. Still she doesn't look up. Her swivel chair creaks as I turn it, leaning on the arms. "How should we celebrate?"

"Sophie." My name gusts against my lips but not in the breathy, lust-filled way I'd hoped.

Amy sits back in the chair. "We shouldn't."

I straighten. "We shouldn't?"

"That's what I wanted to talk to you about, actually."

My face burns hotter than it ever did in the kitchen tonight. "You wanted to talk about how we shouldn't?"

"Sit down." She points to the chair by the door.

I do, because my legs are suddenly weak, the flush of embarrassment apparently sending my body into a state of shock and pulling all my blood back to my vital organs. Not because she told me to.

She takes a deep breath, her chest rising and falling. "I think you should take the other job. The sous-chef job."

"I...what?" My stomach churns. I rack my brain. At any point tonight, did I describe out loud what Amy would wear on her wedding day and scare her off? "But...the show?"

She bites her lip, looking anywhere but at me.

Paul took me to some television event once in New York. There were a lot of high-powered execs and behind the scenes professionals but not a lot of actresses or on-screen talent at the event. I'd always assumed that it was us, the contestants, the actors and hosts, who got the rowdiest when free coupes of champagne were offered up in a pyramid. But that night it was the suits who lost control. A director, drunk from too much whiskey and high from too many trips to the bathroom, pulled a glass from the bottom of the champagne tower and it was all in slow motion, watching the glasses of overpriced grape juice cascade to glittering shards on the floor. That's what this feels like, the realization sinking slowly then all at once, that Amy is letting me down gently.

"There's no point," she says. "In us. In doing the show."

There's no point in us. "Right. Of course." I nod fast; hopefully the action keeps the tears at bay. I fall hard. I fall fast. I imagined Amy on her wedding day, for god's sakes. I should have expected this.

"Sophie."

"I agree. You're right. We should be...circumspect."

As I stand, cool air hits my midriff. This crop top is beyond ridiculous. Who'd wear such a thing after a night of working in a hot kitchen? No one is breezy enough for a crop top after that. There's only enough energy for a beer and bed.

I'm moving too fast and maybe it's good that she's the one letting me down, rather than having me be the one to make the mistake again.

"Circumspect?" There's a playful smirk on Amy's face, completely at odds with the news she's just dumped on me. How dare she look so goddamn beautiful at a time like this.

"Yes," I snap. "Cautious, discreet." With every word now, I can hear my French accent seeping into my English words, which only ever happens when I'm emotional.

I'm blinking too much. Not because I'm crying, I just don't know what to do with my eyes. "It's...smart. Thanks. Whatever."

She winces. In the harsh glow of the single white light bulb hanging from the ceiling, she's washed-out and pale. There are dark circles under her eyes that either showed up spontaneously or I didn't notice until now. "Sophie, don't cry."

"I'm not crying," I snarl, as I dash tears from cheeks. The worst part is she's right. We should be careful. The last thing I want is for the cameras to pick up on how stupidly obsessed I am with her. That would almost be as embarrassing as this moment right now.

"I get it, okay? I know I come on too strong and you're not interested in anything…" I gesture at her. "Serious. But I don't want to take the other job just because of us."

I sniffle, pulling myself together. "I can be professional. I *am* professional."

"No." She stands, coming around the desk. "This isn't because of you." She presses the heels of her hands into her eyes. "I'm sorry. I'm terrible at this."

"What the fuck is happening?"

"I don't think we're going to be open by the time the show airs."

"But…we're doing better, I thought. Right? We did well tonight. We did okay."

She shakes her head. "It's not enough. I need…" She closes her eyes, wincing like she's in actual pain. "I need to come up with some money or else we're going to lose the space. But if I scrounge the funds, we won't be able to pay our vendors next week." She shrugs. "I've done the math a thousand times but unless we get a sudden influx of cash…we're done."

I sit up straight, the sudden burst of inspiration feels like butterflies in my stomach. The fluorescent light buzzes overhead.

"You need an investor."

"I honestly don't know what I need anymore. I can't think."

It all comes together too slowly in my mind, puzzle pieces

that I've turned over and over again until finally they fit. Slowly, I stand.

"Let me get this straight."

She looks up.

"You're such a control freak that you won't even let your head chef look at the numbers on the books. And then, when confronted with a problem of funds, instead of doing what any normal person would do and *asking* for help, you tell me to *find a new job*?"

Amy's eyes are huge, and somehow, she's even paler than before. "Well, yeah. I..."

"You didn't think I could help. You didn't think that maybe *I* might be interested in investing in this business? That I might have some stake in this?" My voice bounces off the close brick walls of the office. Now I'm thankful for my crop top. The built in draft is the only thing keeping me from burning up in flames.

"How much money do we need?" I cross my arms over my chest in what I hope is a power stance.

"I can't let you—"

"Let's be clear." I hold up a finger, cutting her off. "I do not care what you can or cannot let me do. I am head chef of Amy & May's and I want a stake in the business. How. Much. Do. We. Need?"

"Ten thousand."

I nod.

"I can put thirty up front," I say.

"That sounds like your savings."

"It is," I say. "But it's *my* savings. I get to choose what I do with it. Not you. And I want thirty percent of the business."

She really must be at a loss because she doesn't even negotiate. Amy nods. "Thirty percent."

I step closer, so I can see the prism in her eyes, all the ways that brown can hold light, be bright. Her lashes brush her cheeks and I don't—I do *not*—look at her lips, the press of her teeth into the delicate skin.

"And you stop making decisions for me."

"Deal," she whispers.

I grab my coat and bag, opening the office door. "Amy? You better watch it. The next time you tell me to take another job… I might listen."

Chapter Twelve

Amy

The restaurant is loud enough that the sound of laughter and the clatter of dishes makes its way all the way down the hallway to my office. Normally, I'm able to block everything out to focus on the work in front of me, but all I can do now is listen to each murmur, burst of laughter, every scrape of a fork on a plate to try to assess it. Are they enjoying the food? Are they enjoying themselves? Are they going to come back? Will tonight be the night that turns things around?

With Sophie's investment, the back rent I owed is paid. But the rent for next month is still due on the first, vendors are owed at the end of the month. And then, of course, there's payroll. My savings have allowed me to keep this restaurant running without taking home a salary yet, but even that won't be enough. The tiny cursor on my spreadsheet blinks and blinks, judging me.

Even if we are chosen for *Cooking for Camilla*, I don't think we're going to make it.

A wave of heat washes over me, like if emotion, anxiety, fear, and failure had a temperature. I wish my mom were here, that I could crawl under her cumulonimbus of a duvet, that never seemed to lose its volume, after work tonight. That I could just listen to her breathing and hear the soft sound of delight she'd make when she woke up to find me next to her. It wouldn't help any of this, but it would feel a lot better than having to prepare Sophie and my team that we are destined for closure.

If my father wasn't such an asshole, I might ask him for some advice. Lord knows he loves to hear himself talk. But he'd never let himself get into this situation in the first place. The sound in the restaurant comes back to me as someone pushes the swinging door down the hall open.

So apparently, I do still have the superpower of blocking out sounds as long as I'm coming to terms with my own restaurant's mortality.

The sound from the dining room is hectic, as hectic as Maggie's hair, bouncing in a cloud of curls, when she pokes her head into my office.

"What's up, Mags?" When I left the floor, it wasn't busy but it was steady, and I thought it would stay that way. From the whites of her eyes, that assumption was wrong.

Maggie bites her lip, glancing back down the hallway. She cringes as a loud bark of laughter travels down the hall from the dining room.

"Maggie." I throw down the pen I was chewing on. "Spit it out."

"There's...a man? Here?"

"Last time I checked, men are like half of our customer base," I mutter. "Unfortunately."

"The man is asking for you," Maggie says.

I look up. "Wes?" Maggie's met Wes plenty of times, though. She wouldn't be acting so squirrely if it was Wes.

"Not Wes. He says he's your dad?"

"What?" I stand up. "He said he's my father?"

She nods.

I hold my hand up. "This high?"

She keeps nodding.

"Gray here?" I point to where his sideburns would be.

"Yes."

"Grouchy?"

She winces.

"Frig." I've summoned him with my business failure. My fingers get tangled in my hair. "Is he staying?" I ask. "Is he eating here?"

Maggie steps into the office and lowers her voice. "He wants to order food and a bottle of wine. Did you want me to ask him to leave?"

Yes, I do.

Wes and Corrine come in every month or so. They're quiet and they leave a tip even though the gratuity is included in the price of the food. Sometimes when friends and family come in they ask for too much, running servers around because they can drop a name, but not Wes and Corrine. They're exactly the type of guests I want my team to have to serve.

My father, though. He's the type of person who puts the gratuity out on the table and slowly picks away at it, holding servers up to a ridiculous standard they can never meet just to scare them. He's the guest who asks for comps and sends perfectly good food back just because he can. He runs you, over and over. He does it all thinking he's superior because "only college students, actors, and fuck-ups" work in restaurants.

My staff doesn't deserve to have to deal with him and yet, the little girl in me who has always wanted his approval loves that he's here. Even though I know the chances are slim, I still can't help but think *what if*. What if I impress him? What if I show him how good I am at this? What if he recognizes that all my hard work was worth it? What if he actually likes it?

"Of course not," I say. "I'll come out. Who's serving him now?"

"Tony."

"Crap." Dad will eat Tony alive, spit out the bone frag-
ments, and ask for a refund.

With each step toward the door, my heart pounds harder.
That laugh comes again. I don't know how I didn't recognize it before. That sound is so, very obviously, my father's
laugh. The one he uses when he wants people to know that
the room belongs to him.

He sits at a four-top with three other men in expensive
suits. Their faces are shiny, sweaty, and red. Drunk and it's
only eight o'clock.

I intercept Tony and the two-hundred-dollar bottle of red
in his hands. "I'll take care of them." I nod at Dad.

Relief flashes over his face. "You sure, boss?"

Not at all. "I'm sure."

He presses the corkscrew into my hand. "I owe you," he
whispers.

With a deep breath, I approach the table. "Good evening,
gentlemen. We're having the cab sauv tonight?"

Dad glances up at me with the same disdain he gives all
service workers. His tie, the knot loosened, is one that Wes
and I got for him years ago. Some Father's Day or birthday
gift I was positive he'd never wear, and, for a moment, my
heart softens for him.

"This is my daughter," he says, flinging his hand in my direction but not looking at me, like I'm an attraction on a tour,
but not one important enough to stop for.

Never mind. Moment over.

The other men smile but when it becomes obvious that he's
not going to go any further, I introduce myself.

"Amy," I say.

"The Amy in Amy and May's?" asks one of his guests, the
youngest-looking one at the table by at least a decade.

"The one and only." I present the bottle of wine to Dad and he waves it away with a nod.

"Where's the May?"

They all laugh at the dumb joke, except for Dad and me.

I pause, the corkscrew stuck into the top of the bottle. "May was my mom's middle name."

The table stills as they register my use of past tense.

They address their quiet condolences to my father, instead of me, even though he doesn't wear a wedding ring. Even though he wasn't there when she died. I let the muscles in my arms burn as I twist and twist the corkscrew. He grunts and nods and I pull out the cork with a pop when I want to scream that he doesn't deserve their kind words, she died of a broken heart as much as she died of cancer.

Dad taps the base of his wineglass impatiently, a familiar, quiet tick that makes me want to do a kind of impotent, un-identifiable violence. I pull the cork the rest of the way out. Splash a mouthful of wine into his glass. He throws it back like it's a shot. It's meant to be a taste. You're meant to let it sit on your palate, to assess the quality of the wine as well as your enjoyment of it.

"How is it?" I ask, my customer service smile plastered on my face.

"Fine," he says.

Fine. Whatever.

"This is a 2017 from Napa," I say, filling up the others' glasses. "You'll notice ripe cherry, sweet tobacco, and hints of menthol."

They all take the time to swirl the wine, letting it splash up the sides of their glasses, holding it beneath their noses.

"I'd suggest the charcuterie, with our selection of hard cheeses, and the tenderloin or the rib eye as a pairing."

They nod. "That sounds amazing."

"Should I put the orders in for you?" I smile. An order like that would put their bill over five hundred dollars but it's not like they can't afford it. All of them are wearing at least that much on their wrists or feet.

"No," Dad growls. "We'll look at the menu."

The hairs on the back of my neck rise in fear at that tone in his voice; a sound that has always made me want to run.

"Fine," I say, just a little too sharply to be considered professional. That sound always made me want to run, but I never did. "I'll check in on you soon."

In moments like these I question why I attempt to reconnect with our father at all. If it were up to Wes, we'd have cut our losses a long time ago, but when he asks why I keep trying, I can't give him the answer he needs. Because I don't know. I don't know what I need from our father, but I know I haven't gotten it yet. I don't know what he needs but there's no way he has it, either.

Sophie stands in the middle of the kitchen, surveying her meager kingdom. Her cheeks are pink and her hands on her hips, ready to tackle whatever problem comes next. She squints at me but looks away too fast for me to grin at her, to wink.

Which is an asshole thing to do anyway. We've been on shaky ground all week. More due to the fact that she's mad at me because I didn't ask her for help than because of my failure as her leader, her boss. I don't get to flirt with her now when all I wanted was to protect her.

"Amy." Dad's voice thunders over the dining room. I'm a twenty-seven-year-old woman but his tone alone turns me into a kid. For the span of a breath, I'm frozen, twelve years old again, hoping he can't see or hear me, that whatever it is that's making him angry will blow over fast.

The half-filled room goes quiet as everyone turns to either look at me or look at the man who speaks to service staff like they count with their fingers. I smile woodenly and return to the table. I'd much rather be staring at Sophie than be the focus of his glare. "What do you need, Dad?"

"We're going to need more wine."

There's still half a bottle left.

"And the tenderloin." He orders for the whole table but none of them seem to care, sipping their wine and laughing with the kind of smugness that comes with wearing suits that are way too expensive.

"Great. I'll let the chef know," I say, inching away from the table.

"We want sides," he says with a frustrated sigh.

"The tenderloin comes with—"

"Scalloped potatoes," he says. "Broccolini."

I shift on my feet, fighting the urge to look away from him and remind myself, I wanted this. A few weeks ago, I was actually pissed that my father had never come here before. What a sweet summer child that Amy was.

"I'll have to check with the chef about the potatoes," I say slowly.

We probably have the ingredients to make them, but Sophie has an entire kitchen to run on the busiest (for us) night of the week. She's also barely spoken to me, so asking her to make these on the fly is going to suck.

"You do that," he says, the dismissal clear.

I don't even bother to tell him the worst part: we don't have broccolini. Not on the menu, not in the kitchen. And he has to know that since he wanted to study the menu so badly. I suppress the urge to scream, my frustration a fist around my throat. He's doing this on purpose.

The servers grimace in my direction as I walk away. It's the only thing we can do to help each other when we've got a table like Dad's. No one wants to take over for you—not that I'd let them—all that's left is to commiserate.

"Chef." I wait for her to look up at me but she doesn't. "I need four tenderloin."

She barely glances up from where she plates the special a few feet away. "Punch it in."

I roll my eyes. Thanks, boss. "I will. Can you make scalloped potatoes on the fly, though?"

Her hands still and she stares down at the plate. "I have the skills and knowledge to make scalloped potatoes, if that's what you're asking?"

You know that it's not, you beautiful terror. "I'm asking if we have the ingredients? And do you have the time?"

Slowly she turns to me, her jaw clenched. "Did you promise someone scalloped potatoes?"

"I didn't promise." I lean closer. "My father is here," I say, my voice lowered. "And it's a big deal that he's even come. He's…" I blush. Sophie seems like the type of person whose father makes a point to eat her food whenever he can. He probably had a standing reservation once a week at her restaurant in Montreal.

"He's never eaten at one of my restaurants before," I say. Normally, I wouldn't beg, especially not to someone I work with. But I want to be able to give him the things he's asked for not because he deserves them. He won't care what is or isn't on the menu. Dad only cares about Dad. But I care. About this restaurant, about proving to myself, to the whole team, that we're good enough. Just as good as him and his suit buddies.

"He wants scalloped potatoes." I cringe. "And broccolini."

She laughs. Even though it's sarcastic, it's still beautiful. The base of her real smile is there even if it's dimmed. "Amy, I'm sure I don't need to tell you this but we don't have broccolini."

"So let's give him long stalks of broccoli." Even as I say it I know it won't be good enough. I look over my shoulder. Sleet hits the front window, leaving streaks on the panes. The clos-

est grocery store is a fifteen-minute drive away and I'm not
going to send one of my team members out in this weather.
They wouldn't be able to get back fast enough anyway. Shit.

"Amy."

I turn to her. This feels like sophomore year, when I begged
my math teacher for an extra two percent on my grade to avoid
my father's disdain. He never cared too much about Wesley's
grades. If Wes did well, he was happy; if he didn't, Dad was
dismissive at best. But if I brought home anything less than
an A, there was no stopping his sneers.

"Sophie, please." Hopefully, only I can hear the pleading
in my voice.

She sighs and looks out over the restaurant. "That him?"
she asks, nodding at my father's table.

"How can you tell?"

"You frown the same."

Ugh.

"People say I look more like my mother."

She shrugs. "You frown like your father, though."

I can't believe I ever thought she was quiet or soft. She cuts
like a knife. I wish I liked it less. "Can you do it?" I ask.

"Obviously," she says, smug. "Jameela," she calls to our
sous-chef. "Take over here." She turns to me, her face all business, none of the flirtation I've been privy to anywhere to be
found. "But he's just getting broccoli."

"Fine." Maybe he'll be too drunk to notice by the time I
serve them. I cringe at the thought. I shouldn't be overserv-
ing our guests at all but it sure would be a big help.

I bite my lip as I stare out over the dining room. The bartender holds the shaker above her shoulders, mixing a cocktail. No one waits at the front of the restaurant; the bussers
have already flipped the empty tables, making their empti-
ness even more glaring in the dim light of the dining room.

At least, guests smile as they eat. Some take surreptitious photos of their food and of Sophie, afraid to be one of *those* people, using social media for food or celebrity sightings. It's not a terrible night by any standard. It's just not good enough, to save the restaurant, or to impress my father.

A slam on the counter behind me pulls my attention out of doom and gloom and back to the kitchen. Sophie has pressed the flat of her chef's knife over a clove of garlic. She peels off the skin and her blade flashes silver in the light as she minces, the pungent scent wafting up to my nose. She's so good with her blade, so fast as she collects the garlic's flesh and drops it into a sizzling pan then moves on to the broccoli, trimming leaves and using her strong blade to chop the stalk. I'm mesmerized.

"Don't you have a job to do?" she asks, not looking up from her work, which I prefer. I'd like her anyway but especially with all her fingers intact.

"I'm doing it," I mutter, as she squeezes a lemon wedge over the pan. "I'm the supervisor."

She tosses the lemon carcass onto the counter and turns to me. "I don't need your supervision, Amy," she says, her voice low. "I distinctly remember you saying you didn't want to supervise me at all anymore."

"I definitely never said that."

"'You should take the other job,'" she says, doing a terrible imitation of my voice.

"Right." I straighten from the deep drift I was doing toward her. Sweat glistens at the edge of her hairline, her skin dewy and glowing. "Sorry, I'll…"

I start toward the hostess stand so I don't have to finish that sentence. The scalloped potatoes will take the longest and I take my time at the front with Maggie, who doesn't actually need my help. The taps have just been changed, and I don't want to expo food and be accused of hovering again. After a quarter of an hour annoying Maggie, I stand at the back of the restaurant, watching my father start on his third glass of wine and laugh cruelly at his friends' jokes. Or maybe their expense.

Sophie's timing is impeccable. Somehow, she pulls together their family style meal at least twenty minutes faster than she should have been able to. As she lines up the tenderloins, I creep forward.

"Drew." I grab his arm as he drops off some plates for the dishwasher. "Help me bring these out."

His throat bobs as he glances between the food and my father.

"Don't worry. I'll take the lead."

With a heavy sigh, he nods.

I slide the plates to Drew and nod to Sophie. "Thanks, chef."

Her mouth curves in a tight-lipped smile as she chops. I pause on this side of the counter. Something inside me doesn't let me walk away yet. Probably avoidance, because no one in this restaurant wants to deal with my Dad's table. Except I'm still frozen here. The food will get cold. With every second that ticks by the steaks sit past their resting period. *Look at me, look.* I want her eyes. It's selfish, but I can't help it. I broke things off—whatever it was we were doing—to protect her but I don't want to make this walk alone. And Drew doesn't count. I need her. The short, stern fortitude she brings to the kitchen or the bubblier kind of strength she brings to the rest of her life. I'd take any of it, either or.

Just look.

She glances up once, a brief, uninterested scan of the restaurant, and her gaze falls on me. She looks down again, then back up. Like she's finally realized that I've been standing here begging for her eyes. The relief unfurls in me, like the soft ribbon of my old pointe shoes on the bare skin of my calf. It takes everything in me not to throw these steaks on the floor and tell her it was all a mistake. A stupid, selfish mistake. One I made to make myself feel better, like I was selfless, some kind of good person, when what I really want, what I've always wanted, was to take her to bed and make her feel so good she never wants to leave.

"The steaks," she hisses. "I didn't bust my ass for you to let our most expensive cuts get cold." I can't decide if I want to hiss back or kiss her. I settle for narrowing my eyes and telling Drew to hurry up with the rest of the plates. The smell of garlic and cheese wafts up from the tray in my hands and some of the guests turn in their seats to watch our procession go by. I don't blame them. The potatoes are beautiful, perfectly layered and crispy edged. I want to slow down, pause and present them like they're a bottle of wine to hear people *ooh* and *ahh*. Sophie is so talented, and she works *here*.

"Thanks for your patience while we pulled this together," I say as I set the cast-iron skillet in the middle of the table, on a trivet Drew sets down for me. Together we arrange the dishes as the guests move side plates and wineglasses out of the way for us.

Except for Dad.

He sits with his arms crossed over his chest. One long leg sticks out from the side of the table, so Drew has to move around him awkwardly to set the last plate down.

"I think that's everything, gentlemen." I give Drew a quick nod and he scampers away to tend to his own guests. "Is there anything else I can get for you?" I ask, doing a scan of the table for empty water or wineglasses and cutlery. "Our chef made these potatoes special," I say as the silence extends to all of his guests and I pick up the wine bottle to fill up the rest of Dad's glass, which is—surprise, surprise—almost empty.

"What is this?" He points at the plate of broccoli, the greens arranged in long stalks, their color bright, the bunch overflowing on the silver tray. They look truly perfect. Crisp but soft enough to just get the fork through. On the tray, with the antique silver tongs, they could be a home-cooked feature in a Martha Stewart magazine.

He looks at it like it's something a rat threw up on his shoe. I swallow. "Broccoli."

He takes the bottle from my hand and pours the rest of the wine himself. "We asked for broccolini."

I take a deep breath but it shakes. "Right. Unfortunately, we don't have that in restaurant. But our chef put together this dish with garlic and black sesame. I think you'll like it."

"Right." He casts a look to where Sophie stands at the edge of the kitchen. She watches us, unabashedly. "That…" He rolls his eyes. "Actress."

My fist clenches and my thoughts tumble over each other. I don't know where to start with all of the problems with that sentence. The fact that she's not an actress, she's a chef, or that there would be nothing wrong if she was an actress, or the implication that her participation on reality TV somehow made her less than.

He makes a tired, disgusted sound. "You can't even do this right," he says, quietly dismissive. My face burns as his words register with the other guests at the table.

With a shuddering breath, I push down every urge I have to spit verbal bile at him. "As I said, we don't have that ingredient in the restaurant but—"

He throws down his napkin, like he's preparing to get up and leave, and the only thing I feel is relief. Finally, he'll let me enjoy what's left of this night in peace.

"Your brother begged me to come here, you know. Said this dump needed the cash."

He shakes his head. The guests at the next table look over now, the din of the half-filled dining room lowers, and each empty chair seems to prove his point.

Dad is like any bully, something I learned quickly when Dad's behavior mirrored the kids' that gave Wes a hard time in school. He requires a strong hand, firm words. He needs to be reminded that he's not in charge here and if it were anyone else it would be me to remind them. I've always been the one to stand up to bullies, at school, at work—both coworkers and guests. But my throat closes, as if with a few words my father can paralyze me, make me the kid he's only ever seen me as.

His guests shift in their seats, avoiding my eyes. Embarrassed, even though it's him who should be ashamed, a quiet voice in a small place in my heart says. And I know it's true but when he's like this, it doesn't matter what he should be. All that matters is how mortifying it is to be his daughter. It's bad to know your father thinks so little of you; it's devastating for other people to know it, too.

Wes would never have begged him for anything but I'm mad at my poor brother nonetheless, only because in this moment, it's easier to be mad at him than at this man in front of me who's far more deserving but also more terrifying.

"You...you're..."

He shakes his head. Like he has anything to be disappointed about. "You had so much potential, Amy."

I resist the urge to smack my palm against my temple, to dislodge this hellscape dream from my brain. This is about vegetables, right? My father looks like he wants to disown me for a cruciferous veggie. Of course, that's not what it really is. He's looking for any reason to be cruel, to make himself feel better. And time after time, I let him. I open my mouth, praying for words to come.

All the things I've never said but wish I could—*You're a shit dad. I never want to see you again. You don't deserve me*—lie shriveled and brown like the pruned leaves of my plants.

"Mr. Chambers," Sophie says, suddenly beside me. My heart

stutters somewhere near the back of my throat. She leans over the table, taking plates away and passing them to Drew and Maggie, who walk them back to the kitchen.

"Thank you so much for visiting Amy & May's. I heard this was your first visit." She's taken off her cap and stuffed it into the chest pocket of her coat, the strings hang out the top. I focus on them as they dangle. Her long, thick hair is pulled back in its usual tight bun, but a few wisps frame her face. It's probably just the lighting but right now she glows.

"Unfortunately, it will also be your last. We don't tolerate the abuse of our staff. No matter who you're related to."

He glares and for a moment, everything inside me clenches. As I look around, our guests have made a show of going back to their meals, but the quick glances and hushed whispers verify that everyone is staring. The entire restaurant has stopped what it's doing to watch me be reamed out by my father, like a little girl. I've never wanted to throw up from mortification before. I couldn't even have the good luck of being humiliated in front of a full house.

Zero out of ten. Would not recommend.

But Dad does the thing he always does when confronted by someone braver than him. He retreats. "We were leaving anyway," he says, snooty.

None of his friends make eye contact as they leave. One throws a handful of bills on the table. Sophie smiles a plastic, customer service version at them. Chefs hardly ever have to use a customer service face at all. They get to stay behind their stove, scare coworkers away with their knives, and leave the front of the house to deal with people. This smile on her is unbearably strange.

"Drew, can you finish clearing this table?" Sophie asks. "We've got another table waiting."

Without her having to ask, I follow her through the restaurant. I keep my head up, but only to stare at the back of her head and the twist of her hair. To study all the different colors that auburn can actually be.

She turns into the office and rolls the chair toward me. "Sit down."

I sit.

"What were you doing before he got here?"

I blink around my office. Paperwork? No. Accounting. "I was doing…something."

She nods. "Don't come back out unless I come get you."

I scowl at the realization that she's grounding me for the rest of the night. "I'm not a child."

She reaches over the desk, like she's going to touch me, but pulls her hand back, making a fist at her side. "Amy, you're white as a sheet and you let that sad excuse for a father walk all over you. Let someone else protect you for once, okay?" She turns on the heel of her sensible shoes and leaves me lost in a cloud of her lemon scented shampoo. I should go after her and tell her all the reasons I don't deserve this, but now that I'm sitting, this evening, all the tens of thousands of worries it's brought with it, is suddenly too heavy.

As the silence settles so does my heart rate. The blood in my ears isn't quite so loud anymore and my arms and hands don't tingle. I want to talk to my brother; even just hearing his voice would bring me all the way back down to normal. But I'm too afraid of what he'd say. That it will sound too much like *I told you so.* I could call Jeremy. He's the type of friend who never questions why you're calling. He'll just make me laugh and then be totally apologetic, like he was the one calling me. But I don't know where my phone is and the energy I need to find it is bleeding out of me fast. It pumps out of my fingers, evaporating through my eyeballs until the only thing I can do is drop my head onto my arms on the desk.

The worst day of my life was the day Mom died. Leaving her side was like leaving a piece of myself behind. Like I was attached to her and the only way to move forward was to tear myself away, even if it meant losing layers of skin, maybe a limb or two. Dad's not dead. He treats his body like shit but somehow, he's the picture of health, and yet the pain feels the same. I know, in my heart, that nothing he said tonight is true. I know that I am strong and capable. I am smart and confident. I am everything I need to be. But whatever I am is just not good enough for him and now I have to leave another piece of me behind. Because I definitely can't go through that again.

The wound won't be as big or as deep. There won't be much of a scar but I'm not willing to put myself through that anymore. Especially not in front of my team, my guests.

In front of Sophie.

I moan into my forearms. I should be embarrassed that she witnessed that. I froze. I was a complete mess. But mostly I want to hold her. No one, other than my mom or my brother, steps up for me. Mostly because I don't let them. But Sophie did. She does time and again, even though I give her too many reasons not to. Even when it costs her thirty *thousand* dollars.

I want to say thank you to her in a million different ways. Breakfast in the morning, a full seating every single night. I want to make her breathless. I don't want her to choose somewhere else, someone else, over this restaurant, over me. I want to throw myself at her feet. And after that, if she decides she wants to go our separate ways and meet other women or cook somewhere else, so be it.

But right now? I want Sophie to burn herself out on me.

Hands in my hair jolt me awake. I sit up fast and immediately my neck protests the strange angle I fell asleep in. With her hand in my hair, holding the back of my head, I close my eyes again and let her take my weight.

"All set, boss," Maggie says from the doorway. Sophie and I pull apart in the most obvious way possible. She snatches her hand, hiding it behind her back, and I push my rolling chair into the wall behind me.

If Maggie's smile could talk it would say, *oh sweetie, I already knew.*

"All set for what?" I ask, standing up, then sitting down again as all the blood seems to drain from my head.

"We're done," Sophie says. "It's almost midnight."

"Shit. Sorry."

She shrugs. "Turns out all of us professional kitchen staff actually do know how to close without you."

I narrow my eyes. Cheeky.

"See you tomorrow, Maggie," Sophie says, dismissing her. Maggie waves and we both wait in tense silence until we hear the back door close behind her.

"Sorry," I say again. "That you had to close for me."

Sophie hops onto the desk. "You were passed out. Figured you needed the rest."

My brain feels like it's operating through a thick fog and every time I look at her, catching a peek of her profile, I get the feeling that I was dreaming about her.

"I was going to make you go over the finances with me, but I think you get a break tonight," she says, her eyes assessing.

"I'll email everything to you tomorrow," I promise. "Thank you again." I clear my throat. "For handling him. I wish I could say that he's not usually like that but..."

"We can talk about it," she says. "If you want?" Her legs kick, the soles of her shoes swooshing on the linoleum floor.

I shake my head. "Not really."

She looks down between her knees, biting her lip. I catch

her calf swinging in front of me. "Not right now," I amend. "But one day, I'd like to tell you about it."

"You have lines all over your face." She gestures at my cheeks. "And your hair."

I pat it down as a blush creeps up my neck. "Sorry," I croak, for no reason at all. "I'm still kind of out of it."

She hops down and pulls keys out of her pocket. "I'll give you a ride home."

I shake my head. "I'm fine. I don't need special treatment."

She wraps her hand around my wrist, squeezing gently. "Maybe not. But you had a rough night and the weather is terrible. Would it kill you to let someone take care of you for once?"

Honestly, it kind of would, but I swallow down my discomfort and nod. I manage to croak out more of my thanks. We move through the restaurant in silence, flipping off lights and double-checking locks. She holds open the back door for me and I tug my coat tighter as I slip and slide to her SUV. Behind me, the security keypad beeps as she types in the code and locks the door.

It's not until we're on the road, moving slowly through the icy streets, that the hair on the back of my neck stands up and I catch a glimpse of the back seat. If Sophie is acutely aware of the fact that the last time we were in this car together she made me come, she is not giving anything away.

"I told my mom I'm bi," she says as we wait for a stoplight to change. Her voice is perfectly neutral.

"How'd it go?" I ask as I squeeze both my fists as hard as I can. Please let it have gone well.

She laughs. "Well enough. She asked me why I can't find someone to marry me if I have double the population to choose from." She looks over at me and laughs again. "Your face."

"Is it my What the Fuck face because what the fuck, Sophie?"

She sighs, and even with the heated seats and the vents

blasting dry air at us, her breath mists in front of her as she exhales slowly. "Parents."

I guess I can relate to that. "It's the building up here on the right." I point to my three-story walk-up as she turns onto my street. She stops at the curb, putting the car into park.

"End of the line." She tips her head back against the leather headrest and closes her eyes. The console says it's 12:11am, the light turning her skin icy blue, but I know that if I ran my tongue up the path her pulse takes, it would be warm.

"What are you going to do tonight?"

She opens her eyes. The intensity she carries with her in the kitchen has bled out during the drive, so when she smiles at me there's no edge to it. It's completely sweet, like her.

"I'm going to shower. And then I'm going to go to bed."

I nod over my shoulder. "I have a shower."

Her hands grip the steering wheel. "So?"

"You could shower here."

"And sleep here?"

I shrug. "Sleep," I say. Or something.

"I thought you didn't want…"

The thing is, I've always wanted her. But I have no right to play games, to ask and then take away, then ask again. But it's *her* I want. The person that stood between me and my father's rage, the person that let me sleep. I don't want to leave this car tonight without her because I'd leave a little piece of myself with her.

"I don't want to be alone tonight," I say. "Sleep. We can just sleep," I assure her. And it's true. If all we do is fall into bed beside each other and fall asleep, it will be a gift, infinitely better than being alone. She presses her lips together. It's too much to wish for, but god she looks disappointed.

With a deep breath, she says, "Where should I park?"

Chapter Thirteen

Sophie

Amy's towels are softer than I expected. She seems like the kind of person who would never use something as frivolous as fabric softener. But then again, she didn't seem like the kind of person to have a plant named Esther living on the window ledge in her shower, either.

So maybe Amy contains multitudes.

I wipe the fog off the mirror. Through the closed door, I track her movement around the small apartment by the creak of the wooden floorboards under her weight. She seemed nervous as she showed me around, gathering way too many towels and giving me multiple options for clothes to borrow while she threw my work clothes, which smelled of cooked meat and garlic aioli, into the tiny stacked washer-dryer tucked into the corner of her kitchen.

She demonstrated how the shower worked and apologized for the small selection of shampoo and conditioner. After she left—explaining that the door needed to close just so, or it would open again, even if I locked it—I spent a full minute with my nose in her peach scented bath products.

She was too busy being overprotective to realize I only wanted this moment: to be standing in her bathroom, smelling like her. If I were catching feelings for Amy, which I'm not, I'd pretend this was an everyday occurrence. Maybe that I lived here, that we shared shampoo and clothes and a bed. But I'm not catching feelings. None at all.

I look down at the clothes Amy gave me. The sweatpants are too long, of course, but she'd already taken the liberty of rolling up the hems when she gave them to me. Even when she is hurting, she's trying to take care of me. She tries to make it impossible for me to do the same. But there's one way I can care for her. And it doesn't require sweatpants.

Steam billows around me as I open the door. Amy sits on the edge of her bed, her head in her hands. She looks tired, maybe a little broken. Before I can chicken out and close the door again, come crawling back out with my clothes on and my tail between my legs, I step over the threshold. Music plays softly from the laptop propped up on the kitchen counter. A scented candle, something that smells like it would be called Christmas Tree Farm, burns on a small table next to the windows. She's turned off all the lights in the apartment except for the one above the stove and two lamps on either side of the bed.

Between the soft light and the warm ambience, this feels romantic. But it's not. I have to remember that. I walk across the apartment. The rugs that cover the floor make it easier to sneak up on her, so my seduction can't be interrupted. I stop in front of her, press my belly gently to the top of her head, and run my fingers through her hair. She seemed to like that earlier. I don't think a lot of people touch Amy with tenderness. Probably, she doesn't let them.

"Hi."

She sits up and my hand falls away. With her eyes closed, Amy wraps her arms around my towel-clad hips, pulling me into the space between her legs. She buries her face in the towel.

"Hollywood." She says that terrible nickname like other people would curse. "I told you I didn't invite you up here for anything other than sleep. I'm being good."

Good? What's that supposed to even mean? "Did you ever consider asking me if I wanted you to be good?"

"I didn't ask you up here to sleep with me," she repeats. "But you look…" She shakes her head. "So beautiful, Sophie." She says my name softly, like it's delicate. Her hands follow the curves of my hips; her fingers tickle where the towel meets my thighs.

"What, this old thing?" I laugh at my attempt at humor.

"I feel like I keep sending you mixed signals."

I straighten, shaking my head. "Not mixed. There's nothing mixed here. Just friends and coworkers helping each other feel good." I shrug.

In this light she's a study in contrasts. Dark hair and porcelain skin. Delicate nose and eyelashes, strong shoulders. She's sharp angles, with the most vulnerable look in her eyes.

I fall too fast and too hard, and no matter what I tell myself, that will inevitably happen again. But that's a future Sophie problem. Right now, I can't bring myself to care.

It's not until I drop the towel, cool air prickling my skin and pointing my nipples, that I realize I have never been naked in front of Amy before. Pantsless, yes. Shirt askew, sure. But not bare.

I place one knee on the bed and then the other, hovering over her, and for a breathless moment I forget what comes next. There's only my heart beating so hard against my ribs that they'll be sore tomorrow, my hands on her shoulders, her eyes so wide, so open, I could fall inside them. I'm tethered to this moment, floating above her, asking her for everything, for too much, but not having the words.

But Amy knows. She always knows. She tunnels her hands

in my damp hair, giving the gentlest of tugs so I arch my back. Her lips ghost over my collarbone, leaving a trail of heat and frayed nerves in their wake. The silk of her blouse is a crumpled mess in my fist and she's barely touched me.

"Were you hard up, Hollywood?" she asks, smiling into the swell of my breast.

I run my thumb along the sharp line of her chin and jaw, tipping her head back. "Say it," I whisper.

"Say what?"

"My *name*."

Her eyes shutter. "Sophie. Were you hard up, Sophie?"

"Don't look so smug. You know I was."

She wraps her lips around my nipple and tugs me closer by my thighs.

With all the strength training I do, I'm supposed to be the strong one, but Amy flips me easily, her grin far too self-satisfied. She crawls up my body, her hair falling around her face like a dark crown.

"You are very dressed," I say.

She hums, grinning. "And you are very naked."

"Be naked, too," I whine. She rolls her eyes but sits back on her heels to pull her blouse over her head, her bra simple and white.

"Better?"

I grin, stupidly. One of the things I learned about myself when I started looking at women—really looking at women, letting myself feel the attraction I had suppressed for so long— was that I'm really into boobs. Big breasts, small breasts. The way they look in clothes, with bras, without bras, no clothes. I meditated on the feel of them pressed against mine, the taste of the skin between.

"You're staring, Hollywood."

"It's just…" My voice sounds breathless to my own ears. "I love boobs so much."

I giggle, dropping my face into my hands. Amy laughs, too. Her hands wrap around my wrists, pulling them from my face.

"I like them, too."

I cup her jaw with my fingertips. "You have really nice ones."

She huffs out a soundless laugh. "So do you."

Amy hovers over me, serious again. "You're golden," she whispers, her hand curving over my hip and stomach. Her eyes can't find a place to stop. She takes me in with the slow perusal of someone who won't be rushed. "You're glowing. Sometimes, when it's busy and you're just…" She shakes her head as her hand slips down my legs, pulling them apart, moving slowly back up my thigh. "You're in the zone. Totally focused. Your skin is flushed from the heat and there's always one piece of hair…" She tugs at a strand. "That's fallen loose. I thought that was when you were most beautiful, but I was wrong. It's right now."

In the kitchen, I've never had a problem demanding what I want. It's everywhere else in life that I'm lost, trying to make Mom happy, trying to be the person Paul thought I was, to be the woman a few thousand social media followers think I am. But Amy makes me feel brave enough to ask for what I want.

"Kiss me," I say, pulling her down to me.

Her lips on mine are always a shock. The sweet smell of her lip gloss, the smooth expanse of her skin against mine, her breasts small and full. She's everything I never dreamed I could have.

She keeps finding new places that make me shiver: the tip of my chin, underneath my breasts. She guides my arms to the bed, spreading them the width of the mattress, pressing the backs of my hands into the soft down of her comforter.

She pushes my legs apart and vaguely I remember her promise. That she'd do exactly this and make me come with her mouth. Pleasure moves through me like liquid as she kisses the hair between my legs, the soft skin of my inner thighs.

"Okay?" she asks, her breath ghosting over my lips, wet with the lust she's stoked in me.

I press my head into the mattress, lift my hips. "Please, Amy."

She holds me open, gentle but totally in control. "You never have to beg. I promise."

Amy kisses my cunt like she kisses my lips. With her whole mouth.

Her fingers tease and stretch me. Normally, I have to close my eyes to come, relax into the bed and wait for the orgasm to arrive in its own good time. But I can't look away from her dark hair between my legs.

She's right. I am beautiful. When I'm open on her bed, the sheets gripped in my fists, my hair already a mess from thrashing for her, my legs straining around her shoulders. She makes me feel beautiful.

Amy drags her tongue up my pussy, over my thighs, sucking the delicate skin into her mouth until I know she'll leave marks. She sucks my clit and instead of hoping beyond hope that this time, this one time, I'll come fast and hard, I throw my head back and moan, loud and echoing in her apartment, as I pulse against her tongue. She doesn't stop, even when I pull at her hair, bucking my hips, until my orgasm finally ebbs, and I slump back on the bed.

She crawls up my body and smiles against my cheek. "Every time. You're so good."

Pleasure glows low in my belly, an aftershock of her mouth and her words. Compliments from Amy are an addiction I didn't know I had.

★ ★ ★

We lie on our sides facing each other. Amy's body is heavy, her skin warm from the orgasm I just gave her. In the soft light she looks a little angelic, her hair a wild mess of short curls and her lips plump and turned up in the hint of a smile.

"Why do you call me that?" I whisper.

"Call you what?" she asks, her voice husky and warm. Amy drifts on the edge of consciousness, her eyes barely open. Meanwhile I can't stop touching her. My new favorite place is her ass, pulling her hips into mine.

"Hollywood."

She takes a deep breath, like she is making a concerted effort to stay on this side of awake. "Because you went to Hollywood," she says, as if it's obvious. "For the show."

I kiss her because she's cute. Her mouth tastes like me, warm and salty, and mine probably tastes like her.

I've never had a kiss like this, that tastes this good, with so much pleasure on my tongue.

"But I didn't," I say, smiling against her lips. She hums in response, her mouth buzzing against me. "We filmed in Georgia."

She rolls onto her back and flings her arm over her face. "You mean to tell me I have to call you Atlanta now?"

I laugh, too loud for the soft light and the slick feeling between my thighs. "You can still call me Hollywood. Or if you want..." I prop myself up on my elbows. "Sophie."

She grumbles. The music from her laptop is almost too quiet to reach us here, the comforter acting like a cocoon billowed up around us, keeping the world out. I creep my hand the few scant inches between us again. The urge to touch at least some part of her burns in me so that even when she rolls away, I crawl back to her. Always caressing her, keeping her on the edge of awake just to hear the soft, throaty sound of her voice.

"I'm proud of you," I whisper.

She pulls her arm off her face and frowns with her eyes closed. "Huh?"

"The way you dealt with your dad tonight. Don't worry, I won't make you talk about it," I say quickly when her jaw tenses and she opens her eyes. "He doesn't seem like an easy person to be the child of."

She shrugs. "I wouldn't say I dealt with him."

"You did better than you think."

Gently, I brush her hair back from her face. My fingers follow the curve of her ear, her jaw, back to her lips. She's such a tough person, a strong woman, that these little moments when she lets me see, or maybe lets slip these little pieces of tenderness, they almost knock me out.

"He's never been a particularly kind man," she says against the pads of my fingers. I move my hand to her chest, warm between her breasts. "But we're alike in a lot of ways."

She pauses and I have to bite my tongue not to say anything.

First because I get the feeling that Amy opening up about her father is not a common occurrence and I don't want to scare her off with any sudden movements. But also because if I said what I want to say, an immediate and absolute disavowal of the notion that she is anything like the cruel man I met tonight, I don't think she'd believe me.

Amy is not convinced by quick, empty words. Her currency is action.

Silence settles between us.

"I think that's why I keep pushing for a relationship with him." She laughs quietly. "Want to see what I'll be like one day."

I move my fingers back to her mouth, a gentle command to stop. "You'll be like you," I say.

A car sprays slush on the road outside and the sound makes

its way up to her third-floor windows. Just the suggestion of the cold makes me want to burrow into this bed, into her. I want to be her blanket.

"You're the one who should be proud," she says against my fingertips.

"Of what?"

"You're a good leader, Sophie. You're brave." She holds my hand to her face. "You told your mom. I can't believe we haven't talked about that."

I shrug. "It's okay. It was a little scary at first, but it turned out as well as I could expect."

She arches an eyebrow and rolls back onto her side to face me fully.

"Listen, if you want to pretend that coming out isn't a big deal, you can, but don't bullshit me, Hollywood. I've done it. A million times, it feels like now. Every time." She slashes her hand through the air. "It's always a little bit terrifying."

"Okay. Yes. It was scary. It's like, I know my mom loves me and I don't think she's a homophobe but what if it's different when it's her kid? And I'm so *old*."

"Yes," she says, deadpan. "You're ancient."

"She's had thirty years to think that I'm straight. I worried that finding out that wasn't true would be hard for her to accept."

Amy nods. "See?" she says. "Brave." She kisses me, a hard press of her lips to mine as if to seal this as fact.

"I'd say it was my second-best coming out experience. But I've only had three so far."

"Which was your best?"

I poke the freckle on her shoulder. "You."

"Oh." She laughs. "Yes, that was a pretty good one. What was your worst?"

I purse my lips. The sleet has picked up again, hitting the window beside her bed like a thousand tiny pebbles. "Paul."

"Paul?" Slow realization dawns on her face. "Paul. Paul? Your fiancé Paul? The producer Paul?"

I nod.

"You've got to elaborate, Hollywood," she says, her tone hard and her eyes fierce. "Because I'm kind of catastrophizing over here. Did he...did he break up with you because you're bi?"

"No." I squeeze her hand. "No. The opposite, actually."

"He...he dated you because you're bi?"

I laugh. "No."

"You broke up with him because you're bi."

I flop onto my back. "He said...he asked...well, first, I said, that I didn't want anything to change between us but that I just wanted him to know, I guess. It felt like something important to me. I was scared to know this about myself but also proud. To suddenly realize straight girls didn't think about other girls like I did. To finally give a name to what all those feelings were. I wanted to share it and I wanted..." I shake my head. "In the moment, I wanted to hear him say he believed me, that it was important to him, too. But he asked me to keep it a secret. Like if I didn't want to break up or open our relationship, there was no point in taking it public. Why did I deem it important to tell him?"

She sucks in a breath. Her lips press against my temple, soaking up a silly, hot tear.

"He apologized the next day," I say. "But..." I bite my lip. "I'm a forgiving person. Not in my kitchen," I say quickly when she snorts. "In my personal life, I forgive and forgive and sometimes it's bitten me in the ass to give people so many chances. But this thing. This one little thing. I couldn't forgive."

"This one little thing of affirming your identity," she says flatly.

"I know I'm making excuses for him. But honestly, once the hurt wore off, I kind of felt…"

I squeeze my eyes shut. After the first few days, once the hurt and the shock of what I'd done had worn off, all that was left was relief. Relief because we'd gotten together so fast and were hurtling toward marriage and I'd done it again, jumped into something without really thinking it through. There were two paths for my life that bisected that night: on one path I stayed with a man I had truly loved, and we got married. I'd be a bi woman married to a straight man and I'd have been happy.

On the other path I was alone, but I got to explore who I was on my own terms, at my own pace. And neither path was the wrong one. I just know that the relief I felt meant that I chose the right path *for me.*

"That I had made the right decision," I say slowly.

Amy talks about wanting me not to burn out on her but what I think she's really saying is that she doesn't want me to use her for sex and then move on. That's something a flighty person would do. Something a person who, say, runs headlong into relationships, into business partnerships, who throws their savings into the pot to save a business, might do.

She doesn't need any more proof that I move faster than a freight train. And really, it's not my fault anyway. She's the one who's so hot.

And infuriating.

And secretly soft.

She smiles. "Good. Obviously, I am reaping the benefits of that decision, so I support it." She laughs to herself, her eyes closing again like she might decide to drift back to sleep.

Her hand breaks a trail through the goose bumps on my

skin from my hip to my breast. I cover it with my own as she caresses me. She crawls onto her elbows, scooting across the bed to get closer to me. There's something intoxicating about being the object of her affection. When Amy looks at me like this, with her eyes so big they could devour me, her cheeks flushed like nothing excites her more than my body laid out beneath her, it's easy to let myself be distracted by her touch, to let her put her hands and her mouth all over me again.

But Amy yawns, triggering one in me. I close my eyes to the hazy gold that surrounds us, the heat from her body and her sweet murmurs. Her body gets heavy again, and I am tired too, but my heart still races and I keep my eyes closed tight in the hopes that eventually sleep will take me. If I fake it long enough.

Because I can't look at her and keep control of the rest of me. If I look, I'm afraid I'll do something silly, something I'll regret. Like let this moment get the better of me. Because she's beautiful and she makes me want to be a better chef. She makes me feel brave enough to stand in front of a camera again. To put myself on display for everyone to pick apart. She makes me feel so proud to be queer from all the quiet, regular ways she is just herself, every day. Amy takes me apart bone by bone, and I am happy for it. And all these feelings make me want to say something stupid. Something a person who rushes into everything says.

So, I keep my eyes closed and I imagine that under different circumstances I could tell Amy that she makes me want to be as brave as she is.

Chapter Fourteen

Amy

The space where Sophie was sleeping last night is still warm as I slide my hand, with increasing urgency, around the bed. For a heartbeat I luxuriate in that warmth, the knowledge that she was here at all a balm that pushed the embarrassment from my father's reprimands and the fear for my restaurant to the back of my mind.

A floorboard creaks and I sit up, fast. The comforter pools around my waist and Sophie stops, her shoes in her hands, her eyes on my chest. "Were you...are you leaving?" I ask.

She winces, dropping her shoes in a clatter to the floor. "I was going to get us coffee," she says quickly.

I cover my breasts with my hands. If she's going to sneak out after sex, she doesn't get to see my tits anymore. "I have coffee in my kitchen." I point to the coffeemaker but quickly retract my arm when it reveals nipple.

She rushes forward, kneeling on the edge of the bed, her hands out, placating. "I know, but it was going to be loud and you looked so...peaceful and... I wanted to do something nice for you. Get you a coffee and bring you a pastry or something." She shrugs, picking at a thread on the duvet. "I left you a note," she says, like this proves her story.

I hold out my hand palm up, and she runs over to the

counter, where a piece of paper sits tented beside my laptop. My name, written in her loopy cursive, covers the front fold.

Hopefully you'll still be asleep by the time I get back but if not, hold tight. Getting you coffee ;). Don't be grumpy. I'm coming back.

I scoff but place the note on my bedside table, my name up. "I wouldn't have been grumpy."

She stares in deadpan. "You're literally grumpy right now."

I wave her words away. "You're not supposed to get me coffee anyway."

"I'm not?"

"Of course not." I throw off the covers and run to the closet, pulling on my old BU sweater and a pair of joggers. "I'm supposed to make you coffee."

"You are?"

"Yes." I toss a new tank top and sweatpants at her. Sophie catches them with her face and a quiet *ooph*. "Those are the rules. Put those on."

She laughs, looking down at the clothes with what I really hope is frustrated adoration and not just frustration. "Amy, I...usually I meet my weightlifting coach in the morning. I have to go home and get changed and go to the gym and then I've got to work on some recipes." Her voice tightens into a whine. An entirely unendearing sound that she somehow still manages to pull off.

"I thought you were going with the risotto?"

"Maybe. I don't know."

"Do I get a say in this?"

She pauses, her eyes narrowing. "Normally, I'd say yes since it's your restaurant. But I just invested in it so now it's my business, too. Specifically, the kitchen."

A laugh bursts out of me. "You purchased the kitchen? Just the kitchen?"

"It makes sense that the kitchen is primarily my property,"

she says, a mischievous grin brightening her eyes. "But seriously, I want to do this myself. And right now, the risotto recipe is *not* working."

I press my lips together, secretly relieved. Risotto was too safe.

"Fine. You won't hear anything from me." I look her in the eye. "I trust you."

She blooms under the praise.

"But," I say as I measure enough beans into the grinder for two people. "Rules are rules." The grinder covers her reply and I mime not being able to hear her. "Put those on," I shout.

She rolls her eyes but starts to switch out last night's work clothes for more of my own. I smile down at the grinder. By the time the grounds are fluffy and fragrant, Sophie is fully changed, sitting at a barstool along the counter, hunched over her phone. "Lucky for you, my coach canceled our session this morning because of the weather. The roads coming into the city are bad, apparently."

I nod like this was all a part of my plan. The triumph I feel at having her here makes me feel at least thirty percent responsible for the inclement weather.

"So who makes these rules, by the way?" she asks, setting her phone on the counter. "These supposed you-make-me-coffee rules?"

Well, it's me. I make the rules. But I know a trap when I see one and I'm about to walk into the you're-being-pushy-again trap. "Sappho," I say with all the authority of a lesbian on a power trip.

She grumbles something that sounds like, *it's a good thing you're cute.*

As the water boils, I scoop grounds into the French press. "Rule number two is that I make you breakfast." I pour the water and put the lid on. "I was thinking bacon or sausage, depending on what I have in the fridge, and ricotta lemon pancakes?"

Sophie's face falls as I turn around. She puts a hand on her stomach. "I don't really eat breakfast."

"I'm sorry." I laugh. "I thought you said you don't eat breakfast."

"I did."

I frown, replaying her words again. "Do you mean...you don't feel like eating breakfast right now?"

She shakes her head. "I'm not really a breakfast person." She shrugs.

The windows along the east side of my apartment create a hopscotch grid of sunlight on the floor and furniture, creeping along the counter toward her hand. All the plants in the room are permanently turned toward the windows and I turn to them now, too, to contemplate how someone so beautiful can be so terribly wrong.

"Wait. What about before you work out? You have to eat before you do that."

"Not really. My body has learned to adjust. I generally don't eat before I work out since I go so early in the morning. I'll eat after, though."

"You eat nothing? That can't be healthy."

She looks down at herself. "I don't know. Do you think I look unhealthy?"

She grins because she knows she has me. She looks like a fucking bomb went off in a hot girl factory.

Sophie rolls her eyes. "Sometimes when I'm on my period I'll have some fruit before I go to the gym. My body needs more help processing the carbs during that time, so I'll give it a bit of a boost with the extra sugar."

"Why don't we just pretend you already worked out," I

say brightly. "Then you can eat breakfast. Beautiful, delicious breakfast."

She twists her lips in a pensive pout. She seems like maybe she wants to. Maybe I've convinced this woman of the absolute necessity of breakfast food. "I really don't like it."

I push the plunger on my French press down a little harder than necessary. But it's not like I'm going to force-feed her. Sophie hops down from the stool and comes around the counter. For a moment, she stands behind me, a warm presence at my back, one I've felt a million times before in our work kitchen, but one that feels far more intimate here, in the morning light, in the green haze of my apartment turned nursery.

Sophie slips her arms around my waist, pressing herself to my back; her head rests between my shoulder blades. "But I'd love to stay and help you cook for yourself," she says, the sound of her voice traveling through my rib cage into that warm place around my heart.

I put my hand over hers where they link around my stomach.

None of this is what I should want: waking up together, cooking outside our professional kitchen. Sophie should be meeting other people, learning about who she likes, what she likes, exploring all the amazing ways she gets to be herself. But I'm selfish, in more ways than one, since she absolutely should be off testing recipes. And I'm stupid. Because part of me hopes that somehow, after all is said and done, she won't want anything to do with anyone else.

She'll only want me.

"Just so you know." I squeeze her hand. "I own one hundred percent of this kitchen."

Her laughter shakes my back. "Yes, chef," she says quietly, kissing me through my sweater.

I could lie and tell myself it's hearing her hand over her

power in the kitchen to me. That I'm still drunk on the lingering scent of her lemon shampoo or the way her lashes fan her cheekbones as her eyes flutter closed. That I'm just intoxicated by the goose bumps I get when she presses her laugh into my skin. But the least I can do for myself is be honest. And honestly, I'd hand over my chef's knife right now if she asked me to. I'd never cook again.

I'm too scared to think about what that means.

Despite my assertion that I'm in charge in this kitchen, it's hard not to be distracted by Sophie. She approaches this meal with the same seriousness that she does our work, tying her hair back and glaring furiously at pancake batter when it's runnier than she expects.

"Hey," I say, as she carefully slices the lemon zest into a twist. "You're kind of good at this."

She flushes. "Cooking?"

I wait until she puts down her knife before I set the tongs against the pan of sizzling bacon and kiss her neck. "Being my sous-chef."

She laughs, throaty and a little bit evil. "Just this once." And I know she means being my sous-chef, and not she'll cook in this kitchen just this once. But the thought sucks nonetheless. I turn back to the bacon, laying the strips down on a paper towel to soak up the fat.

Sophie has asked me, more times than I deserve, to stop protecting her. Maybe I should stop being so dumb and just listen to her.

"How's this?" she asks, pulling me out of my head.

She's piled the pancakes high on the plate; the blueberry coulis I made dribbles down the side. The dish is topped with extra ricotta, whipped and drizzled with a lemon reduction.

"That is…gorgeous."

She smiles, obviously pleased.

"This is sort of like recipe testing," I say. "Maybe we should serve Camilla pancakes."

She rolls her eyes. "We don't even have a breakfast menu."

"You can eat breakfast food any time of day."

She shakes her head. "It has to be something special. Unique. I can't just throw any dish in front of her," she says, her voice teetering on a sharp edge.

"Are you nervous?" I ask. "About cooking for a celebrity chef."

She shrugs, folding and unfolding a dish towel. "Not really."

Which makes sense. She's cooked for a celebrity chef before, for eight weeks on *Pop-Up Kitchen*. "So, it's just the show in general," I say. When she doesn't respond, I ask, "What happened there, Sophie?"

Frost patterns the kitchen windows and she looks there instead of at me. "I thought the show was going to be about food. Cooking. Maybe that was stupid of me."

"You're not stupid."

"Naive, then. But it wasn't about the food at all. It was about the drama and getting yelled at by the chef and strategizing in order not to get kicked off for another week. When I cook in a restaurant, it's not about me. It's about the food. But it feels like it hasn't been about the food for so long now. Sometimes it feels like it will never be about the food again."

"It sounds like you lost yourself on that show."

She looks up at me. Her eyes seem greener when she's here, surrounded by all my plant babies. "Can we talk about something else?"

My first instinct is to say no. To sit her down and tell her about how *obsessed* I was with her because of that show, because of her *cooking*. Her laser focus, her creativity. I can't reconcile that ferocity with the lost soul in front of me now.

But I'm a new Amy. I'm not bossy anymore. At least, not with her.

"Sure." I shrug like this is exactly what I want to do, as well. She adjusts the garnish on the plate, and I follow her gaze.

"Where'd you get mint?" I ask, pointing to the sprigs of mint leaf. "And are they…" I squint. "Candied?"

"I sprinkled them in a little sugar. I got it from that plant over there."

"Ursula?!" I shriek.

Sophie puts the stack of objectively gorgeous pancakes down. "I'm sorry. Is your mint plant named Ursula?"

I turn and transfer the bacon to my plate to hide my red face. "Some studies show that naming plants helps them grow."

"Was I not supposed to use Ursula's leaves?"

"It's okay. She was having a bit of trouble growing recently, but she's doing better. It's fine." I will simply spend some extra time with her today for some post-pruning recovery.

I smile to prove it. "Thank you," I say. "Breakfast has never looked more beautiful."

"This was fun," she says, like she wasn't quite sure it would be until just now.

"Are you sure you don't want any?" I ask. *Are you sure you don't want to talk about this?*

She stands on the edge of the kitchen. Suddenly, she seems so far away, remote.

"The next time you make eggs Benedict, I'll be here, but I should go. My cat has probably eaten through all her kibble by now."

"Sure." I didn't even know she had a cat.

After a moment of me nodding she steps forward, placing her hand on my hip, and reaches up to kiss me, just under my jaw. "And listen." She takes a deep breath. "I want you to know that I'm happy to keep this casual. I get that you want to keep things cool between us for the show. So you don't have to worry about me, okay?"

I swallow twice, a third time. My mouth is so dry. "Right," I say. "Cool."

"Is it okay if I wear these home?" She plucks at the sweats. "I'll wash them and bring them into the restaurant tonight."

I nod. I don't think I'll be able to get any more words out without at least a liter of water. I'm not even upset with her. She's only doing exactly what I said she should.

Sophie grabs her stuff and blows a kiss from the door. It clicks shut behind her and I'm left alone in the middle of my kitchen, the bacon cooling on the plate, the whipped ricotta losing its form, the coulis pooling at the base of the pancake stack.

At certain times of day, when the sun hits all the plants in the windows just right, the room gets a hazy green quality to it. It's fitting now because I feel a bit hazy. What the fuck did I do?

"Well, shit," I say to my plants. Rule number one of fucking your business partner is not to catch feelings. But if the pain shooting through my chest is any indication, I've caught something. "Now what am I going to do?"

But of course they don't answer.

Chapter Fifteen

Sophie

This is for the best.

I tell myself that when I pull up to the restaurant. Amy's car is already there, without snow tires—a death trap in weather like this.

It's for the best, when the first thing I hear when I walk in is her laugh, a hard cackle that sounds mean, sharp, and unkind to an unfamiliar ear but is actually the most unrestrained version of herself.

This is for the best, but I don't quite believe it even as I push open the door to the front of the house, grocery bags filled with seafood paella ingredients banging my knees. Amy stands in the kitchen with her back to me, and I take the opportunity to stare unabashed at her strong shoulders and the slight curve of her waist. Her undercut always thrills me. It's edgy and irreverent in a way I've never been able to be. But mostly it's the feel of the short hair against my fingertips and the way it sends goose bumps down her neck when I trail my fingers through it that I love the most.

My grin could crack my face in half as I stroll up behind her. This is for the best but it's completely casual to run your fingers through your business partner's hair, right? It must be. I even lift my hand, the grocery bag obstructing any chance of me touching her, until she throws her head back and laughs again and I see the person making her make that sound.

"Paul?" I stop, the heavy bag pulling my arm back down. He straightens from where he was leaning against the bar.

"Hey, Soph." He smiles. "How are you?" We do that awkward dance, shuffling then stopping until he takes the initiative and closes the gap between us, holding me gently by my biceps and kissing each cheek. "Good to see you," he murmurs.

"You, too. What are you guys…" I gesture between them. I got the distinct feeling that Amy didn't like Paul the last time he was here. But she laughed her real laugh, her big laugh, with him just now.

"Paul stopped by while I was doing some paperwork." A two-top is strewn with her binders and her old brick of a laptop. "We've been chatting."

"About what?" My fingers pulse as the plastic bags cut off my circulation and I swallow a quick shot of shame that I didn't pick up my fabric ones on the way out the door.

They wouldn't talk about me? Would they? Somehow, I've gone thirty years without ever having two lovers in the same room at the same time. I've quite possibly never felt so awkward in my whole life.

"Restaurants," he says. He smiles strangely, his face asking, *why are you being weird?*

"Right. Restaurants." Turns out I'm not the only thing they have in common; arrogant of me to think so, frankly. There's hours of conversation in restaurants.

"But now that you're here…" He pauses dramatically, ever the showman. "A lot of people don't know this, but Camilla has been quite involved in our selection process. She saw your application tape and read up on this place." He looks around approvingly.

This place has good bones. I felt it the moment I walked in. The decor is bright, and even with the lights off and the seats empty, I could tell it was special.

That's because of Amy.

She'd never admit it but it's her heart in here that makes it feel this way, like you've been here before, like you're coming home.

"Camilla insisted that we include Amy & May's in our first season."

The words hang in the silent dining room for a moment until, like we're both on a timer, Amy and I turn to each other. She doesn't squeal or scream or throw her hands in the air. She just smiles, a little crookedly, and says, "Holy shit, Hollywood."

I laugh. "If I'm Hollywood, then what should I call you? Boston?"

She cracks her knuckles. "You got us here. You can call me whatever you want."

Every cell in my body is tuned toward her. I want to hold her face in my hands and tell her that it was her, all her. I thought I'd feel dread when this moment came, that I'd be terrified of being back in the spotlight, if only for a moment. And I am scared, especially about what I'm going to cook because now the pressure is on, but there's also joy and excitement. Joy because she's joyful and excitement because this time I'm not navigating this alone. There's no strategy or backstabbing. I have a team plus a force of nature: Amy Chambers.

The way I feel about her is probably written all over my face. I can't decide what's worse: my ex-fiancé seeing that I'm hopelessly gone for my business partner or my business partner noticing that I'm stupidly obsessed with her after promising her that this was, that I could be, casual.

"What now?" I turn back to Paul. "I mean, what's next?

What do we need to do?" He looks at me like I've lost my mind but hopefully he chalks it up to excitement and nerves.

"We'll send you an itinerary in the next day or so. There will be paperwork to sign."

I nod. If it's anything like *Pop-Up Kitchen*, it's a lot of non-disclosures and privacy agreements, filming and ownership rights for the content.

"Scripts," he says, casually.

"Scripts?" Amy says. "I thought this was reality TV?"

Paul shrugs, looking a little uncomfortable. "You won't have to memorize lines. But there are themes that get pulled from your backstory to create..."

"Drama," she finishes for him.

He nods once and she clenches her jaw. For a moment, I want to tell her to fuck it. We don't need this show if it makes her uncomfortable—especially the idea of drumming up her past, her mom or dad, or her sexuality—but then she smiles again, effortless. I could have been imagining the tension.

"So be it," she says.

"And you'll need to start recipe testing," he says, his voice teasing because he knows exactly how much I love to tinker in the kitchen.

"I've got that covered." I gesture to the bags.

"What's this?" Amy peers into the first bag and slowly frowns. "You're making..." She pokes her head into the next bag. "Paella?"

I glance between her and Paul. Is he even allowed to hear this information?

He holds his hands over his ears and lets out a high-pitched scream. "Keep it a secret." He jogs for the door and grins over his shoulder as he leaves.

"He's a peculiar fellow," Amy says slowly, very clearly trying not to insult my former lover and our current television producer.

I giggle. "Yes. He is."

"Paella?" she asks again.

I shrug. "I thought it might be a better a dish to serve. Better than risotto at least." I definitely do not imagine the look of relief on her face at my mention of the now unfashionable risotto. "Camilla probably prefers paella to risotto, right?" I ask, pulling ingredients out of their bags and organizing them on the counter based on when they'll be used in the recipe.

Amy closes her eyes, shakes her head. The day outside is the kind of dull gray only possible in mid-March, and the restaurant is dark and gloomy wherever our moody overhead lights cannot reach, casting her face in deep shadows.

"You're making a classic Spanish dish. For a Spanish chef?" Her voice has that same tone she uses to call Paul peculiar or speak to guests on the phone.

"Well…" It seemed like a good idea as I stood in the middle of the produce section of the grocery store this morning. "Yeah."

Amy hums.

"Just say it."

She shakes her head and presses her lips together, her eyes too big in her head. "Say what?"

"Whatever it is you want to say," I growl.

"This is the kitchen. This is your domain. I'm staying out of it."

I sigh. "Just tell me. I know it's killing you."

She leans her hip against the counter, a pensive look on her face. "I've never seen you eat paella, or cook it, or talk about it. Are you making paella for us?" She gestures to the restaurant. "For you? Or are you making it for Camilla?"

"Obviously I'm making everything for Camilla." I pull a kitchen knife out of the block and start in on a Spanish onion.

"This is your chance to express yourself through your food. At least with the risotto it was something you *like*, right?"

"That's easy for you to say." I turn my back to her and crush a garlic clove against the flat of my knife. It's not that she's wrong. In fact, she's almost categorically right. I don't even have that much experience making paella. "It's been great these last few weeks, okay? The whole team feels like it's coming together. But as much as I have this team behind me, you behind me, this time, there's only one person in the kitchen when it comes time to start filming."

"This time?" A line appears between Amy's brows. "You mean like when you were on *Pop-Up Kitchen*?" She closes the space between us, holding my face in her hands. "This will be nothing like last time. I promise you. Whatever you need. I'll do it."

My heart pounds like when I lift something heavy or run to the top of Mont Royal. I crave her touch, aching for it, and kiss the soft skin on the inside of her wrist. "Are you saying this as my business partner or as something more?"

She drops her hand.

"I'm not trying to put you on the spot," I say quickly, stepping away to give myself space and at least the illusion of control. "But you say you want me to spread my baby queer wings and then I go and burst right through that and…" I close my eyes when she opens her mouth and she must take it for what it is: a request, a pause, the time for me to think through what I want to say next without interruptions. "I like this *casual* thing we have," I say and it's only a little bit of a lie because it's very much not casual for me. "But when we're at work we need to…"

"Work," she finishes.

I nod.

"I can do that." And she puts more space between us. "But I meant what I said, Hollywood. Whatever you need."

She pushes through the swinging doors to the back hallway. This kitchen has never felt so cold, like she took the fire with her. I turn back to my paella ingredients.

"This is for the best." If I say it enough times, maybe eventually it will be true.

It becomes believable as the night goes on, the idea that this is for the best. Specifically, the show is for the best. Even if we don't get Camilla's stamp of approval, the exposure will do so much for us. The chance to cook for Camilla Vargas feels like redemption for all the people who stopped coming here after Paul and I broke up. If only I can get this recipe right.

"When are we going to tell them?" I ask as Amy wipes down a four-top at the end of the night.

"Tell who what?" She doesn't look up from the spotless table as she rubs the cloth over the surface until it shines.

"The team." I edge closer until my hip accidentally brushes hers and we both step back. "When are we going to tell the team about the show," I whisper.

Her mouth twists. "What decision would support you best?"

I blink, processing the sharpness in her tone. *Okay, then.*

"I guess we tell them soon. It's not like they'll have to do too much. But hopefully they'll be excited."

She nods like she's listening, but her gaze is focused on the already clean tabletop and her mind seems far away.

"Hey, you're excited about this, right?" I ask. "You want to do this? With me?"

She nods quickly. "Yeah. For sure." She looks at me from the corner of her eye. "Have you had a chance to review the finances I sent you?"

"Sorry. Not yet. Did you have action items for me?"

"No. I'm just concerned, I guess. Take a look and then we'll talk."

I wait for the span of a few exhales but she doesn't say anything else. Amy is so regularly unflappable that when she is, for lack of a better term, flapped, it's noticeable.

To me at least.

"Are you upset?" I ask. "About the...boundaries?" I gesture to the kitchen behind us where we had our last conversation that wasn't about eighty-sixing fish tacos.

"I'm fine, Hollywood. Promise." She walks to the large table in front of the windows, leaving me alone at the back of the restaurant.

"Should we celebrate then?" I ask, following her.

She glances over my shoulder, where Jameela finishes a scrub-down of the grill. "Tomorrow," I say, closing the gap between us. "Why don't you take me out for drinks and I'll take you out for dinner."

Her eyes narrow. "Are you asking me out on a date, Hollywood?"

"No," I say quickly. But my heart flutters like the silly schoolgirl I am whenever I'm around her. What would a real date with Amy be like? Would she pick me up in her little red car? What kind of restaurant does a restaurant owner take her head chef to anyway? Maybe we wouldn't go out to eat at all, maybe we'd go to a hockey game or a museum or the theater.

"No." I shake my head to punctuate how very much I am *not* thinking about dating her. "Of course not. That would be...confusing."

She makes a sour face like she's disappointed.

"I'm just saying we should celebrate. Right? Why not tomorrow since we're closed on Mondays. We have nowhere to be."

"Can't," she says, absently. I'm certain that she's already polished this table based on the high shine of the wood. "I have plans."

"What are you doing?"

"Going to a drag show with my brother and a couple of our friends."

"Cool," I say into the silence, where she most definitely did not invite me to tag along. Not that she should. She's allowed to have her own life. And plans. And people. And I don't want to be one of them. Not at all. "Well, maybe I'll pop a mini bottle of champagne or something."

I leave before I can say anything more, like beg to be invited or ask her if it's just me or if she's being rude. I toss my chef's whites in the restaurant linens bin and pull on my coat. Our commercial landlord has sprinkled salt and sand on the pavement out here, but I still pick my way carefully to my car, frowning at each new foothold but not really seeing them. Instead, I'm trying to decipher what that face meant when I said I wasn't asking her on a date or the one she made before she assured me that she was excited.

I throw myself into my car and turn on the engine, letting it warm up and closing my eyes, and jump seconds later at the sound of three sharp taps on my window. Amy stands at my car, the back door of the restaurant open and spilling a perfect rectangle of yellow light onto ice and snow. "Open," she says, muted through the glass.

"Bossy," I mutter, but push down the button for the power window. "Please?" I ask for her.

She smirks. "You want to come tomorrow?" she asks. "To the drag show?"

Yes. "No. I'm fine."

"Come on, Hollywood. Sorry I was being cold in there. I'm just..." She shrugs. "Thinking."

"It's fine," I say. "Thinking about what?"

"You. Me. My brother and his girlfriend. Like eight of our closest friends. And the most gorgeous drag queens you'll ever meet. I'll buy our first bottle of champagne." She holds the door, her fingers curling over the edge of the window, and I want to curl them around my own fingers and bring them to my lips. Her breaths and mine mingle in a cloud between us.

This is for the best.

"Fine," I say. "Since you're begging me."

Her smile turns real and wide. "Cool. I'll send you the details tonight."

"Great."

She hovers there, her mouth a few inches away, the open door beckoning behind her.

"Great," she repeats and it's probably wishful thinking that she leans closer. I adjust the heat on the seat warmers, turning away from her to focus on the dashboard, instead of embarrassing myself by closing the gap between us.

"Later, Hollywood."

I watch her walk back to the door, unafraid of the ice and the cold, like she's unafraid of everything.

"Bye." I sigh.

Chapter Sixteen

Sophie

Amy & May's is going to be on TV! Catch us on the first season of Cooking for Camilla. *Our superstar head chef, Sophie Brunet, dusts off her show knives to cook for the best in the business. Want to know what we'll be serving Camilla? You'll have to watch to find out ;)*

Amy's post went out to the meager few hundred Instagram followers on the Amy & May's account. I reshared it. Then Paul. Then *Camilla Vargas*. The *Cooking for Camilla* Instagram account, *Pop-Up Kitchen*'s account. Now the fan accounts are running away with things.

My phone is constantly vibrating, and I've wasted most of my day off engaging with our audience rather than cooking. My kitchen is an explosion of unused ingredients, but at least Amy & May's has a few thousand more followers tonight. I turn the phone on Do Not Disturb and drop it in my bag. I am officially signing myself out of duty.

The Hideaway Club makes no attempts to hide itself from anyone on Columbus Avenue. The first story is done up like an old movie theater, the glittering marquee filled with the names of the drag queens performing tonight. Every possible iteration of a Pride flag hangs from the second-story balcony, the windows plastered in portraits of more queens.

The Canadian in me doesn't want to walk past the long line of people stamping their feet and blowing into their gloved hands—on a Monday of all nights—waiting to get into the booming noise of the club, but Amy said my name was on a list. As politely as possible, I march past them, my chin raised and my mouth clamped shut to keep from apologizing.

The bouncer has short dark hair and deep dimples and looks like she could hold her own on a wrestling mat, but her pom-pom hat diminishes the overall scary vibe. "Name?"

"Sophie," I say. "Brunet."

She arches an eyebrow as she towers over me. "ID?"

Right. Shit. I fumble with my wristlet and pull out my driver's license. I haven't been ID'd in years. I also haven't gone to a bar or restaurant where I didn't already know the owner or most of the staff. Walking in here feels a little like the first day of high school.

The bouncer unclips a red velvet rope from a golden post. "Welcome to the Hideaway."

Collectively, the line grumbles as I walk past, and I tunnel into the collar of my coat to hide from their judgment until I'm safely inside. There's a lineup for coat check, and music booming so loud I can feel it in my back teeth. I stand on the periphery of the club, rows and rows of tables laid out in a grid before me, stopping at a stage where techs set up lights, props, and stage markers. It's dark, except for the bright flashes of colorful lights that streak across the space every few seconds. It's like every other club I've ever been to. From the noise to the faint whiff of vomit coming from the bathrooms.

Except it's also nothing like any bar I've been to before. For a Monday night in the dead of winter, it's absolutely packed to the seams. Even bars that host industry nights can't get this kind of turnout on a Monday, the only night of the week when most restaurants are closed so restaurant workers can go out and let their hair down. Above the bar there's a neon sign that says *kiss the girl* in hot pink letters, and many of the patrons have taken this message to heart. Girls kiss on the steps to my right, at a table for two pushed up against the mirrored wall, underneath the mirror ball. Boys kiss in the line for the bathrooms, too. They do shots and take lime wedges from each other's mouths. Queer folks as far as the eye can see, kissing other queer folk. I can't believe it's taken me this long to step inside a bar like this, even before I knew I belonged here, too. There's so much joy, so much love, in this hot, sweaty space.

I never want to leave.

"Are you Hollywood?" asks a drag king in suspenders and a white tank top with a serving tray loaded with drinks.

"I...yes...well, my name is Sophie? How did you...?" He points across the room to a table near the front of the stage. An Asian man in a Sox ball cap stands on his chair waving at... me, I think. Even though I'm sure I've never met him before in my life. I do, however, recognize Wes and his girlfriend, Corrine, seated beside him. Even from my spot on the stairs, I can see the bright pink nail polish on his fingernails as he tucks hair behind her ear. Finally, my eyes fall on Amy sitting opposite them and the sight of her almost makes me turn and run from the room.

She's had her hair touched up since last night, the fade on the undercut smooth and the lines crisp. Her hair swoops to one side in a tangle of ringlets big enough for me to stick my finger through. Her cheeks and brow line shimmer in the flashing lights and reflection from the mirror balls hanging from the ceiling; her lips are a deep, shiny plum. She looks like a combination of the kind of faerie that exists to tempt humans to eat and drink and dance until they die and all of my Kristen Stewart as a Twilight vampire fantasies combined.

"They asked me to grab you. You can follow me." He tosses his slicked back red hair into place and moves through the crowd, somehow getting jostled by the crush of people but failing to spill a drop from his tray. My legs follow him, or more accurately, they go to Amy. But I stop a few feet from the table, even as she slides a chair toward me with the toe of her combat boot. She wears a strapless white crop top underneath a leather jacket. Her black jeans are skintight.

Amy might be trying to murder me. Between the blood draining from my head and the words I'm trying to come up with, my heart can't keep up. I can feel my pulse in my throat, the tips of my fingers, lower.

"Sit down," she says.

"I'm underdressed." I look down at my black T-shirt. The fanciest thing about my outfit is my cuffed jeans. Her eyes do a slow, circuitous route down my body before she meets my gaze again.

"You look good to me." She has to shout the words over the music and the crowd, but she has a way of saying it like it's just for me. Like no one else could even hear her.

How am I supposed to pretend to be casual now?

"Sit," she says again. I do and she hooks her boot around the leg of my chair and pulls it closer to her. I close my eyes for just one deep breath. *Get it together, Hollywood.*

She throws her arm around me. "Everyone, this is Hollywood."

"Sophie," I say. Corrine waves across the table. She's the only other one not covered in glitter or something bright. Her red lips are the only pop of color on the black silhouette of her outfit. She looks like she came straight from work.

"It's nice to see you again," she says.

Wes reaches over the collection of half-full pint glasses to offer his fist for a bump. "Hey, Sophie."

The others go around introducing themselves. There are so many of them, I know I'll forget half their names by the end of the night. The other half, I can't hear over the cacophony in the room. People shout and squeal and sing along to music that I don't recognize but that sounds cool and hip nonetheless.

"I'm Jeremy." The tall man who had been waving from his chair reaches across the table to shake my hand. Someone has painted a Pride flag onto his cheek and it crinkles into his deep dimple.

"Jeremy?" The Jeremy she experimented kissing boys with?

He looks between Amy and I. "Has she told you all about me?" He looks exceptionally pleased with himself.

"I might have mentioned you once or twice," she assures him. They launch into an argument over who is Amy's best friend, him or Wes—Wes, it's obviously Wes—but I'm too distracted by Amy's hand, curling the ends of my hair between her fingers, to pay much attention.

I glance over at her again and again and she responds with a gentle tug at my hair or a squeeze of my shoulder. Eventually, the conversation moves down the table and she turns to me.

"Do you want something to drink?" She leans in closer than necessary, to whisper in my ear. I shudder, closing my eyes. Her voice travels through my body like an electric current. I thought I'd like to have a celebratory glass of champagne to-night, maybe a cocktail, but now I think I need every single one of my wits about me.

"Just water," I croak, my throat dry. "What are you hav-ing?" I nod to her tumbler glass filled with something clear and bubbly, a slice of lime wedged along the rim.

"Keep a secret?"

I nod. She could make me do just about anything right now.

"It's just sparkling water. Normally, we get a little rowdy on drag show night, but I wanted to keep things low-key."

I nod. "Smart."

I have no idea what I'm saying; I'm too busy getting high on the smell of her. I've never cared before, how much the skin of a peach resembles a person's skin, when you put it on your tongue. I think she wears the peach scent on purpose, just to remind me. "Do you come here a lot?"

"We started in college. It's harder to get together now with everyone's different schedules, though."

The table jostles, interrupting her, and she covers her glass with her hand to keep her drink from spilling. Jeremy has migrated down the table to sit on the lap of a white woman with short choppy hair in a mesh tank top.

"So that's Jeremy, eh?"

She bites her lip. "Yeah."

"Your first kiss?" It's meant to come out teasing. Half an hour is not a lot of time to collect data about a person, but so far, my top three descriptors of Jeremy would be: goofy, tall, and goofy again.

But somehow, I end up sounding short. He's handsome and their history is obviously deep and strong. It's not that I'm jealous of that goofball. He's her friend, her good friend, her almost best friend if it wasn't for Wes, but there's a silly part of me that imagines a world where Amy and I were sixteen together. And that silly part wonders what it would be like to be her first ever kiss. If she'd make the same quiet sounds that she does now, if her lips tasted the same, or her cheeks turned the same rose tone they do now.

Amy's smile slowly fades. She searches my face, her eyes stopping at my lips again and again. "Not my last though," she says.

I grab the tumbler from her hand and gulp down the rest of her drink as she smirks.

The music stops and all the lights go out in the bar. I jump but no one else makes a sound. The room goes almost silent, a feat for such a rowdy group. A spotlight illuminates the stage and a white drag queen dressed in a black top hat and red circus ringmaster bodysuit steps into the circle of light.

"Welcome to the Hideaway." She swoops her arms grandly, smiling coyly, and the crowd whistles and stomps. She struts around the stage, explaining the show through a combination of stand-up and song. More queens join her on the stage and in no time I'm sitting forward in my chair, giggling. I'm drunk on the crowd and the pageantry and the music but mostly, Amy. Every point on my body that touches hers burns, the sweet kind, like the smoothest whiskey, or ginger root and chili. The club is packed but it might as well be the two of us here with the drag queens.

It's the way her laughter moves through me, skipping a beat on my heart, her voice that's the loudest when we cheer. Whenever she looks over at me, I feel it, the weight of her dark gaze like a blanket I never want to throw off. I sit taller instead; let her see more of me if she's going to look. In the dark of the club, with everyone's attention on the show, I'm brave. There's nothing casual about us here because there doesn't have to be. In the dark, I'm not a chef celebrating an opportunity for my newly invested restaurant and she's not my business partner and majority owner.

Right here, right now, she's a beautiful girl in glitter.

As a Black queen vogues in a sequin bodysuit, I inch my hand from where I've been white-knuckling my own thigh. Before I can think too hard about it I slide my hand under hers on her lap, twining our fingers together.

My rib cage is a butterfly sanctuary, filled with paper-thin nerves as delicate as wings, but as Amy looks at me, my smile is big, and my hands don't shake or sweat. Her cheeks and mouth shimmer in the glow from the stage, like a target for my lips.

"Are you having a good time?" she asks.

"Yeah." I lean in closer. "Are you?"

She shrugs. "I was thinking."

"About?"

"It's hard to celebrate here."

I nod. "You're right. It's very hard to celebrate here."

"I can barely hear you," she says, scooching to the edge of her seat to get closer.

"Maybe we should go somewhere quieter." I lower my voice.

"You always have great ideas, Hollywood. I should listen to you more often."

Amy stands as I laugh, shouting something soundless at her brother on the other side of the table. He looks between us and gives her a thumbs-up and then she's pulling me out of my chair, leading me between tables, before I can do more than wave goodbye to the group. We stop on the stairs, stuck between servers and the mingling coat check and bathroom lines spilling out of the hallway. Amy turns to me, standing on the step so that her already tall frame simply towers over me.

"Where should we go?"

Her hand has never left mine this entire time. We could get a drink somewhere quiet, do a proper cheers, start planning beyond the show, to leverage this opportunity. But with her hand in mine I'm braver still.

"My place." I swallow. "I have…vodka there." There's a good chance I have not a drop of alcohol there.

Amy rubs her thumb over my lips. She pulls at my lower lip and slips her thumb in my mouth. I close my eyes and press my teeth gently into her skin. When I open my eyes, Amy's gaze burns into me. She pulls her thumb from my mouth but keeps it on my lip, holding my mouth open.

"I'm going to kiss you," she says, her lips inches from mine. "Is that okay? Because of, you know, boundaries?"

"Yes." I nod. "You know, you can probably kiss me at work, too."

"I can?"

"Maybe not when I'm freaking out about recipe testing."

"Deal."

She tastes like lime, tart and sweet, and the berry flavor of her lip stain. I tunnel my hands into her hair, ruining her careful curls, dragging my fingers through the short, buzzed sides. She drags her thumb down my chin, over my jaw, with just a bit more force than necessary and I'm grateful to these queens and their music and their fans, who are so loud no one can hear me moan. The sound moves between the two of us, one of mine melting into one of hers. She slips her tongue behind my teeth. Despite my brief history on television, I've never been one for public displays of emotion, including affection, but I want to reach under her shirt and cup her breast right here. I want to drag my thumb over her nipple the same way she drags hers down my throat, to slip my hands beneath her jeans and pull her hips into mine. I want to drop to my knees on these stairs and give back to her all the ways she makes me hot.

Once upon a time, Amy might have looked at me and seen a silly woman who'd let the pressure of *Pop-Up Kitchen* and the loneliness of a breakup get to her. A woman who'd lost a piece of herself. Once upon a time that assessment would have been true. But that ended when I figured out who I really was. Realizing I was bi was a gift, the greatest gift I could have ever given myself. It was the first chance I'd ever had at loving myself authentically, to love others the same way.

Once upon a time, Amy might have needed to protect herself from me. I might have not been able to love her the way she deserved. But when she looks at me now, I hope she sees. The decision to kiss her the very first time was all mine; to make her come in the back of my car, mine. The decision to sleep next to her, to cook with her, to slip my hand into hers, to kiss her on these steps and let her spread me wide-open later. All of it belongs to me because I finally gave myself permission to love everything about me.

I don't really care anymore if she wants to step aside, or I promised that I could be casual.

I break away from her mouth. Our chests heave together and from somewhere nearby someone whistles, the sharp, shrill sound of a catcall. "Take me home," I say.

There's glitter on my fingertips, glitter in her hair. My mouth is sticky from the deep red of her lips.

"Take me home and let's celebrate the right way," I say.

She says nothing, just takes my hand and pulls me from the bar, hails a cab, and gets in. I stand in the doorway and she ducks her head to catch my eyes. The street is dead except for right here, in front of the Hideaway. Music and other sounds of joy mix, light bursts from the building like a little sun.

"Are you coming?" she says. "What's wrong?"

"Nothing." I smile. "I just really, really love being bi."

She laughs, the head thrown back cackle that I love, and pulls me into the cab. And by the way that her smile catches me off guard, like an unexpected dip on a fast, winding road or the first drop of a roller coaster, I think I really, really love Amy, too.

Chapter Seventeen

Amy

If it were up to me my hand would be halfway down Sophie's pants right now. But I don't want to traumatize this cab driver and besides, Sophie doesn't seem like the PDA type. She trembled in my hands on the stairs in the club, even as she licked at my mouth and nipped at my lips and clutched my jacket in her fists like I would float away without her. As if there was anything in this universe that could tear me away from her then or now.

She stares out the window as the cab pulls away, her eyes huge and sparkling in the Hideaway's spotlights. Her hand inches toward me on the cracked leather upholstery until it finds mine. She twines our fingers together.

"Hey." I tug on her hand because I'm selfish. I want to feel the weight of her stare without having to share it with anyone or anything else.

Sophie's cheeks and lips are smudged with the remnants of my makeup. Even her hair has touches of glitter in the roots around her face. But it's not enough. I want to leave glitter everywhere, cover her in it. I want to make a map of her body with my fingerprints and the six-dollar makeup I got from a kiosk in the mall.

"Hey." She smiles. Every time she lets me see this part of

her, this starburst version of herself, it knocks me on my ass. When I'd only gotten snippets of her from the show, I wrongly assumed she was the same kind of angry girl that I was. She's so much more than that. She's layered with more complexity than I have in my pinky finger.

Sophie rests her head on my shoulder, foregoing the seat belt to be closer to me. I can't think of a way to tell her to put one on without sounding like an overbearing billionaire or her mother, so I reach around her instead and click her into the center seat.

She pats my hand and returns her temple to my shoulder. "Sorry."

Warmth fills me like she's turned on a tap. And I don't know why. I don't know what kind of hold she has on me. Until she pulls my arm around her, tucks herself in against me. The warmth filling me from my chest outward is the feeling of being known, of being seen and understood.

Sophie knows me. At some point I let her see.

"I'm proud of us," Sophie says.

This late and this cold the streets are quiet, hardly anyone out. The Common glows faintly from the streetlamps lining the walkways but even it looks frozen to this moment in time.

"How come?" I ask.

"We're different. We approach things differently. And we could have let that dictate our relationship." She pauses. "Our professional relationship. But we communicated with each other. We *listened*. It's such a simple thing to do. And it's so obvious. But so many people just...don't."

"You're right." I lift her hand to my mouth and kiss each knuckle. "People don't communicate." I settle back in my seat. The car's heater is on full blast and despite the intensity with which I wanted to completely consume her a few minutes ago, between this heat and her warm body pressed against mine, I'm almost sleepy. It's only Sophie's hand on my knee, stroking softly back and forth, keeping me on the right side of wanting. Her touch is so casual, so ordinary. It's something a couple would do, when they know they have equal and pre-consented access to each other's bodies. When they know the boundaries of what the other person wants and needs.

"I'm happy we communicated. Well, you communicated with me mostly."

"Don't do that." She presses her head into my shoulder. "Don't sell yourself short like that."

The cab stops in front of a slick-looking condo building in Back Bay and Sophie pays the cab driver before I can get any money out. I growl at her and press my nose into the spot between her neck and shoulder as he passes her change. She holds the door open for me as I climb out of the car and takes my hand as we walk in.

"You're not allergic to cats, right?"

"Oh yeah. You have a cat."

"Fifi," she says, pushing the elevator button.

"I'm not allergic."

The elevator is one of those with mirrors on all three sides so it's Amys and Sophies as far as the eye can see. In the garish fluorescent light overhead and with every version of myself looking back, I can see what I thought was only obvious to me.

The makeup is almost completely washed from my face, my lipstick more of a purple-ish smudge than an actual stain. My hair is a mess from her hands and the sleeveless crop top beneath my jacket is dangerously close to slipping beyond public decency.

I'm keyed up. On the edge. I'm completely feral.

"What are you looking at?" she asks, as the elevator rises slowly, the button for the ninth floor lit up. She pushes me against the back wall and slips her arms around my waist. She kisses my chest, a chaste press of her lips to my sternum, then my collarbone. But she looks at me the whole time, making it not so chaste at all.

I look at her, against me. Then at the her in the mirror. "I'm looking at you."

"And what do you see?"

I see a woman who went so far outside her comfort zone for *me*. To make me happy. To help me achieve the things I want. Who invested in me, in our dream. I see the woman I'm totally gone for.

I push my fingers into her hair and swallow down the sweet taste in my mouth, the absolutely wild urge I have to tell her that. Even if I can't *tell* her that. Not after she had to save my restaurant, after all of her insistence that we be casual.

"I see… I think you're hot for me, Hollywood."

She closes her eyes, pressing her head into my hand. "I think you are, too."

"Another secret?" I whisper the words across her lips, and she nods. "I know I am."

The doors open before I can kiss her. Probably for the best. I might not stop. She pulls me out, both hands wrapped around mine, walking backward down the hall, her cheeks flushed, eyes bright. I want to remember her like this forever.

She lets go of me only to open the door, to pull her coat and boots off. Then she's on me, helping me with my coat, throwing it on the floor. She drops to her knees to tug off my combat boots and tosses those aside, as well. She tries to un-button my jeans and wrestle them down my hips, but I pull her back up.

"Hollywood. Sophie." Her hands slow their frantic undress-ing beneath mine. "What are you doing?"

"You said we could celebrate," she says, matter-of-fact. "I'm celebrating."

"But I want to see your apartment. I want to meet Fifi." I peer over her shoulder into the dark apartment. She's shaking, almost frantic. "And I want to talk to you. About the show… and the restaurant."

"After," she says, her fingers teasing my rib cage as she tries again to pull my shirt off. This time from the bottom.

I squeeze her to me. "How about this?"

She closes her eyes and presses her forehead to my shoulder. "Amy," she whines. She even wiggles against me; the brat.

"Let's talk about the show." I tip her chin up, waiting for her to look at me before I say another word. "And then I'll make you come."

She narrows her eyes. "Weren't you going to do that already?"

I roll my eyes, knocking my head against the door. "Fine. Talk to me about the show—specifically, your fears about it—and I'll make you come. Fast. Or don't show me around and you might not come for hours. Maybe not even at all."

"You wouldn't."

I shrug. "Who knows what I'm capable of."

When she glares, looking up at me through her eyelashes, her nostrils flare a little bit. This seems like a bad time to call her adorable, though.

"Fine. I want to have sex and she wants to talk," she mumbles. "I guess as a compromise, we'll have talk."

She drags me from the door and pulls me down a short hallway, flicking on the light to reveal a white and dark gray kitchen. It's large but the decor is nothing like what I imagined for her. Professional Kitchen Sophie is structured and meticulous. But out of the kitchen she's warm and inviting, and this kitchen is anything but.

"What are those?" I point to a row of jars along one counter, many covered in cheesecloth or filled with murky liquid.

"I'm fermenting."

Like I've flipped a switch, suddenly, she's completely forgotten the fact that I am standing here, my pants half open, or the fact that thirty seconds ago she wanted to be in them. She launches into a description of the fermenting process for miso.

"There's two kinds of miso. And I have a rye vinegar." She lifts up a jar filled with a deep amber liquid. "And in here." She peels back the cheesecloth on a container. "Root vegetables with penicillium candidum."

Slabs of what I assume used to be food sit in the container. All of it covered in a fuzzy white film.

"What the hell is that?" I press myself against her kitchen counter, holding my hand to my nose.

Her face falls and she covers her mold collection like their feelings might be hurt. "I've been experimenting with fermentation for foods. And as the weather gets better, I want to start foraging."

"For what?"

She shrugs. She remains very dressed while goose bumps prickle along my exposed stomach. "Lots of things. Like, you can use wild rose petals to infuse flavor into different desserts and ice creams. Even drinks."

"You're a mad scientist."

Sophie cocks her head to the side, studying me for a moment. "I can't tell if you're making fun of me but if you are may I remind you that you're standing in my kitchen with your fly down."

"I'm not." I close the space between us. "It's sexy. I promise."

"Mold is sexy?" She sounds skeptical.

"Not the mold specifically." I kiss her, a slow brush of my tongue. "But how excited you are about it. That's sexy."

She wraps her arms around my neck to deepen the kiss. "Can I come now?"

"You said you're alone out there when you'll be cooking for Camilla. Do you really feel that way?"

She bites her lip, looking away. She's only turned on some of the overhead lighting, half of her lit by that and the other half of her face in darkness. "No. Not exactly. This feels different than last time. There's no backstabbing. No one is getting voted off. But that doesn't make this any easier to do."

"To be on TV?"

"To put yourself out there," she says, her voice high. "To volunteer to be judged. You said I should cook for myself but... I don't know what that means for me or what that looks like?"

She glances around her kitchen, at the fermenting foods and a bag of rice, a collection of spices, like she'll find the answers in them. If I could, I would gather up all the pieces of her that I love and put her back together, bit by bit.

Her softness, her loyalty. The way she seems to say yes to everything, like being my head chef and kissing me and investing in a restaurant that's failing because she loves it. How smart she is, her hard work, and the way she can take a few basic ingredients and make them into something nourishing and beautiful and most of all delicious.

"I wish you could see what I saw when I watched you on that show."

She covers her face with both hands, groaning. "I can't believe you watched that."

I pull her hands down by her wrists. "How could I not watch. I'd watch it again right now." The whisper of an idea murmurs in my head. "What would you make right now? If you could make anything. Like the most comforting food you can think of."

"For Camilla?"

"For yourself."

"Poutine, I guess." She says it like *poo-tin*. Her lips pouting the word. "It's best to eat it at this time of year, when it's freezing out and the chips are piping hot and you and your friends are all huddled together to keep warm before you take the Metro home."

"Make some for me," I say. I pull out my phone, looking for the best spot in the kitchen to set up the camera.

"What are you doing?"

"You're going to cook something you love, on camera."

Sophie laughs until I hit play on my phone and start recording her by propping it up against a flower vase.

"I thought we were going to have *sex*."

I kiss her, probably out of frame but that's okay. This part is just for me anyway. "I will. After you cook."

"I don't even know if I have all the ingredients." She's snarky and frowning but that doesn't stop her from opening drawers and pulling out pots and pans. And of course, she does have the ingredients; like any good French Canadian there are cheese curds in her fridge. "My mom brought me some," she mumbles when I laugh. And without much prompting at all she starts to wash potatoes.

"Not because you told me to," she says, scrubbing at the root vegetable with a hard bristled brush. "Because I'm hungry."

She pours me a glass of water and pushes me onto a kitchen stool with a growl and the tease of a kiss but no actual contact. The she rolls up her sleeves and puts her hair up, like she would in our kitchen, and gets to work. Sophie has an almost industrial-sized deep fryer that she muscles up from the depths of a cupboard, refusing my offer of help. Soon, the kitchen is filled with the smell of deep-fried potatoes and gravy made from actual animal protein because she also has three kinds of stock in her fridge.

I consider myself a skilled cook but poutine from scratch would take me, at minimum, an hour, and yet within thirty-seven minutes Sophie presents the most elevated dish of French-Canadian street food I've ever seen. She sprinkles rosemary and Maldon salt on top.

"You wouldn't get it with any garnish on the street, but I think it adds to the flavor." She hands me a fork. I hand it back to her.

"You first." My phone's battery is almost dead, but I frame her in the shot just for this bite. "How is it?" I ask.

Sophie's eyes close and she hums a content, happy sound. "Perfect," she purrs. "It tastes like home."

I lean forward, my mouth open, and she feeds me a forkful. And I thought her vegan version of this was delicious, but this. It's to die for. The gravy is smoky and warm, the cheese just soft enough to pull as I take it off the fork. The potato actually crunches between my teeth but the inside is velvety smooth. Without ever having to be there I suddenly know exactly what Sophie meant, can feel the cold pushing in against my coat as I stand with her on a sidewalk, surrounded by people speaking a different language and sharing a cardboard box filled with potatoes, cheese, and gravy.

"You're amazing," I say around my mouthful. "This. This is what you should make for Camilla."

Sophie smiles, takes another bite, chasing gravy off her lip with her pink tongue. "It's street food, Amy. It's too plain."

"It's you," I say. "And this is anything but plain. You just think that because you've been eating it your whole life."

She hums, like maybe she is contemplating this.

"Well?"

"I'll think about it," she says, finally meeting my eyes. But her cheeks are flushed, and her shoulders are set back. She's proud. "I should clean up." She looks around at the mess I insisted she make.

"Take off your shirt," I say.

"Amy."

"Take it off. Well..." I pause as her eyes get too big to hold in her excitement. "Take it off then show me more of your apartment."

"Amy," she growls.

"Then you can come," I say in a singsong voice.

She presses against me, her chest expanding on a long sigh, the soft knit of her sweater brushing my too hot, sensitive skin. She steps back and in the overhead track lighting, the windows behind her uncovered, she pulls her shirt off in one quick movement. Underneath, she wears a simple black bra with a small bow in the center. Her breasts strain against the fabric; the straps have pulled tight against her shoulders.

"Next room," I say, and she grabs my hand and takes me out to the living-dining room. This room reflects a bit more of her. There's a throw blanket on the couch that hasn't been folded, cookbooks stacked on the coffee table, and the dining table has a collection of half-burned pillar candles in the center. Fifi the cat sleeps in middle of the couch, black with white feet and a little white snip on its nose.

This room looks lived-in even if the decor itself is still nothing like her: different shades of gray with abstract art on the walls.

I come up behind her and lift the strap on her bra, kissing along her shoulder. She moans at the contact, soft and pained, and I push both straps from her shoulders.

"Take off your pants." I bite the back of her neck and she shudders. She pops the button and wriggles out of her pants, leaving them in a puddle of fabric on her dark hardwood floor.

Sophie turns to me, slipping her hands into mine and kissing along my collarbone, along my neck and chin. "You said I couldn't come yet," she says.

Instead of letting me answer, she covers my mouth with hers. The windows along two walls are uncovered and the light from the hallway behind us creates a perfect silhouette to anyone looking in.

"Someone might see," I whisper but I don't stop kissing her back. Not when Sophie is like this, hungry and brazen.

"Let them," she says. Standing in front of me so I'm blocked from view, she slides her hand up the inside of my denim-clad thigh.

"What are you doing?"

"You said I couldn't come yet. You didn't say anything about you."

I moan against her mouth at the pressure of her fingers through my clothes. I'm so revved up from sitting beside her in that club, from kissing her on the stairs, from watching her display of competency porn in action. There's so much I want to do to her, do with her, and not all of it involves my mouth between her legs. But between the stress of the show and stress of our looming debts, it never feels like there's enough time. The end of Amy & May's feels like it will mean the end of all this, too.

"The tour isn't over yet," I say.

"There's nothing else to see. My apartment is small."

"Bathroom? Laundry?" I ask. "A den?"

She pulls her fingers away but it's the loss of her mouth that pulls me forward for one more kiss, two.

"Yes, yes. I have all those." She wipes at her mouth where the last of my lipstick has smudged along her chin. "This way."

I follow her down a short hallway, past a bathroom with a stacked washer and dryer set to a small office without a door. While her bra was simple cotton, her panties are black lace, the kind of cut they call "cheeky." The curves of plump, muscular ass flex as she strides into the small room ahead of me. The back panels of the underwear are held together with satin ribbon, crisscrossed into a small bow at the top of her ass. I want to pull the knot apart with my teeth.

"Were those comfortable to wear in those pants?"

She doesn't respond, just holds her hand out in a Vanna White pose. "The den."

She makes no move to turn on the lights so the small desk and chair are bathed in silvery moonlight. There's a bookshelf along one wall, filled with more cookbooks, memoirs and biographies of famous chefs, a novel about a chef of the Roman Empire, and different variations of *How to Ferment for Dummies*. On another wall is a bulletin board and it's covered in little Sophie-isms: a cocktail napkin from a restaurant in Quebec, photos of family, and friends I've never met, and her with the kitten version of Fifi in her lap, and one of the full cast of *Pop-Up Kitchen*. I recognize the set from the night of the finale—I've watched the episode enough times that her hair, her clothes are imprinted on my brain. The entire cast had been flown back in for the finale and Sophie stands next to the winner and celebrity judge, wearing the kind of smile you wear when you're trying to pretend you're happy. Everyone else in the photo looks at the camera, except for Paul. He stands at the edge of the frame with a few other people I never saw on-screen. He looks at the group; he looks at Sophie.

"Hey." She presses her breasts against my back, wrapping her arms around my waist. "Are you happy now? Was the tour all it's cracked up to be?"

I cock my head to the side, pretending to ponder. "I don't know. Maybe you need to show me your duct work."

Sophie laughs and grabs my hands, placing them on the wall.

"What are you doing?"

She tugs my pants down, not stopping this time until she's pulled them off. I start to turn, but she places a firm hand on my thigh. "Unless you are truly uncomfortable, you better put those hands back on the wall."

Slowly, I turn away, a hand on each side of the bulletin board. She kisses up the back of my legs, from the soft spot behind my knee, up my thighs. She tugs at my underwear with her teeth.

"Do you have any idea how hot you looked tonight?" she asks, pressing open-mouthed kisses to my cheeks. Her hands find their way up my thighs. My body strains for her touch. I have to lock my muscles down to keep from arching into her mouth and hands.

"I almost had to leave," she says, rubbing her knuckle back and forth over my underwear, against me.

"I'm...sorry?" I'm half confused and half overcome. "I'll never do it again."

"Are you kidding?" She slides her fingers over my clit and I cry out. "Do it again. Do it always."

Sophie kisses over the seam of my ass through the fabric. She follows the line of my plain bikini-cut underclothes with her tongue. She sucks marks into the backs of my thighs and my biggest regret is that I won't be able to see them without a mirror or some yoga classes. I drop my forehead against the bulletin board, my hips following the rhythm of her fingers. "God, Hollywood."

Underneath my arm I can see her shoulder, her hair, silvery-white in the moon. "Let me turn around," I beg. "Wanna see you. Kiss you."

Her fingers and mouth disappear and with quick hands she turns my hips so my back is against the wall. I try to reach for her, to pull her up to my mouth, but she presses her forearm across my hips, staring up at me as she gives my pussy the same attention she gave to my ass.

"You look…" I tip my head back. Just the heat of her mouth, the pressure of her tongue and fingers has gotten me so close. "You're burning."

It doesn't make any sense, of course. She's the color of a statue in a dark room, but she's lit me on fire. The wet slide of her tongue on my cunt would be the only relief I could take. I want to burn with her.

"You fuck me so good." I gasp as she pulls my underwear aside, blows softly on my heated skin. "Please."

I come bent over her, my hands in her hair, my voice echoing in the quiet room, as she licks between my legs, until I have to beg her to stop.

She sits back when I finally straighten, looking up at me with a happy little smile. I drag my fingers over her lips but the only things I can think to say right now are too heavy for us, for what I've asked her to be for me. "Come here, baby," I say instead.

I help her up and taste myself when I kiss her. I trail my hand down her curves, nuzzling her jaw and neck. She opens her legs for me when I finally get to where she is hot and wet. With one slow swipe of my finger along her lace, I say, "The tour isn't over yet."

Sophie steps back to assess my level of sincerity.

I shrug. "I want to see your room."

She stomps her foot and turns on her heel. "Fine." And walks into the next room at the end of the hall.

Finally, this is the room that seems the most Sophie-like. The walls are a light green. Gauzy white curtains cover the windows and a soft golden light from a tall lamp, next to a plush armchair covered in athletic gear, turns the space hazy and warm.

"Who decorated for you?" I ask, pushing aside one of the

curtains to catch a glimpse of her view, which is of the red-brick exterior of the building next to hers.

"Amy," she says dryly. "Is that really what you care about right now?"

I turn around and a part of my brain explodes. That's the only explanation for the way every word I've ever known disappears from my vocabulary. If I had to right now I could maybe make sounds. I can't move, either. I'm rooted to this spot. I could stand here forever, in fact, if I had to. As long as I can have this view.

"Because the last thing I want to talk about is the decor in my apartment." Sophie lies reclined on her bed. Her bra has been discarded on the floor and her hair over her shoulder brushes the tips of her nipples. Her hand rests on her belly, three fingers tucked underneath her lace underwear.

In college I took an art history class with my brother because he insisted I needed more culture in my life. It was mostly a class about old white men who drank too much and thought too highly of themselves and their paintings. I hated it and barely managed a B. But god did those men paint some beautiful women. Sophie is a real-life Venus, nipples pink and skin soft. But far more erotic than anything that ever hung on the walls of the Grand Salon.

Slowly, her whole hand stretches the black lace, her head falls back on her neck, her hair pooling behind her. She gasps.

"What are you doing?" I ask. My voice feels fragile in my throat. I look from her to the mirror on her wall where she gasps again, her hand moving. It feels like I can't look directly at her. Like my vision will fractal. "What are you doing?" I beg.

"Touching myself."

My heart beats in my throat. I'm wet from just her words, her quiet sounds, the liquid shine on her fingers when she pulls her hands from her panties and says, "You made me wait so long, Amy."

I've always been good at sex, knowing what my partner wants and needs, how far to take things, and when to stop. With Sophie, I know. But then I turn my back for a few seconds and she starts to finger herself on her bed. So, also I know nothing. And I like it a lot more than I ever thought I would.

My nipples push through the stretch fabric of my top as I walk, on legs that feel far too unstable, to the edge of her bed. I wrap one hand around her ankle, pushing her legs farther apart.

"Take those off." I nod to her panties.

She stares up at me. "Take that off first," she says, mimicking my careful tone.

I shake my head, spread her legs a little wider. "I promise I'll make it good, Sophie. Do you trust me?"

She pauses for a moment like she's really considering it then she nods once and pushes her panties down her thighs. I help her once they get past her knees, dropping the sopping wet fabric on the floor at the end of the bed.

"Okay," I say, pulling her legs apart again. "What are you waiting for?"

She makes a whining sound. "I want you to do it."

"I am touching you." I squeeze her ankle. "And you were doing it so good, baby," I say softly.

A small, proud smile teases her lips.

"You make me so hot when you fuck yourself for me," I whisper. "Show me again. So I know how to keep you happy."

There's danger in words like these. They speak to a future where Sophie has not rightfully tossed me aside. But I'm past the point of trying to pretend I'm not too far-gone for her.

She starts at her collarbone. Her fingers trail along the dip and curve to the space between her breasts. She brushes along the soft skin beneath. The phantom feeling tingles along the backs of my own knuckles. Sophie circles her nipples, then takes herself in hand, plucking at the tight buds. She watches herself in the same mirror I did earlier and I want to scream out the window that my lover *knows* how hot she is. My lover can't look away and neither can I.

Soon, though, playing isn't enough. Her hand moves between her legs and she slips two fingers into her pussy. Her head falls back and she releases an anguished moan.

"What are you thinking?" I ask.

"That it's you," she says, without hesitation. She paints her vulva with her wetness, draws her fingers in tight circles around her clit.

"You're pretending it's me touching you?"

She nods, her eyes clenched shut.

"Are you going to come?"

She shakes her head. "Not unless it's you," she says, but her voice wavers, high and tight like the last time she came all over my face.

I hum. "You did do exactly as I asked," I say, pretending to ponder my next move even as I crawl up the bed and settle on my knees between her legs. "You look so beautiful, baby," I croon, running my hands down her inner thighs.

Sophie opens her eyes, relief passing like a wave over her face when she sees me. She's so slick when she slides her fingers into herself again. "Can you take more?" I ask.

"Please," she says, breathless.

I lean over her, slipping my middle finger in with her. Her inner thighs and ass are soaked with her arousal. She's hot and snug around me.

"Another one."

"I don't want to hurt you."

"Another." Her tone is commanding, even as her chest heaves. "It will hurt more not to feel you."

I take her nipple in my mouth as I slip another finger inside her and she cries out.

"You want my mouth too?"

She nods. "Hurry."

I crawl down her body, sucking her clit, and watching her as she watches me. A flush moves like a wave up her chest and neck as her thighs tighten around my shoulders. She's supple in my hands. The way she gives herself over is the strongest, bravest thing I've ever seen and I know I should strike the iron while it's hot, lick her and fuck her and make her come, but I'm a little too selfish for that. She's beautiful and trembling as I slow my fingers against hers, blow softly across her hot flesh. I want to keep her here, on the edge of everything, for a moment longer.

She releases a frustrated growl. Her fingers keep moving, fruitlessly against mine, her legs thrash. "Amy," she says against the back of her teeth.

I laugh into her skin, sucking and leaving gentle bites along the insides of her thighs.

"Don't be mad," I whisper. Slowly, I give her what she wants and the frustration leaks from her body. Anticipation curls her toes, tightens her thighs. "You look so beautiful when you fall apart."

But it's so much more than that. Because soon everything will start to change—our little restaurant will be in front of television cameras—and I want to hold on to us, just us, as tight as I can for a few more moments.

Now that we have the chance at everything we've ever wanted laid out in front of us, I'm starting to realize, maybe I didn't want it at all. Maybe I just wanted her.

I curl my fingers inside her, press down on her stomach, suck at her clit and she's so close I can taste it.

"Amy?" She gasps. "I'm gonna… I think… Amy." She grabs at my hair, my hand on her tummy, the bed cover. "I think I'm gonna…"

And when she comes it's everything. The long column of her throat, glistening in sweat, her body clenching my fingers so hard. She comes all over me, screams a sound I've never heard before. Like if pleasure was a noise. She comes forever, until she's nothing but soft skin and liquid muscle. The bed-sheets are soaked and so is my chin.

Is this what being a superhero feels like? Because that was fucking awesome.

"Let's do that again."

She shakes her head, her hair a mess around her. "I can't. I need a break. I can't."

I fall beside her on the bed. My heart pounds and my thighs are slick for her but I can feel her exhaustion, making her heavy and warm.

"I've never done that before," she says, a little breathless.

"You mean you've never squirted?" I kiss her cheek.

She laughs, throaty and satisfied. "I don't think so."

"You'd know."

"I should change these sheets," she says.

I roll onto my side, pushing her hair back from her face. "You rest. I'll change them."

It might be the light or the color of the walls but her eyes look especially green, the same color as the glass of my favorite bottle of red wine.

"No." She heaves herself onto her elbows but I push her back down with an easy hand on her chest. "I want to make you squirt, too," she whines.

"Remember when you told me that you had a hard time coming." I laugh when she scowls at me.

"I do," she says. "You just have a magic mouth."

My grin could crack my face. "Thank you. I take my cunnilingus skills very seriously." I nod to the bathroom. "Take a moment. I'll change the sheets." I kiss down her chest.

"Fine." She stops me with my mouth against her palm. "You take good care of me."

If I were the type of person to gloat, I'd gloat about that. I bite the pad of her finger instead. "I thought you didn't like that."

"You know that's not what I mean."

"I do." I pull her up into a sitting position. "I like taking care of you."

I'd like to take care of you forever. The thought feels illicit. Like the worst kind of secret. Not because it's wrong but because she deserves more than a grumpy woman who's married to her job.

"Can I stay the night?" I ask instead.

"You'd better."

Sophie slides off the bed and wobbles, fawn-like, to her bathroom. I find fresh sheets on a shelf in her closet, pull the soaked ones off and throw them in the washing machine in her spare bathroom. She returns looking fresh and far more awake than she was before. I'm warm under the covers, in nothing but my underwear. She takes a sip from the glass of water I placed on her bedside table and smacks her lips. Sophie hurries under the covers, smiling and so fucking beautiful I could drop dead.

And maybe I am a grump who spends too much time at her restaurant that is on the cusp of failure. But maybe I'm also not as much like my father as I try to convince myself I am.

And even if I am, maybe I deserve Sophie.

Chapter Eighteen

Amy

A wad of rolled up straw wrapper lands on my keyboard. I flick it away without breaking rhythm typing. Wes huffs from the other side of my laptop, his grumbling blending into the coffee shop sounds.

"Amy, look."

I stare harder at the screen, numbers jumbling together. Anything to avoid my brother and his face.

"Look, Amy."

"You put your straw up your nose, didn't you?"

I cringe at the squeal of the cappuccino machine across the coffee shop.

He huffs again. "How'd you know?"

Finally, I look up at my brother, who has indeed stuck a paper straw up one nostril. Like a loser.

"I'm pretty sure you shoved your umbilical cord up your nostril in the womb."

He pretends to be offended. "That's disgusting."

I shrug and wave my hand at him because he is the one with the nasal fixation here, not me. "Bro."

He shifts in his seat, jiggles one leg where it's crossed over the other. "We've been sitting here too long."

"I'm working. You said you wanted to work."

"I think I have to pee. I've had too much coffee."

I close my laptop. Balancing the books isn't going to happen with this chatterbox in my ear. "Stop talking."

He opens his mouth to argue and I point at him. He snaps his mouth shut.

"Go to the bathroom. Order me a soup and get a sandwich. It's…" I check the time on my phone and am distracted by a message from Sophie where she's sweaty and smiling, posing in the mirror with her booty popped and her bicep flexed.

Her: *Instagram-worthy? ;)*

Me: *ok but what if. And hear me out. That one was just for me.*

Me: *also what if you sent me another one but with fewer clothes on* 😇

Her: *LOL nice try. And fine. I'll take another one. That one is yours* 😏

"Amy?" Wes waves his hand in front of me. My grin could crack my face in half. "Who are you texting?" He peers over the table and I click my screen off.

"Ahh." He sits back in his chair, reclining with his hands behind his head and looking too smug for a guy wearing Bert and Ernie socks. "You're in love."

I almost drop my phone, catching it then bouncing it between both hands. "I am *not*."

The woman sitting at the table beside ours gives me a dirty look. Fair. I was yelling. Putting my phone facedown on the table, I lean forward to give my brother my full attention. "I don't know where you got the impression that I'm even dating someone, let alone that I am in love with them."

"Corrine loves to remind me that she and I weren't dating when we fell in love but the other night at the Hideaway? You and Sophie sure *looked* like you were dating."

Siblings were a terrible idea, as a concept.

"We're…" It's not a lie to say we're just fucking. We have

sex and we run our business together and I think about her almost constantly. So, okay, maybe we're not *just* fucking. We're doing something together, something big.

"How did you know?" I ask him instead of finishing my sentence. "How did you know you were in love with Corrine?"

Wes's face turns serious and he props his elbow on our small table. He works for a start-up that promotes a "flexible work-life balance" but so far all that seems to mean is, he can fuck around with his sister at eleven o'clock on a Thursday but keep his laptop open for any incoming emails.

"That's a good question." He rolls the straw that had previously been stuck up his nose back and forth over the table.

We're going to need someone to come wipe down this whole place with bleach.

"It's hard to say. When I look back on it now, it feels like I was always in love with her. From the very first meeting when she thought I was a total asshole."

"That's not very helpful."

He laughs. "No. It's not. I don't know how I knew that I loved her. I just know that one day I woke up and I wished Mom was alive. I mean, I always wish Mom was alive but that morning I wished she was alive so she could meet her."

I nod. My stomach hurts. "Yeah." I shrug. Of course I'd want Mom to meet Sophie.

"I know how I know I'm still in love with her though," he says. "Corrine makes me feel like a Saturday in July at Fenway. When I've had exactly one beer. And one hot dog with mustard." He gets a far-off look in his eyes. "And you're there and Jer's there and the Sox win." He shakes his head, smiling. "Yeah. That's how I know."

"Wesley," I say, my face gravely serious. I cover his hand

with mine. "Never tell your girlfriend that she makes you feel like baseball, okay?"

He laughs, throwing his head back. At least three people stop to watch him be obnoxious. "What's your favorite thing in the whole world?"

"I couldn't possibly pick one favorite thing in the whole world. My favorite what? Favorite food? Favorite sport?" But even as I deny it, I can see it. Or feel it, more like. Warm sun, the green haze of my apartment in the morning. Breakfast.

"Baseball, a beer and a dog, and Fenway Park. That's my favorite thing in the whole world. Corrine makes me as happy as my very favorite thing. Happier, actually. She's like..." He rubs his chest. "Hot dogs and a sunburn and laughing and that..." He clucks his tongue in an audible imitation of a bat hitting a ball. "Crack the bat makes. She makes me feel what all those things feel like, right here."

The back of my throat burns, the first warning that I'm going to cry on this uncomfortable wooden bench in a chain restaurant. "Don't you have to go pee?" I ask, looking out the steamy coffee shop window.

He sits for a moment before he gets up, leaning across the table to kiss the top of my head, because he is a good brother despite being a little bit gross and obnoxious. He knows when to leave me to have my Emotions.

In the whole wide world, my favorite thing would be a stack of pancakes, the tinny sound of music coming from this crappy old laptop, the humidity in my apartment fogging up the windows. Maple syrup and a full stomach and all the leaves pointing toward the sun. That's what Sophie makes me feel like.

My stomach hurts again but not because I'm missing Mom. It's the same feeling I had before. Butterflies but worse. So much worse. It's the entire monarch migration happening in my diaphragm. Of course, realizing that I'm in love with So-phie Brunet would make me feel sick to my stomach.

Because that's completely normal.

"Amy?" I jump at the sound of my name. "Hi," Paul says.

He stands behind Wes's chair. His expensive-looking pea-coat, and a scarf that is undoubtedly cashmere, are sprinkled with snowflakes. "How are you?"

The only good thing about the fact that my face almost al-ways exists in a state of Resting Bitch is that Paul probably can't tell that I'm scowling at the sight of him since I already looked this way. Regardless, it takes me a beat too long to plaster on the smile one would expect when they see the executive pro-ducer of the TV show that's supposed to save their restaurant.

"What are you doing here?" I ask. Over his shoulder I search for Wes but he's nowhere to be seen. Of course.

Paul laughs awkwardly. "I work in a building down the street."

"When you're not on set."

"Right." He glances over his shoulder then leans in. "You're not here with Sophie, are you?"

The petty part of me wants to whip out my phone and tell him: *no but she did send me this photo. This very beautiful photo. Because we're a thing. Together. And also I'm in love with her.* If I'm going by my brother's standards, which normally I wouldn't do. Except for he's definitely the least emotionally stunted between the two of us.

But Sophie is not a plaything to be fought over or put on display. "She's at the gym. I think," I add to make it seem like I'm not totally attuned to her.

"Listen, Amy." This can't be good. Whenever someone tells me to *listen* I almost never want to hear what they have to say. "I hope I'm not overstepping. But Sophie mentioned that the restaurant was struggling. I wanted to offer my help or expertise any way I can."

I swallow down the taste of bile, the absolute, sudden livid rage trying to crawl its way out of my mouth. This is exactly the thing I hate most about myself. The way I am most like my father. We let anger take over, until we don't just see red. We *are* red, hot ire.

To have to sit here as this man sticks his unwelcome nose into what is very much not his business. I remind myself that he's just trying to be helpful. And he is, in fact, a successful restaurateur. He likely has plenty to teach me. He also holds the keys to an opportunity he knows Sophie and I very much need. So no matter how badly I want to laugh in his face and tell him to stick his "advice" between his ass cheeks and invert a fart, I don't.

I remind myself of the real reasons I'd rather gargle broken glass than get advice from him: because I see him as a competitor for Sophie's affections—even though she broke up with him. Because of the careless way he treated her when she gave him one of the most precious gifts she could give him: better insight into who she truly is.

"Thank you, Paul." My voice shakes. But that's the only outward sign of how very much I hate this man. "I think we have it under control."

He makes a pleasant face as a barista calls his name. He holds up his finger, asking them to wait. He's completely polite, nodding when they place his order to the side on the counter.

But the audacity.

"It's my pleasure. Just know I'm here if you ever need me. I only want the best for Sophie. And you, obviously."

My smile is the kind of toxic plastic that can never ever be recycled. "Of course."

"But you two are going to do great on the show. I'm sure

you won't need me at all. Sophie especially, she was made to be in front of the camera. Don't you think?"

"You've mentioned that."

I can't do any more than bare my teeth, nod as he walks away. The worst part is not that I kind of hate Paul, or that Sophie told him something private about our business. Though, I'm probably going to be mad about that later. The worst part is, he's right. Sophie is beautiful but she's also kind. In the face of an industry built on hardness, rigidity, she's gentle. She sucked me in from my small laptop screen. Before I even met her, I was hooked on her blush, her grin, that curl her hair does when the kitchen gets hot. She shines on camera.

Wes thuds back into his seat. "Sorry." He runs his hand through his hair. "Corrine called." He pauses, watching me. He's always been able to see too much. "You okay?"

"Fine," I say. I open my laptop, stare at the numbers on the screen that tell me what I already know. My restaurant is failing. My dream is dying.

I'm dead weight. Just like my dad was to my mom, leading her on all those years. But Sophie could flourish. At another restaurant. Or even on TV. I've rewatched the video we made last week. Maybe it's just me and the Sophie-colored glasses I wear but she's breathtaking, the serious face she makes as she's chopping and the way she pauses over her words when she's talking about flavors and palates. Sophie is as much of a star as he thinks she is.

She's Hollywood, after all.

Chapter Nineteen

Sophie

Fifi winds figure-eights through my legs as I walk in the door after my gym session.

"Miaou miaou, Feef." She chirrups back and I drop my gym bag to replace it with her. She's getting a little heavy in her later years. "Let's get something to eat."

She pats at my hands as I collect chickpeas and goat cheese, red onion and pepper and cucumber from the fridge. A vinaigrette I whipped together a few days ago gets a sniff and a sneeze and eventually I have to put her down to put it all together into a salad, but she hops onto my lap as I sit down to eat and open Amy's email with her spreadsheets. I guess now they're my spreadsheets, too.

Fifi's purrs vibrate along my legs as I stretch out on the couch, my phone screen propped up against her back, but my food sits forgotten on the coffee table as I slowly scroll.

I whistle low under my breath and the sound makes Fifi's ears twitch. "Okay. So it's tight."

We're on a razor's edge, even with my investment. Not that I was under any impression that thirty thousand dollars in the restaurant industry was a lot. At a time like this, I miss Paul for his counsel. I don't know much about the administration side of running a restaurant. Ask me to close a kitchen? Keep the appliances up to the health code? I'm your girl. But this is my first time running an actual business. And I can only imagine Amy's fear. This restaurant is everything to her.

I should call her. We can figure this out together, like we have everything else so far.

The numbers on my phone screen disappear and Paul's name flashes instead, as if I summoned him. He and Fifi were great buds so I answer the call with video, picking her up off my lap so her disgruntled little face will be on-screen.

"Fifi," he exclaims as he registers us.

He's somewhere on the street, his earbuds poking out of his ears and his nose red. I lift her paw in a wave. "What's up?" I ask, bringing them both back into the kitchen. I set Paul up on the counter, leaning the phone against the fruit bowl so I can clean up, and Fifi on the ground, which gets me a disgruntled meow and a tail flip as she stalks from the room.

"How was the gym?"

I pat at my hair in its loose ponytail; my sweat has long since dried but left my hair frizzy.

"Great. What's going on, Paul?" I ask again.

"Hold on." The phone screen goes dark for a moment, then he reappears in his car. "Sorry about that. I was wondering what you were doing tonight?"

I frown and laugh at the same time. "Working?" I take a bite of leftover cucumber as my stomach starts to eat itself.

"After that."

After that I'll probably be with Amy. We've spent every night together this past week. But I'm not ready to tell Paul that. "I…don't know what I'll be doing…"

"Have dinner with me."

My knife clatters to the countertop. I pick up the phone to see his face but of all the questions running through my brain

I can't pick one to ask. I settle for, "I won't be done until ten. Maybe later."

He waves his hand because of course that's not a problem for a man who owns multiple restaurants and knows many more owners. He could get a five-course meal at two in the morning.

"How about Frank's place?" he asks. He doesn't refer to a restaurant by its name. It's always the name of the owner, the head chef, his friend. Maybe one day he'll call ours just Amy's, or Sophie's place. "Ten thirty? Eleven? I won't keep you too late. Promise," he says quickly. "I know you need to be at the gym early."

I drag a hand down my face because this is awkward, but it needs to be said. "This...isn't a date, is it?"

Paul sobers. "No. I wouldn't do that to you. It's business related."

I study his face through the screen. "Is it about the show?" I ask, relief washing through me. If it's about the show I could bring Amy. Even if it's not a date, having dinner, alone, with Paul will feel strange. Like putting on an old sweater that doesn't quite fit in the shoulders anymore.

He winces. "Not exactly. But it is entertainment industry related."

"O-okay." It's not that I *want* to go, exactly. I don't not want to go, either. But I can't really turn down "business" opportunities. Not after looking at those numbers.

His answering smile could reflect the sun. "I can't wait."

The screen goes dark, and I set the phone back down. I survey the mess I've made from food prep, the full bowl of chickpea salad getting soggy sitting out on my coffee table. Without bothering to put anything else away, I open the pantry and pull out a sleeve of Oreos. I don't need tangible proof to know that telling Amy I'm having dinner with Paul is going to upset her. If she had dinner with one of her exes—all *none* of them—I'd be upset.

I shove a cookie into my mouth. This is going to suck.

Amy's spreadsheets are visible again on my phone now that my call is over. My spreadsheets. Our spreadsheets. And our alarmingly depleted funds. Except... I lean over the counter, crumbs leaving a trail to my phone, and navigate to the payroll spreadsheet. Fifi winds through my feet again, my earlier offense forgotten.

"I think I know how to fix this, Feef," I say.

She rolls onto the floor and licks her butt.

"There you are." Amy kicks the door to the staff room shut behind her and has my face in her hands before I can say a word.

She tastes citrusy, like the lemon water she's been mainlining all night, and for a moment I just let myself cling to her. Her black knit sweater soft and warm where I clutch it in my hands.

"Service went well tonight, yeah?" She tucks my hair behind my ear. Her eyes are bright and excited, and I know she wants to debrief, like we've done every night for the last many nights, at my house or hers. Then she wants to topple me onto the bed and make me come two or three times. I want that too, especially with the smell of peaches in my nose. The other day while looking for a phone charger, and absolutely not snooping, I found a large, practical Tupperware storage bin underneath her bed filled with sex toys and lubricant. Things I'd never considered trying when I was only having sex with men but that the thought of now make me squirm with anticipation. I'd pulled the box out while she was in the shower, and she'd found me surrounded by her collection of synthetic debauchery. She'd promised me that we'd play soon, when we had more time, and now it's kind of all I can think about.

"Sophie?" Her indulgent smile starts to fade as she steps back and takes in the wide-legged slacks and black button-up I brought with me for dinner at Frank's. A far cry from the athleisure leggings and sweater I usually pack for after work. "Do we have plans tonight?"

"I..." I turn away from her to slam my locker shut. "I have plans."

This shouldn't be such a big deal. It's not a big deal. I'm meeting Paul for dinner to discuss a business opportunity... or something. And then I'll go over to Amy's.

"With who?"

I pop the top off my lip balm and slather on far too much, but even that has to end eventually and I'm forced to say, "Paul."

Amy's face shutters. All the excitement lighting up her brown eyes fades between one blink and the next.

"He called me this morning," I say quickly, taking advantage of the vacuum of sound her silence has created. "And asked if we could meet tonight for a business meeting."

Her eyebrows jump into her hairline. "This morning?"

I nod.

"What kind of business? About the show?"

"No. He said it was entertainment industry related, but no. Not the show." I swallow past my tight throat. Amy is not the type of person who would ever want me to ask for permission, even though we're terrible at boundaries. We're not even dating. Whatever this is between us, I'm sure she's chalking it up to improved interpersonal communication. But it's taking everything in me not to ask for her blessing.

"I asked if you should come, you know?" I pull her sweater between fingers. "For show related stuff and he said..." I shake my head. "It's not..." I wince. "It's not...you know."

"A date," she says flatly.

"Right. Are you…" I wait for her to answer, at least fill in the blanks, but clearly I forgot who I'm speaking to. Amy isn't going to let me get away with avoiding this. "Are you upset that I'm meeting my ex for a business related meeting?" I ask in one hard breath.

Her face stays blank, infuriatingly so, since I'm pretty sure mine is red from nerves and some sort of unidentified embarrassment. "Why would I be upset?" she asks.

I blink because I'm a little shocked but also not. I knew that Amy wouldn't react well. No one would, certainly not me. But still. It hurts to hear her question this.

"Because you and I are…"

I stop myself when the staff room door opens and Carly shuffles in. Her eyes widen as she takes us in, standing close together but somehow also miles apart. "I'm just getting my stuff," she squeaks.

Amy smiles, back to her role of the professional, if not aloof, boss. "Go ahead, Carly."

The only sound is the squeal of her locker door opening and the jangle of her keys. She slams the door and leaves with a quick goodbye, not even bothering to put her jacket on.

"You know why I think you'd be upset. I'd be upset, too. I just want you to know that I'm not…this is not anything but… courtesy." I step in close to her now that we're alone again. "I'd much rather be with you tonight." I press my nose into the soft skin of her throat but her arms don't come around my back like I hoped they would.

"I saw him today."

"Saw who?"

"I saw Paul. At a coffee shop."

"So?"

She shakes her head. "Don't you think it's weird that I saw

him? We talked *about you* and then he sets up a meeting with you?"

"I guess the timing is a little strange..."

She makes a frustrated sound in the back of her throat.

"What are you insinuating?"

She paces back and forth, shoulders hunched. "Nothing. I don't know."

I try to catch her sleeve as she paces past. "Is it okay if I come over after?" I ask. "I took a look at the numbers today and I want to talk about a plan for moving forward."

Amy stops, folding her arms over her chest. She's like the three raccoons in a trench coat version of herself. Twitchy and uncomfortable and unable to stop fidgeting. "Yeah, it's fine, just don't..." She slams her mouth shut and looks away, so I wait.

"Don't what?" I say. Without realizing it, I've crossed my arms, too. I shake them out, but I have the sinking suspicion that this is our first fight.

"Don't tell him any more about how our business is failing."

Amy doesn't wait for me to respond. Her lips are still curled in a snarl as she leaves, letting the door fall closed with a loud clap behind her. For far too long, I'm just confused. I've never told Paul that this business was failing. We've barely spoken for any length of time since...since I told him that we were applying for the show.

"Shit." I pound my fist against my locker, not very hard, and not out of anger. Just because I'm really that dumb. In the moment I knew it was the wrong thing to do. I knew she'd react exactly like this.

Amy's car is gone after I close up, and I make it to Frank's ten minutes late, but Paul sits at the bar, nursing a scotch. The restaurant is all dark wood and low lighting, leather seats and the kind of staff uniform that immediately makes them noticeable if you're looking for them but helps them fade into the background if you're not. It's the kind of place that you can tell serves every cut of steak imaginable, without ever having to look at the menu.

I don't look at him when I climb onto the stool beside him. I can't decide if I'm angry at him or not and I can't look at him until I decide. Why would he mention it to Amy at all? He'd have to know she'd feel embarrassed. Unless that was his purpose?

"I haven't ordered any food yet," he says by way of greeting. "But I told Alex you'd probably want a red, something Italian."

With a sigh, I turn to face him. "Thank you."

As if on cue, the bartender—Alex—sets six ounces of red wine in front of me.

"Salut." Paul lifts his glass and I do the same.

The wine is earthy and oaky, with notes of cherry. It warms me from the inside and coats my tongue and throat when I say, "You saw Amy today."

Paul takes another sip of scotch before he answers me. "She was at the coffee shop near the office."

"And then you called me?"

He shrugs. "We spoke about you."

"What did you say?"

He sighs. "Honestly, Sophie, I think I made a fool of myself. I told her how well suited you'll be for the show."

I take another sip of wine. "Why would that make you a fool?"

He frowns into his glass and like with Amy, waiting him out gets me nowhere.

"Why would that make you a fool, Paul?"

"I didn't come here to talk about this."

"About what?"

He slings back the last few fingers of his drink. His voice

is deeper, guttural as he turns to me and says, "It makes me a fool because I'm obviously in love with you, Sophie. But I told you that tonight isn't a date. I'm not here to talk about that."

I open my mouth, but I don't know what to say. There's nothing to say. Other than, "I'm sorry."

He shakes his head. "Don't. It's not... I fucked up. And I know that. I'm not asking for second chances. I'm trying to give you an opportunity."

"It's not just that you fucked up. I fucked up, too." He shakes his head but I press on. "I rushed into things with you because...well, because of my mom if I'm being honest. You know how she is. She's always wanted me to get married, have a family. That wasn't fair to you. I'm sorry."

I rushed into things to try to make other people happy but even if we didn't know each other for long, I know Paul and his eyes plead with me to drop it. "What's the opportunity?"

"You probably noticed an increase in activity on your social media accounts after we announced you'd be on the show?"

I nod.

"The producers noticed. You were a fan favorite on *Pop-Up*. And you're going to be a favorite with *Cooking for Camilla*, too. They want to offer you a job, Sophie."

"But... I already have a job."

He laughs. "We need a host for a documentary style show. Think Bourdain but you don't just go and eat all around the world, you cook there, too."

"But... I'm a chef."

Paul's smile is kind. "Exactly. That's why we think it should be you."

"You want to send me around the world to cook in different restaurants?"

"In restaurants, night markets, scratch kitchens, farms. Wherever the food is."

When I found out I was going to be a contestant on *Pop-Up Kitchen* I felt nothing. No heart beating out of my chest or cold sweats. I was numb. Excited—beneath the nothing I knew it was what I wanted and I was ready—but numb.

That's how this feels. Except this time, there's no excitement underneath the nothing, waiting for its big reveal.

Paul must feel it, the flat oozing numbness that's seeping out of me like molasses, because he grabs my shoulder and gives me a gentle shake. "Are you hearing me, Soph? This has the potential to catapult you to the top. Everyone is going to want to work with you after this."

After? "How long will this take?"

"Right now, we've got a twelve episode season planned. You'll be going all over the world. Buenos Aires, Sicily, Nairobi, Seoul, Auckland."

"That sounds…" Long. It sounds like a long time to be gone. "But the restaurant."

He shrugs. "You'd probably have to quit your job at the restaurant."

The numbness vanishes, replaced with the kind of panic that has me fighting tears. He takes my hand in his, squeezing. "I'm telling you this as a man who's been in this industry for a long time and not as your former fiancé. You are a talent, Sophie. You have the potential to do great things and this opportunity can make that happen. I need you to ask yourself if you really think you can reach your full potential at Amy & May's. Does it have the funding to grow with you? I know you're loyal to Amy but at some point you've got to put yourself first."

Maybe the wine is getting to me. My stomach churns and I'm lightheaded. "It's not just about loyalty," I say. And it's not just about potential. It's about what I *want*. Not what my mother wants or what Paul wants.

Me.

I don't aspire to the type of greatness that Paul is talking about, even if it's flattering to know he thinks I could reach it. The things I want are quieter than that, closer to my mother's dreams for my life than I'd ever really care to admit.

I want a kitchen that's mine. I want the freedom to create. And Amy. I want Amy.

"I know you like Amy," he says and I blush so hard I can feel it in my toes. "Oh." He drops my hands. *"Oh."*

"No," I say, though why bother denying it.

He presses the back of his hand to his mouth, smiling against it. "I should have known."

"What?"

"When we spoke about you today, it was obvious."

"What was, Paul?" I want to grab him by his artfully rumpled collar and shake him.

"How she feels about you. But it just never occurred to me that you might feel the same way."

"How does she feel about me, Paul?" This time I do grab him. I pull him around to look at me. If there was anyone who might know what Amy is thinking, the last person I would go to would be him. And yet, here I am.

"You love her," he says instead and he's lucky I don't strangle him. The way he's looking at me, it's like he's never seen me before, not until right now.

"Yes." There's no point in denying it. Not now that I have to untangle my fingers from his Hugo Boss. At some point between getting her off in the back of my car and kissing her on the stairs at the Hideaway, I went from being obsessed with that one shirt she wears to obsessed with her, to wanting to hear her laugh, performing better as a leader and a chef not just because it's my job but because of what it means to have her be proud of me, proud of our kitchen. "Yes, I love her."

Paul picks up his scotch glass and peers into it like another mouthful might magically appear. When one doesn't, he sighs. "I'm sure you'll be suspicious of anything I say. But you chose me because it's what your mom wanted. Make sure that if you're choosing to say no to the opportunity of a lifetime, it's for you, Sophie. And not Amy Chambers."

Chapter Twenty

Amy

When the knock comes, I almost don't answer. Even though I'm not exactly sure what I'm upset about. All Sophie did was tell Paul a truth that is more embarrassing than it is hurtful. It's my ego that's taken a hit.

By the time I roll off the bed, pull on some sweatpants, and slouch over to the door, my apology is ready for her on the tip of my tongue. Along with all the ways I'll make it up to her. Also with the tip of my tongue.

"You're not Sophie," I say, after I pull the door open and stare dumbly at my guest.

Jeremy smiles crookedly, leaning against the door frame. "I know. It sucks, right?"

"What are you doing here?"

"Sorry. I should have called. I just…" He runs his hand through his hair, making it stick up in a black wave. He takes a step back then another. "I can go. You're expecting company."

"No." I open the door farther. "I don't think I am." I'm fairly certain Sophie won't be coming tonight. It's way past late at this point. "I've got beer."

He nods, sheepish. "That'd be great."

Jeremy toes off his sneakers, snow melting from the treads onto the rubber mat by my door, and tiptoes through my apartment on his stocking feet. He launches himself onto my bed, the mattress springs bouncing and squeaking under his sudden weight, and throws his arm over his eyes.

"What were you watching?" he asks, nodding at my now-dark laptop screen. I hand him a bottle of beer and take a sip from my own, closing the laptop so he can't shake the mouse-pad and watch Sophie's face appear on an old episode of *Pop-Up Kitchen*.

"Nothing," I say. "So what's up with you? Why are you derping around my house at..." I make a show checking the time on my phone. "Midnight?"

"I saw your lights on," he says. "I was just driving around being derpy alone. I couldn't go see Wes. That's not true. I know I can. But he's so happy all the time. And, like, I'm happy for him. But I can feel the true love wafting off him like a noxious gas. It's too much."

I laugh at the visual of my brother walking around like a twitterpated Pig-Pen. "So you decided to join me over here on the Dark Side. I'm honored."

He pushes my shoulder. A gentle reprimand for the nega-tive self-talk. "You're not as Dark Side as you like to think you are."

"Yeah, yeah."

Jeremy reaches out, playing gently with the delicate leaf of the fern hanging beside my bed. He says to it, "Actually, I came because I might need..." He takes a deep breath. "I need a favor. A job, specifically."

"A job? At the restaurant?" My first instinct is to say yes. Jeremy is like a brother to me. Some days I even prefer him to Wes; he doesn't get as emo about the Sox losing. "But what about law school?" I ask. "Can you juggle law school and a part-time job?"

He picks at the label on his bottle. "I would need full-time."

"You're going to work full-time *and* finish your second year of law school?"

He continues to look anywhere but at me. "In this scenario, I wouldn't finish law school."

I take his hand in mine, squeezing tight. "Jeremy. What's happening?" I wince. "Are you…flunking out?"

He shrugs. "Not exactly. I'm doing fine, I guess. I just…" My friend's brown eyes are glassy when he looks up at me. "I *hate* it, Amy. I knew it would be competitive but everyone is so…well, they're assholes, honestly. The research is fun and the work is whatever. But I feel like I don't belong there and maybe I should just try something else until I figure my shit out."

Jeremy has always been the kind of smart that's a little terrifying, so it's not a surprise that he finds legal research "fun" and the heavy workload of a second-year law program "whatever." It goes beyond memorizing facts and formulas. He's the human personification of galaxy brain. But success and excellence have never been a priority for him. He's compassionate, kind—overly so in my opinion, he lets people walk all over him, though he's never asked—so it's no wonder he's not exactly flourishing in the hyper-competitive environment.

I look around at all my plants, some of the leaves curled in, but flourishing, thriving nonetheless. Because of the environment they've grown into.

"My restaurant is failing," I say. I don't really talk about this at all, unless it's with Sophie. Wes knows things aren't going great, but not the specifics. Dad knows nothing at all; we haven't spoken since Sophie kicked him out. But saying it out loud now doesn't feel as terrible as I thought it would. "My dream is dying."

"I'm sorry, Ames."

"Our landlord gave us three months to come up with the

money we owe, and Sophie invested. She saved my ass. But next month's rent is on the horizon. Vendors are starting to make noise about their bills." I bounce my head off the wall behind me. "I don't think we're going to make it." The beer has gone warm but I drink it anyway, adding moisture to my dry mouth. "Overhead costs are the kiss of death for a new restaurant. I knew that going in and yet…" I shrug.

"See," he says. "I knew you were the right person to come to."

"Yeah, Wes would only try to be cheerful and, like, solve things for us."

"Gross," he agrees. "So what are you going to do?"

I sigh. "We've got this reality TV appearance. But it's a last-ditch effort. By the time it airs, I think it will be too late."

"You're going to close?"

I turn to him. "Now?"

He nods.

"No. Never. I'm…the captain. Going down with the ship and all that. Besides, you wouldn't believe the number of restaurant owners who've failed. It's like…a rite of passage or something. I'm *supposed* to fail." But saying that out loud doesn't make it feel any better. My stomach aches at the thought of closing the doors to that restaurant and never opening them back up again. "If anything it was inevitable," I say quietly.

A tear falls down my cheek. I rub at it with my shoulder. But it does nothing to stop the next one. "I wanted it so bad. You know, Jer?"

He murmurs his agreement, his big palm petting the back of my head.

"At first it was like, look what I can do. I'm twenty-six and I'm opening a restaurant and it's going to be amazing. And then, all these young queer kids found their way there. And we fought so hard to get the staff the things they deserve, like a livable wage, for god's sake. And Sophie took a chance on me, on this kitchen, when she probably had so many better offers. She's turned down offers to stay with me, she's bought into the business. I failed her. I've failed all of them."

The bed dips as Jeremy gets up. He shuffles to the kitchen, rummages around in my cupboards, and comes back with a glass of water. "Drink this," he says, exchanging it for my beer. "Alcohol is a depressant."

"Thanks." I sniffle and take a big gulp of water. Like an alarm, I can hear my father's voice when I cry, telling us to stop our sniveling. To buck up. It's why crying in front of my mother's house feels like the only safe space. Mom encouraged crying, the painful body-racking sobs kind of crying. She said those kinds of cries released hormones that make you happy. It was science. Even Wes was known to get a good crying jag in when he thought I couldn't hear him.

Apparently, Jeremy Chen is the exception to the only cry in front of Mom's house rule. Or maybe Jeremy just has the same energy. He and my mom always got along well.

"I'll still give you a job if you want it. But I just thought you should know you might not have the job for very long. I'm a failure, Jeremy."

He makes an angry noise, ducking into my field of vision. "That's the last thing you are. You only fail if you give up. And you're not doing that. I'm so fucking proud of you, you know that, Amy?"

I bury my face in my sleeve until the urge to cry again passes. Then I wrap my arms around my friend. "Thank you, Jer." I squeeze him until he squeaks.

"Please. Release," he croaks, tapping out on my shoulder.

We separate laughing. "This has been helpful, Amy. Thank you."

"Did I do anything? I think you ended up helping me."

"Naw." He stands up, shaking out his arms, bouncing on the balls of his feet. "You inspired me. I'm going to keep going. Push through. It's only failure if I give up, right?"

"Are you sure? If you're not happy..."

"No, you're right. I'm not happy but this is something I've wanted since I was fifteen years old. I can't give up when it gets tough."

I follow Jeremy to the door with my hands tucked into the sleeves of my sweatshirt and lock it behind him. I don't know what's going to happen to my restaurant next. I only know what I can do about it.

Not give up.

No matter what happens, I'm not going to give up. I'm going to keep doing what I've done since before we opened: make the best decisions I can to protect my restaurant and staff. And Sophie.

Sophie steps into my office, closing the door behind her even though it's far too early for any of our staff to be here yet. She's come straight from the gym, her hair curled from sweat and in a bun, messy from movement and exertion rather than artfully so, but she's already changed her clothes into the comfortable, practical kitchen wear I'm used to seeing her in. She sets a to-go coffee cup on the desk and sits in the chair by the door.

"I'm sorry," she says. "About talking to Paul about our business."

"No. I'm sorry." The sudden rush of relief that we are making up takes my breath away. "I was embarrassed, and I took it out on you. You didn't deserve that."

We smile, shyly.

"You didn't come over last night." I try not to make it accusatory but it sounds that way regardless.

She peers down into the hole on the lid of her own coffee cup. "There was a lot to unpack after my talk with Paul. I needed some time. To think."

I take a deep breath, sitting straighter in my chair. That sounds ominous.

"What did Paul want to talk about?" My pulse thrums in my throat, like her answer could make or break me.

"He offered me a job," she says, so casually, like her taking another job wouldn't just ruin me professionally but would devastate me personally more than I care to admit.

I will not bad-mouth her ex to her face. I will not bad-mouth her ex to her face. I will not…

"That motherfucker *poached* you? Right out from under my nose?"

"He only poached me if I said yes."

I don't move, as if that will help me hear better. "You didn't?"

She shakes her head. "No. Of course not."

She sets her cup down on my desk, rising out of her chair and scooting between my legs and the desk. She perches on the edge and runs her finger along my bottom lip.

"I work here, Amy. I'm your head chef."

I reach for her, pulling her mouth to mine. She leans into me, her arms coming around my waist as I stand between her legs. The relief at hearing her affirm her place here, beside me; I don't have the words to tell her what it means to me. That she trusts me despite us staring down the barrel of closure.

I kiss her again, brushing my tongue along her lips. I pull at her hair until it falls down her back.

"What are we doing?" she whispers into the skin over my heart. And I think she's asking more than her words say. But with her in my hands, cheeks flushed and pink, lips bee-stung, a gift only for me, I don't think I can say the words that I want to. I'm afraid once I start speaking, I won't be able to stop.

Her eyes close in my silence.

"Hey." I brush my thumb over her cheekbone. "Look at me."

She blushes as she meets my eyes. "You're beautiful," I say. The words are too simple for what she is. But they're all I have. "You lay me out, Hollywood. Every time I get to touch you. To work beside you. That you chose…" *Me.* "This restaurant over…" I shake my head imagining what kind of gig Paul could have lined up for her in some swank, five-star, à la carte restaurant. "What was undoubtedly a better restaurant?"

She pulls me down to her mouth again, presses her forehead to mine. "*This* restaurant. You. You're worth it, Amy."

I close my eyes, on fire from her. How she can go from shy to strong in moments. "Amy, I…"

I kiss the words out of her mouth, far gentler than before. Her face is sweet and flushed as I pull away and we right our clothes where we've pulled at them. She stays on the edge of my desk as I sit again, planting her feet on my thighs.

"I want to come out on the show." She reaches for my hand, entwining our fingers. "I want us to come out on the show."

"What do you mean?"

"You know what I mean." She squeezes my hand. "This. We tried boundaries for a hot minute and were terrible at them, but we can't keep pretending that we're just business partners. And I know I run headfirst into things, but this feels right. Doesn't it?"

It scares me. Not just declaring us, but how brazenly she wants to show herself to the world. It's incredibly brave, how vulnerable she's willing to be.

"What was the offer?" I ask because while she is brave, I am a coward who can't admit to the woman I love that she is, in fact, my girlfriend. "Paul's offer? Is he launching a new restaurant or is it one he already owns?"

"Oh. That," she says flatly. She rolls her eyes and lays it out for me: the travel, the cooking. The absolute celebrity of it all. Her voice is unexcited but a small smile tugs at her lips as she talks about the destinations, the opportunities to cook and learn from locals.

And I can see it. See her on the streets of packed cities. The glow on her face from the heat and her excitement as she cooks in a hundred different types of kitchens. The way she'd charm her hosts, the chefs, the audience.

The same way she charmed me.

"And you said no?" I clarify. My stomach rolls, my skin too hot. "To this?" My arms fall away from where they hug her thighs.

"Yeah. Paul made his pitch, saying I should choose for myself and not let you factor into it but..."

"Wait." I push my desk chair back until it hits the wall behind me. "You said no to the job, not because of a professional obligation. You said no to the job because of *me?*"

She frowns. "Well, it's a bit more complicated than that but...yeah."

I shake my head. "Sophie, that's..." I trail off. No thoughts, just confusion.

She laughs, a little cruelly. "What?"

"It's stupid, honestly."

"Excuse me?" She hops down from the desk. "My choice to stay here and cook in *our* kitchen as opposed to gallivanting across the world is stupid?"

I stand now, too. "Can you hear yourself? Of course it is."

"I thought you'd be happy." Her voice rises. "I thought you, of all people, would be happy, not just for yourself but for everything we've worked for. I've sunk my money into this place now, Amy. I can't just walk away."

"Happy? You thought I'd be happy that you turned down an opportunity to be a fucking chef superstar to stay here and…and…fucking close this restaurant with me? You know that's what's going to happen, right, Sophie? You looked at the numbers. You know Amy & May's isn't coming out of this alive." My voice breaks on the last word and for a moment so does she. Her face falls.

"We will, though. That's what I wanted to talk about last night. I know how we can fix this."

"I've run these numbers a million times. Unless we somehow get another influx of cash—"

"Or we cut costs elsewhere."

I shake my head. "There's…there's nowhere to cut costs."

"I'm taking a pay cut," she says. She smiles like the words she's saying aren't earth-shattering. "That's how we save this place. I'm a partial owner now and I know you aren't taking a salary yet, Amy. My salary is one of our biggest expenses."

She holds her arms open.

I want to fall into them, into the softness of her body, her strength. I want her to be the one to hold me up for a while, just a little bit. But if she does that for me, I'll break. I know I will. I'll let her choose Boston and me and our restaurant. I'll let her choose to take far less than she's worth, over the world.

The literal world.

And it's not the same, the relationship my father had with my mother. But it is, too. Because he kept her around, strung along, long after he'd fallen out of love with her. He kept her here under his thumb when she could have been flourishing instead.

I won't be that for Sophie. She'll hate me for it. But this is one last decision that I have to make.

"I'm not going to let you choose me over the opportunity of a lifetime. Not when you'll resent me for it later."

She tilts her chin, bites the inside of her lip. "Well, it's not your choice to make," she says.

I make myself hard, the way I did when I was a kid and my dad made my mom cry again, or when Wes found me after school, his nose running with blood and his glasses cracked. I make myself the girl with weapons for feelings because it's the only way I can get her to see, to make the right choice.

"It kind of is, though." I walk around the desk to the door, holding it open so I can make a quick getaway. She doesn't turn to follow me, showing me her back as she stares at the white painted brick wall.

"You should come out on the show, if that's what you want." It hurts to breathe right now, to say these words, like I've taken a bite of something far too hot and it burns all the way down my throat. "But you and me? There's nothing to… come out about. There's nothing to announce. We're not together."

Her shoulders reach her ears by the time I'm done. Slowly she turns. The green in her eyes is vivid from the tears that don't fall.

"You are so selfish."

I've never had to take a punch, but her words hit like one anyway. I have to fight to stay upright. Not to let the pain in my stomach keel me over entirely.

"I chose this." She points at the floor, at this restaurant. "I chose us. I chose you. But I also chose *me*, too." She turns her finger on herself, hitting her chest so hard I can hear it from here. "I love you, Amy. I love what we've built. And that's for me. Not just you. But obviously *you* know what's best for me. You know what I want out of my career. Out of my life. Have you ever bothered to think about that? To ask?"

"You could be a star." My voice echoes down the hall. From the corner of my eye someone moves, freezes.

"Maybe I don't want to be a star." Her tears fall. I track each one because I'm the person that put them there. "Maybe the only Hollywood I wanted, was to be yours."

My escape plan is unnecessary because Sophie moves quickly, pushing past me and running down the hall, past Maggie frozen in the doorway. She runs through the back doorway and is gone.

Chapter Twenty-One

Sophie

After Paul and I broke up I lost something. An indefinable something that made me a good chef. I spent my hours in the kitchen trying to play catch-up but always falling a little bit short.

That's not what this feels like. After I left earlier today, I drove around for a while, until my face was so tight and my head ached from crying so hard I had to go home and shower. I changed and lay on my couch, Fifi purring on my chest, until the absolute last minute. Then I came here.

Amy has spent all her time in the office or at the hostess stand. Maggie has sent concerned glances my way every thirty seconds or so. I cook. When I'm cooking, it doesn't feel so much like I've lost an unidentifiable thing, some spark that I can't catch. As I chop and sauté, plate and garnish, nothing is lost. I know exactly what to do and how to do it, and I even get it out on time.

I just...don't care. I haven't lost something. I've lost everything. I'm numb.

"You okay, chef?" Jameela asks. I look over at her, suddenly aware of the knife in my hand, the mushrooms on my chopping board.

"Yes," I say. "I'm fine."

I am. I am fine. I'm fine with this. I'm fine with the way Amy's hunched over that hostess stand like a dragon protecting a stash of gold. I'm fine with how she hasn't looked me in the eye since I left. I don't really feel anything at all. It's kind of nice, after feeling too much, too strongly, too soon, for so long.

It's nice to not have to care so much about this job, to not have to worry that I'm doing it well. It's like going on a little brain vacation even though I'm here. At work. With the woman I love. And she dumped me. So I could take a job I don't want.

Because if I had to feel that? Any of it. It would fucking suck.

"Chef?" Jameela asks again.

"Sorry." I look over and smile, pick up my knife and start chopping the mushrooms left on the board. "Fine," I say. "I'm fine."

Jameela's face falls along with her gaze. I follow it to my hands, my knife, my mushrooms. I must be really numb. Well and truly numb. Because my first thought is *mushrooms don't bleed*. And then, *so whose blood is that?* And finally, *oh it's mine*.

"I'm bleeding," I say like one might say *it's raining*. Like I am reporting the weather.

"Shit," Jameela says, loud enough that the patrons at the tables closest to us on the other side of the open kitchen stop and stare. She grabs my hand, flinging it over my head. The blood pools on the board, on the food—those poor mushrooms are inedible now—and drips down my arm. Jameela presses a clean cloth to it and I look up, watching where her dark skin surrounds mine, where the blood leaks into the white fabric on my sleeve.

It should hurt. But it just…doesn't.

"What the hell, Hollywood?" Amy asks, suddenly beside us. And *ow*. That hurts. That name on her lips, the concern in her eyes, the absolute fear as she looks between me and Jameela and the blood on the counter, is like a switch flipped in my nerve endings, and the pain comes rushing down my arm.

"I... I'm bleeding," I say.

"Yeah, no shit." She grabs my hand from Jameela's grasp, sending searing hot pain through my forearm. I hiss and her face crumples. "Are you okay? Did it hit the bone?" She turns to Jameela. "Did she hit the bone?"

Her voice is frantic, her face white as a sheet.

"I don't know." Jameela herds us toward the back of the kitchen. We're undoubtedly causing a spectacle but it's too hard for me to tell. My vision starts to close in, a fuzzy blackness encroaching from the edges of my eyes.

"I think I need to sit down."

Amy continues to swear, repeatedly and angrily as someone procures a chair and someone else shoves a glass of water in my uninjured hand and everyone else stops what they're doing to watch their head chef potentially pass out next to the sink.

"Get back to work," I say, though it has none of the authority I'd like it to. But they listen, at least.

"I'll take over," Jameela says to Amy. She looks down at me. "I think she'll need stitches."

As I look between them, it dawns on me. "You want *her* to take me to the hospital?"

Jameela frowns but takes my spot at the counter, her back straight and tall but also kind of fuzzy. That's probably not good.

"Come on," Amy says. She wraps her arm around my back, pulling me up while keeping my other arm above my head.

"I don't want to go with you," I say, dead weighting into the chair like a toddler throwing a tantrum.

Amy huffs, her jaw squared. She looks down at me, her lips pursed. "Too bad. You cut your fucking hand open—"

"Why do you care?" I whisper-hiss.

Amy rocks back on her heels, her eyes transform from angry concern to hurt. From the corner of my eye, Carly stops to stare at us both.

Amy shakes herself, literally shakes her head, squeezing her eyes shut like she's resetting her own router, and bodily lifts me again. For a skinny chick, she's actually quite strong. Or I might be losing too much blood.

"We can argue in the car, but you need stitches now and I'm not wasting another second for your hand to get more fucked up."

She pushes me through the back hallway door, stops outside the staff room to find my coat and throw it over my shoulders, ducks into the office to grab her own coat and keys.

"I want Jameela to take me," I say. "Or Maggie."

"You know they can't. They have to stay here and run the kitchen and the floor." She opens the back door and holds up her key fob. From outside, her car beeps, the lights flashing through the doorway.

My arm throbs, from hand to shoulder the muscles ache from keeping it elevated. Without Amy to put pressure on the wound, blood streams through the cloth. A deep, teeth gritting kind of pain pumping with my pulse. It hurts enough that I do as she says, walking out into the snow in my practical indoor work shoes, letting her open the passenger door for me and do up my seat belt.

"Why would you do this?" she says, as she jams her keys into the ignition. The engine squeals and she throws the car into reverse, maneuvering out of the cramped parking spot like she's a Formula 1 racer.

"You think I did this on purpose?" I use the dashboard as a prop to hold my arm up, pressing my other hand against the wound hard enough to make me see stars, then backing off a little.

"I think you weren't paying attention and you put yourself in danger." She makes a wide turn onto the street, driving entirely too fast for the amount of snow coming down.

"Slow down," I snap. "And why do you think that is? What could have possibly been preoccupying me?"

"I don't like seeing you hurt," she says, clenching her jaw. Her skin looks washed-out and pale, especially in the headlights of oncoming cars, the greens and reds of the traffic lights.

"And why do you care?" I ask again. My heart pounds too hard for someone with an open wound, but this pathetic part of me wants to hear it. I want to hear her say she cares because she loves me, too.

Amy glances at me and back at the road, once, twice. At some point my blood has landed on her, smeared against her cheek. The cuff of my jacket is soggy and cold. She can probably read the desperation on my face because in the span of a few short breaths her face changes from panicked to neutral, numb.

"Because you're my head chef. I need your hands."

The hand in question throbs again but then so does my chest. "No, you don't." My hurt at her words sounds angrier than I actually feel. I'm not angry at all. I'm sad and slowly going numb again. Numbness in my hand—which can't be good—and in my head and in my heart. "If you needed these hands you wouldn't have told me to take that job. You would have heard me when I said I wanted to stay and fight for this place. Our place."

She stops the car, pulling up the parking brake, and I look out the window to an urgent care center on the other side of the parking lot. Light spills from the wall of windows onto the snowy cement; a handful of people sit huddled in chairs inside.

"Come on," she says, opening her door.

"No. Pass me my bag." I nod at my backpack she threw in the back seat. Slowly Amy pulls it out and dumps it in my lap. I thread my good arm through the straps. "I'm going in alone. Please don't follow me."

"Hollywood," she says, like she's tired, weary of my bad attitude. Like I haven't spent this whole time trying to get her to listen to me. For once.

"You don't get to call me that anymore," I say, rage shaking my voice. "You don't get to pretend to care about me or this expensive hand of mine. You gave up on us. You didn't listen, when the only thing I asked you to do," I hiss. "Was fucking listen. So hear this: Don't follow me into that building. Don't talk to me at work unless it's *about* work. And don't. Do not. Ever. Again. Make a decision for me."

I push open the door and start to climb out.

"Hollyw—Sophie," she stops herself.

I look over my shoulder.

"I'm sorry."

"Don't be. You get what you wanted, Amy. I'm going to take the job."

I slam the door shut and walk. The cold keeps my wits about me; the blood seems to have slowed to a leak. I don't look back, not when I hear a car door open and close again. Not when the engine starts and certainly not when it drives away.

Chapter Twenty-Two

Amy

She shows up the next day. And the next. She's almost useless with her stitches and her hand wrapped in a huge bandage. But she shows up and tells everyone what to do. She ignores me unless she has to speak to me, and then she says as few words as possible.

Every time I look at her, all I can see is the hurt in her eyes when she said I gave up. How much it hurt to hear, because it was true. I gave up on her and this restaurant when I told her to leave, after I'd promised I'd fight.

There was no doggie bag of food waiting for me on the counter when I left after service tonight and I punished myself with a stop at a fast-food drive-through instead. The smell of the deep-fried saturated fats permeates the fibers of my car upholstery but I sit and eat it anyway, looking at Mom's house and waiting for tears. But they don't come. I'm a well, run dry. Instead I'm filled with fire. The angry kind. The kind that needs to be let out in a good old-fashioned yelling match.

Throwing my leftover fries back into the greasy bag, I start my car and drive across town. I haven't been to my father's house since I was a teenager. I expected it to look different, or to at least feel different, as I approach the front door. But it doesn't, and I don't feel different, either. I'll always be the scared kid I was when we last stayed over here, before Wes and I decided together that we wouldn't go back. Mom never made us choose, she would never. But it didn't feel right when she was sick and heartbroken to give our time to someone who seemed so indifferent.

The doorbell echoes on the other side of his front door. The front light isn't even on. He's probably not home. He's probably out with clients. Maybe he has a girlfriend we don't know about. I wonder if I can get her a message. She needs an escape plan.

I'm halfway down his icy front steps when the door opens. My father stands in the doorway, a glass of something amber in his hand, the house dark except for the glow of a television coming from a room down the hall. His tie hangs loose from his neck; his pants look floppy in his stocking feet.

"Amy?" I haven't heard him say my name like that in a long time, maybe ever. Without frustration in his tone, anger, boredom. His voice is softer, lighter. I could almost convince myself he's happy I'm here. That he wants to see me.

"Hi, Dad."

He blinks like he can't believe his eyes. "Do you want to come in?" he asks, stepping aside. He sounds tired. He looks it.

Do I want that?

"When I decided to come here, I was going to yell at you," I say.

His jaw tightens. It's almost imperceptible but it's loud as a scream to me. The first sign that I have acted in a way that displeases him. The clock has begun its countdown to when I will be told why I am what's wrong with this family, with our relationship.

"So, I guess I'd better get this out quick." I stomp my feet in the cold because I don't think I'm going to get invited in now. "I could never figure out what exactly it was that I did.

Is it because I'm gay, Dad? Is it that cliché? Because I don't think it is. Or maybe I just don't want to believe it. Could you tell I was gay before even I knew?"

"What are you talking about?" he asks, voice flat. He takes a sip of his drink, the ice clinking against the glass.

"You don't love me, Dad. At least, not the same way that other fathers love their kids. I've always been too loudmouthed, too argumentative, too quick to anger. I've never been able to stay..." I hold up my hand, thumb down. "Under your thumb. Not the same way you could keep Wes or Mom there."

He scoffs. "Stop with the dramatics, please. Of course I love you. You and your brother."

I nod. My ears are so cold and I don't know where my hat is. "You love us, in your own way. The best you could, I guess. I was going to yell at you, but yelling is too much energy. And I've wasted so much energy on you, Dad. You don't deserve it. Not my energy. Not Wes's. You didn't deserve Mom's." I laugh. Not because any of this is funny. More of an if-I-can't-laugh-I'll-cry situation.

"Mom wasted her *life* on you. Her fucking life. You get that, right? Waiting for you to love her enough? To be good enough for you? And here you are, living a life after Mom. But where is she? She doesn't get the chance to live a life after you, after the wreckage you left. A life where she realizes she was better than you this whole time. If I were to yell, it would be about that. That she doesn't get the chance to come out of the other side of your pitiful version of love."

I dash at the tears on my cheeks. Dad is made of stone but I don't know for how long so I keep going. "I've been so terrified of turning out like you. Too angry, too tired to give a damn, that I dumped the first woman I've ever been in love with. Can you believe that? I'd rather be alone than put anyone through the things that you put Mom through. And I don't mean the cheating. I mean the hours and *hours* alone. She was alone while you worked and worked and only cared about the legacy you were building."

I press the heels of my hands to my temples as the weight of what I've done hits me, fully. The mental gymnastics I had to do, all because I was...scared. Scared of disappointing her, of not being good enough. Scared that one day she might not love me anymore while I loved her forever and ever.

I rush forward, wrapping my arms around my father. His remain stiff at his sides. "You were scared, weren't you?" I say over his shoulder. From here, I can smell that smell that every house has. The one that will follow you on your clothes when you leave it. It smells like laundry detergent, fabric softener.

The same brand Mom used growing up.

"You were scared." I pull back. He's red-faced, his throat working but his jaw tense. "I'm sorry for you, Dad. I'm sorry that you don't love yourself enough to love the people who love you back." It's such a strange feeling to feel sorry for your parent, to pity him. "I'm going to learn from your mistakes, though. I'm going to be scared and do it anyway. And I'm going to fail at my business, probably. But I'm going to love her. And maybe I'll suck at that, too. But maybe I won't."

I turn down the steps. It's the middle of the night and I won't see her until tomorrow when filming starts, but suddenly I can't wait to go to bed. Every second brings me closer to seeing her again.

"Amy," he says, his voice rough.

"This is going to be the last time I seek you out, by the way," I say, not giving him a chance to speak again. I was on a roll but I can feel the control slipping. I'm going to need to have a good cry in my car soon. "If you want to have a relationship with either of us, the ball is in your court. I can't speak for Wes but if you think you'd like that—respectfully, kindly—you know where to find me."

We stare at each other, me teetering on the edge of a breakdown. The only clue that he is affected is the way his Adam's apple bobs over and over.

"What's her name?" he asks.

"You've met her," I say. "Sophie. She kicked you out of my—out of our—restaurant."

Chapter Twenty-Three

Sophie

The first text I've received from Amy in a week comes in at three in the morning. I don't see it until my alarm blares at 7:00 but I stare at the time stamp for far too long, trying to figure out what she was doing to be awake at the ass-crack of nighttime. I want to believe that she was sleeping in her bed and woke up because of some dream, about me maybe, and the memory of the dream made her think of me.

But the more gut churning answer is that she never went to bed. Maybe she went to the Hideaway, maybe with her brother. Maybe she met someone there and danced the night away with a woman who was beautiful and funny. A woman who knew where she stood. Someone strong.

The rational part of my brain knows this is absurd. If Amy were out with someone else, why would she text me at 3am:

I think you should make this for Camilla.

Followed by photos of a smorgasbord of quintessential Boston cuisine: Boston baked beans, clam chowder, lobster roll.

All good, delicious food. But food that isn't me. Or even really us. And by us, I mean Amy & May's because *we* are not anything. My thumbs hover over the screen, ready to argue that this is our chance to set ourselves apart when plenty of restaurants will take this traditional route. I think.

Maybe…she's right? Maybe we should just do something classic, something expected even, and do it well. But I don't know if I can do it well. I haven't made a lobster roll since before *Pop-Up Kitchen*. What if I can't even do right by the classics? I'll be run out of Boston for sure. At this point, I'd go willingly.

I mull over our menu options all the way to the gym. I don't have much time left to choose. Filming begins tonight. Just prep shots, interviews. Paul said Camilla would be here for a meet and greet and I'm excited enough about shaking her hand that if I think about it for too long, I might throw up. I'm thankful for the loud clank of the weights, the heavy metal playing over the speakers, the smell of chalk mixed with underlying but constant sweat, at the gym. It's a perfect distraction for my nerves, and the perfect place to get rid of all this excess energy. I can shut my brain off and just lift, just run, just feel like my heart might explode out of my chest, my lungs might shrivel up into raisins. Feeling like I'm going to die in a controlled panic attack is—strangely—usually very helpful for moments like this.

Except for today, when I can't lift even close to my former max. My stitches are out but my hand throbs, weak and sore, every time I wrap my fingers around a bar. I keep asking my body, telling it, to go harder, faster, waiting for my muscle memory to take over and just go. But it's like trying to start a gas stove without a spark. There's nothing there. I'm running on empty and by the end of my session with Natalie, I'm frustrated, exhausted, and close to tears.

"Why don't we stop?" She turns down the music, stopping the timer on the giant digital clock hanging on the wall.

"No," I say, preparing for another deadlift, even as my legs shake.

She puts her foot over my bar. "You're not in the right headspace today. That's okay. You're not always going to be."

I shake my head, shake out my arms, and finally fall back

on my ass. I drop my head between my legs, trying to catch my breath. She places her hand on my back, even though I'm covered in sweat. "You want to talk about it?"

"No," I mumble to the floor. Then say, "I got dumped."

She pauses. "By Paul?"

"No. My business partner. Her name is Amy."

Natalie crouches beside me. "I'm so sorry, Sophie."

I thought talking about it would make me want to cry more but saying it out loud feels a little bit better, actually. "You'd think that after getting involved with someone I worked with last time, I wouldn't do it again. But this...felt different. I thought, at least. I don't know anymore."

My shoulders shudder as I try to push the tears down. I've gone this long without crying about it. I should be able to make it through this, but the tears leak through anyway.

"Weak," I mutter. "I'm weak."

Natalie tips my chin up. "Listen, I don't know anything about your personal life. Or very much about your professional life. But there's one thing I know about you for sure. You're fucking strong, Sophie." She taps the plates on my barbell, then my temple. "It takes strength here to do anything in this gym. And I'd bet it takes strength to be one of the best chefs in the city, too. Just a different kind."

Maybe it's only because I'm heartbroken, and everything reminds me of her, but that sounds exactly like something Amy would say. And it makes me feel better.

Camilla Vargas is, implausibly, more beautiful in person than on TV. Even without makeup, dressed in the clothes she came from home in, she glows. Her smile is huge, her hair shines. She's real and also a little surreal. Amy stands on one side of the kitchen, pretending to busy herself with cleaning that doesn't need to be done while I stand at the other end, pacing. But when Camilla arrives, I stop. She claps her hands, walking around the restaurant, which the crew has cleared of most tables and chairs, her smile huge.

"Sophie," she says, holding her hands out to me. Instead of shaking one of mine, she takes both and squeezes. I hide the wince as a shot of pain goes through my healing hand. "I've heard so much about you. It's such an honor to meet you."

She's full of shit. She has to be. As if Paul mentioned me to her. But I blush nonetheless. She's even prettier up close. I look away and immediately meet Amy's eyes. She scowls and turns away.

I don't know what she expects. It's impossible not to be a bisexual having a panic attack in the face of one of my biggest celebrity chef crushes.

"I'm so excited to see what you're making for me tomorrow," she says.

My smile feels shaky. "Yeah. Me too."

She pauses, most likely hearing the nerves in my voice. Camilla takes my hand, just the one, like through chef-to-chef ESP, she's realized my other one is fresh from a deep cut. "The first time I got to make my own menu, everyone told me what to cook. It was all anyone could talk about, the things *they* would cook if they were in charge. But they weren't in charge, were they?"

I shake my head like a starstruck kid talking to Big Bird for the first time.

"That's right. I was. So I cooked for myself."

"That...that's a good idea," I say. My throat is dry and embarrassingly tight, like I might start to cry right here in front of Camilla Vargas. This time when I look at Amy she doesn't turn away, and neither do I. All of these people are saying the things Amy would say, the things she has said, when what I really want is to hear it directly from her. But I'm the fool who told her to leave me alone.

Chapter Twenty-Four

Amy

"Have you seen Sophie?" a PA asks. I think her name is Tamara. She looks like she should have stopped drinking coffee three ventis ago. She takes a long swig out of a paper cup then crumples it like a frat bro crushes beer cans. "That chef?" she clarifies.

"Yay high?" I hold my hand to just below my chin. *Great tits? Hates my guts?* "No, I haven't seen her. Are you…?" I look around. The kitchen is empty but the dining room is a mess of people preparing to film. "Is she missing?"

"We need to go over some of the shots. She needs to start the prep. Camilla is nice but she does *not* like to be kept waiting." The PA speaks as if from personal experience.

"Okay." I hold my hands out. "I'll find her. Why don't you have some water or something."

She looks at me, confused. "I'm not thirsty." She stalks away and I go in the opposite direction, checking the office, the staff room. Both are empty. We'll have a few staff come in later. Friends and family are encouraged to come in and sit as "diners" and a few servers will bring them food and drinks from a set menu that Sophie has already prepared and that Jameela will cook, to make the restaurant look busy and give the impression that we're filming during regular service. She's not out back hiding in her truck and when I text her a short *where are you?* she doesn't respond.

Things are starting to get louder out front. I ignore the twisting in my gut, the fear that she's bailed, that she's given up. The fear that she's done exactly what I told her to do: she's gone to find Paul and tell him she wants that job. I go back out to the kitchen, hoping that she'll be there as I push the door open, chopping or seasoning or washing something. That she'll be her old self, a little snarly, a kitchen goddess; that the grill will already be hot and she'll already have some kind of protein defrosting on the counter.

Oh.

Oh.

"I know where she is," I say to no one.

The door makes that suction release sound, sticking a bit as I open it. At first glance the freezer is empty but as I step deeper inside, I hear her. A soft sniffle. She leans against a rack of shelves at the back, her cheeks and nose absurdly red. Her arms are wrapped around her chest, her shoulders up by her ears. It could be from the cold or the nerves or both.

"Hi."

She swipes at her cheeks. The only person I've ever been able to cry in front of, until recently, was my brother. Because he was the only one my tear ducts would perform for, he got all of my tears. Right now, just seeing her crying makes me want to break down.

She looks small, scared. My hands and arms feel empty, useless. There's nothing to do. Nothing I can do, or at least, nothing I know how to do to make this better.

"Do you want me to start...the prep?" I ask. That's something I can *do*.

"I can do it."

"They're looking for you, is all."

"I figured."

"Are you..." She's probably nervous. That's all this is. Nerves. It's terrible of me but god I'm curious if she's sad, too.

I don't actually *want* her to be sad. But it would be nice to know if this is as hard on her as it has been on me. "Do you want to talk about it?"

Her chest expands, her breasts pushing against the structured fabric of her apron. "Yesterday I felt…ready."

"And today you…don't?"

She looks up at me, her eyes searching. "What if it's not good enough? What if… I'm not good enough?"

I reach for her, only realizing how cold I am when I touch her cheeks. Objectively they're freezing but they don't feel that way to me. "I have questioned a lot the last few months. Whether we're going to make it. The restaurant," I clarify. "Whether I'm doing enough for the staff or if they're happy. If the menu is good."

She laughs.

I tip her chin up. "The one thing I will not question is if you are good enough. You are…" I could list all of her fine professional attributes. That she is hardworking, that she has good taste, a smart eye for pairings. But when I say she's good enough, that is not what I mean.

"You make me want to be a better person, Sophie. You make me want to be kinder, more patient. And yes, work harder. You push me to succeed."

Her chin trembles and our breath mists between us. I realize belatedly that I have not shivered once in fear of a velociraptor with humanlike dexterity.

"Not good enough? Sophie, you're the best of us."

She slips her arms around me, pressing her chest to mine. If I close my eyes hard enough, I can feel her heart beating with mine. She fits just under my chin. Her weight in my arms, the smell of her shampoo, the steadiness of her breathing, all of it is a relief. Proof that it was real, once, not that long ago at all. Even if I was the one to ruin it.

"I'm sorry," I whisper. "I…" I swallow.

This is a bad time. The wrong time to rehash everything. But now that I've got her here I might not be able to let go if I don't say this.

"I love you."

Sophie shifts in my arms but I hold her tighter. This is a balancing act and the slightest shift will send me crashing to the ground. "And I…wanted you to do what I thought was best for you and I know," I say quickly. "That you hate it when I make decisions for you. And I'm sorry. I did the one thing that you have *repeatedly* asked me to stop doing."

Sophie says, her voice muffled by my shirt, "Can I move now?"

"Oh. Yeah." I step away, brushing casually at my own eyes. "Sorry. Again."

If I didn't absolutely have to be here right now, I might go sit in front of my mom's house.

She lifts up on her toes and presses a soft kiss to my mouth. I don't move, my whole body on alert, every cell has its ears perked toward her like tiny golden retrievers.

"What you said? About me being the best of us. That's…" She shakes her head. "No one has ever believed in me like that before."

"Well, that's dumb of them."

She laughs.

"Do you trust me?" I ask.

"Yes," she says, without hesitation. It feels like I've swallowed something warm, light.

"Then go out there and cook whatever you want. Because I trust you, too."

The door opens and the frazzled PA sticks her head in. "There you are. We need you to start prep."

Sophie looks from her to me. "Let's do this."

Chapter Twenty-Five

Sophie

Camilla Vargas is gracious and kind but she's also an internationally recognized executive chef and her entire demeanor changes when filming starts. Butterflies go wild in my stomach just watching her; she's powerful and a little scary and exactly the kind of chef I want to be. But that doesn't make it any less vomit-inducing to cook for her.

My friend Cara had a baby last year, and I expected her to talk about the pain and how terrible delivery was. She'd refused all the drugs. But when I visited her and the new baby, all she talked about was how wonderful it was, how she couldn't wait to do it again. The pain and the fear of the pain that she'd been obsessed with before birth was gone. All she could remember was the joy.

That's how it feels, to cook for myself again, even if it is on camera, under a deadline, for entertainment. I forget the fear in the form of sweat down my back, the nerves that make me want to throw up. My brain must have made me forget in order to allow me to agree to do this at all.

The premise of the show requires Amy to seat Camilla like any other guest and Camilla is encouraged by the producers to walk around the restaurant after she's seated, to explore the space, to speak to "guests"—our own friends and family—and to enter the kitchen. She peers over my shoulder, her mouth turned down in a speculative frown. She silently tastes sauces with a disposable spoon, studies my knife skills, pausing my chopping once to run her finger along the puckered red scar on my hand. Once her first beverage is served she sits back down again; she chats with Amy and I strain to hear what they're saying.

Natalie smiles at me from her seat in the dining room. It's so strange to see her in clothes that aren't meant to get sweaty. "You got this," she mouths as Maggie sets down a plate that Jameela prepared, the poor woman relegated to a small corner of our kitchen. I nod, my smile tight. I'm more grateful for her presence and her belief than I'm able to articulate right now. Somehow my knife hand doesn't shake, nothing burns, and soon I'm putting the finishing touches on my plates.

And this? This might be the best food I've ever made. There wasn't a lot of skill involved. They're simple dishes, some elevated, some not. It's so cliché to think it and I smile to myself as I lift my eyes and meet Amy's gaze across the restaurant. But this food was made with love. Love for my job, for this restaurant. For her and for myself.

As I set the dishes in front of her, Camilla's lips twist and I can't tell if it's a face of distaste, disappointment, or confusion. But it's not positive.

"What is this?" she asks, the echo of her accent smoothing her words even if her tone is skeptical.

"It's a little..."

"Messy?" she asks.

"Rustic," I counter. A smile pulls at her lips. "I know. It might not be the fanciest dish you'll see but it tastes..."

"Good?"

"Amazing." *You're the best of us.* "I think so, at least."

She leans back in the booth that runs the length of one

side of the dining room, and props her elbow in her palm, tapping her finger against her lips. It's a defensive, nervous pose—one that I would read too much into if I was standing on the *Pop-Up Kitchen* set, but a smile remains on her face. "Tell me about it."

Amy shifts beside me. She's been quiet since I stepped up, and it takes everything in me not to turn to her, to give her this speech. "This dish is inspired by Amy and me."

She straightens.

"Amy was born and raised in Boston. I'm from Montreal. One of the things that we've struggled with..." I grin ruefully. "Is agreeing on what should go on our menu. Amy leans toward classic menu items, especially ones that stay true to her hometown. Cuts of red meat, potatoes, and...crustaceans." I laugh when Camilla makes a funny face at my intentional misuse of the word and feel Amy's gaze on my face. "Montreal food—in my opinion—lends itself to experimentation. It's a place where many different cultures come together, to learn from each other, and turn into something new. So that's what I did here. It's a love letter to our homes but also to...us."

I look to Amy and she's staring at me, her eyes intense. My hands shake at my side and I open them, just a bit, hold one out, just a bit. I don't expect her to take it or even see but she looks down and looks at me and looks at my hand again, short nails that can never keep a polish for long, scars from burns and knives gone rogue. And she takes it, her palm warm, and a little sweaty, but then so is mine.

"It's a bit messy, but at the end of the day, it's exactly what I want. Seafood chowder poutine: the fries are crispy, seasoned with Old Bay. The seafood you'll find in the dish includes shrimp, lobster, and clams. We have a creamy Parmesan sauce with porchetta, and of course classic cheese curds, topped with green onions. It's quite rich so it's a smaller serving, in fact it's something best shared. On the side and to cut the heaviness of your meal, you have a medley of vegetables that we've pickled in house: dill pickles, red onion, spicy carrots, and daikon pickles. And I'd suggest pairing this with a pinot blanc, which I've taken the liberty of ordering for you."

On schedule, Maggie sets a glass of white wine in front of Camilla.

"We'll leave you to your meal," I say.

As I walk away with Amy, her hand squeezing mine, Camilla says, "Paul, you heard her. This is meant to be shared. Why don't you join me?"

I know they're here, Wes and Corrine, Jeremy, Natalie, but their faces are blurred by my excitement. I wait until we get back to the kitchen, the muscles in my face burning from the strength of my smile. Even though it's an open space and the cameras are still rolling as Camilla and now Paul eat my food, I turn to her, hold her face in my hands.

"Just so we're clear, I love you, too."

"You're hijacking my apology."

"You already apologized."

"Yeah but…" She stops to kiss me, a quick peck of her lips to mine. Something so normal, so everyday. "I was going to ask you if you forgave me. If you'd want to give me another shot."

"You have to know that I do."

Her arms come around me, our hips pressed together. We've never really kissed like this before, in the open. At the Hideaway, it was dark, loud, and we were in a space that was totally, comfortably queer. Here, it's public, without the safety net of an entire community at our backs. It feels brazen and brave, proud. It makes my love for her stronger, that she'll share this with me.

"I know I told you to take that job, and if you ever decided you wanted to leave, to take another, to go wherever, I would go with you if I could. And if I couldn't, I'd miss you and wait for you."

"Amy, I'm not going anywhere."

"I know but I'm just saying—"

I kiss her again, to shut her up. "I love you."

Epilogue

Sophie

Six Months Later

A good morning starts with three things: sweat, coffee, and breakfast. I don't eat the breakfast unless it's after I've sweat and had coffee, but Amy doesn't mind. She's just gleeful that she's brought me over "to the light," she says. Normally, my sweating involves a trip to visit Natalie at the gym and coffee comes in the form of to-go cups that I pick up on my way home, but today it's more like the sheet-grabbing kind of sweating. The only lift happening is the way my back bows off the bed, and despite having to make the coffee myself once I've caught my breath, it's my new favorite.

Amy sings in the shower as I crack an egg into the pan, the sizzle and the smell a warm comfort. Her laptop sits open on the counter, the schedule for Amy & May's fills the screen because she was working on it late last night before I was able to convince her to come to bed. She exits the bathroom already dressed in sweats and a T-shirt, her hair wet and curling.

"Smells good," she sings as she spritzes plants and cuts dead leaves.

"So do you," I say, the smell of her peach shampoo wafting from the open bathroom door.

"What are we having for breakfast?"

Before I can answer, the music on my phone cuts out and starts ringing with a call from Paul.

"Good morning," I say, accepting the video call.

"Hello, darling." Camilla's face fills the screen and so does her laughter as Paul's hand pushes her face away.

"Excuse me," he grumbles, pretending to be annoyed by his fiancée.

"How's Paris?" I bring the phone with me as I flip my egg. Amy likes her eggs sunny-side up but I'm over easy.

"Terrible," he says dryly. "Have you given any more thought to our offer?"

"Hi, Paul." Amy props her chin on my shoulder, stealing my coffee mug from me and grinning at the phone.

"Hi, Amy. So?" he says, ever impatient. "Tell me you've thought about it at least?"

On the screen, Amy looks at me. "Well," I say, drawing out the word.

He sighs. "You got Camilla's stamp of approval on the show," he says, as if this should convince us.

"Her approval was more because of a grudging respect and not because she was or is a fan of poutine," I counter.

"I do not love cheese curds," she protests from somewhere off screen.

"But it all worked out in the end, right?" he says, trying to sound charming. Paul is technically right. They used clips of us kissing in the kitchen—with our permission—as part of the teasers for ads and social media promotion, drawing tons of attention to the restaurant, especially among the queer community in Boston. That, combined with our new seafood poutine, has made Amy & May's busier than it's ever been.

But before that, it wasn't *Cooking for Camilla* that got us through. It was us. I took a pay cut and it was hard for a while.

It will be hard for a while longer, but when we do it together it doesn't feel that way, like work. It feels like the perfect recipe.

"It did. It's not that."

Amy pops the sourdough out of the toaster oven, slathering on butter, layering lettuce, tomato, and strips of bacon.

I bite my lip, unsure of how to say it. But Amy takes care of it for me. "It's not us, Paul," she says. "It's you." She winks to soften the blow.

I flip the eggs onto our sandwiches and she tops them with the other slab of toast.

"That's not *exactly* it." I pick up the camera. "We thought about it and we like the offer, we really do. Doing a TV show would be great for the restaurant but…" I look over at Amy, who's already got egg yolk on her cheek. "What would it mean for us?"

Paul smiles, like he was expecting that answer. "I understand."

We say our goodbyes and hang up. Amy watches me as I take my first few bites of breakfast sandwich. "Okay, but are you sure?" she asks.

I blink at her, my mind already a million miles away from Paul's offer. We have to clean this whole apartment, which between the two of us won't take long, go grocery shopping, reserve a table at the restaurant. My parents are coming to visit, both of them, to meet Amy.

"Sure? About being on TV?"

Amy was more into the idea than I was initially. She says I almost look as pretty on camera as I do in real life. Privately, I think she's a little worried that I should be destined for greater things, but she fights the instinct to make the decision for me.

"I'm sure," I say. Leaving my plate on the counter, I step into her arms. Her eyes go wide, and she leans down, expecting my kiss, but I lick the yolk off her cheek, my mouth filled with salt, catching the sound of her squeal.

I laugh as she scrunches her nose. "I don't need to put our love on camera to know it's real."

★ ★ ★ ★ ★

Acknowledgments

It is time once again to write my acknowledgments and I am, once again, emotionally unprepared for this. But here we go: this book, like the last, and like the ones that will come next, would not have been possible without my mother, father, and mother-in-law. In this year, especially, when alone time was so precious, you all made it so that I never had to worry about my daughter. I had the luxury and privilege of pursuing my dream because of the three of you and I will never be able to say thank you enough times, in enough ways. But thank you, nonetheless.

To the book bloggers, bookstagrammers, YouTubers, and book community that has accepted me and my stories, you not only help this industry thrive on your unpaid labor but you have helped my heart grow. Thank you for your love and excitement. Thank you for letting me into your fold and trusting me with your time, your money, your imaginations. I hope my words will always be deserving of you.

Danielle, thank you for keeping me young, for teaching me TikTok, for opening your heart to me, and for letting me open mine to you. Thank you for letting me go on this journey with you of realizing later in life, who we are. You, my dear, are the very best thing that ever came out of That Place, and I wouldn't change a second of my time there, if it meant I wouldn't get to have you in my life.

Courtney, thank you for taking the time to read an early

version of this, when I was terrified I'd get it wrong. You gave me the courage to keep going.

Kiki, it's coming on three years since I got your first email and in those three years you have done something miraculous: you've made my dreams come true; and I don't think you give yourself enough credit for that. Thank you for your belief in my stories. It's an honor to work with someone as insightful, intelligent, kind, and hilarious as you.

Stephanie, you have made my debut and sophomore book experiences perfect. You take what we'll generously call raw material, and make sense of it in a way that feels like magic to me. Thank you for your guidance with this story and for helping me to give Amy and Sophie the love they deserve.

Slackers, I continue to vow to do murders for you (for legal reasons, this sentence remains a joke). Thank you for letting me be a part of your lives and for sharing your beautiful words with me. Each of you makes me a better writer and person.

Rosie and Meryl, thank you for being the types of people that I can share my secrets with. Thank you for sharing yours with me. Your friendship is my proudest, most precious accomplishment.

Even though I'm certain you'll never read these books, it's important that this book have your name in it, Karou. No matter how old you are, no matter what you do, no matter who you become, you can turn to this page and know, I love you, unconditionally, forever and ever.

I always save the best for last: my husband. Thank you for letting me ignore you for the people in my head. Thank you for understanding me better than anyone else, for being the funniest person I know. Thank you for your unwavering confidence in me, your unconditional love. Thank you for letting me live this wonderful life with you. "Baby, you're the end of June" (Styles, 2019).

Julien Doran arrived in sleepy Maudit Falls, North Carolina, with a heart full of hurt and a head full of questions. The key to his brother's mysterious last days might be found in this tiny town, and now Julien's amateur investigation is starting to unearth things the locals would rather keep buried.

Perhaps most especially Eli, the strange, magnetic manager of a deserted retreat that's nearly as odd as its staff. When an old skeleton and a fresh corpse turn a grief errand into a murder investigation, the unlikely Eli is the only person Julien can turn to. Trust is hard to come by in a town known for its monsters, but so is time…

Keep reading for an excerpt from Pack of Lies *by Charlie Adhara!*

Chapter One

It was exactly the sort of place you'd expect to see a monster. A lonely mountain road, a forest so old it creaked. Hell, it was even a dark and stormy night. Or dark and snowy, anyway. But the way the wind was hurling restless flurries against the windshield as the trees swayed vengefully overhead was enough to put even the most assured traveler on edge.

Julien Doran had never felt less sure of anything in his life, and he'd hit that edge at a running jump about two weeks and two thousand miles ago. Right around the time he'd turned his back on everything—the shambled remains of his family, career and common sense—at the suggestion of a dead man.

He might still get lucky. He might never make it to the elusive Maudit Falls and instead spend the rest of eternity driving up and down these mountain roads until, eventually, he'd become just another one of the dozens of urban legends the area seemed to collect like burs. They could call him Old Doran. The Fallen Star. Forty-four years of carefully toeing the line distilled down to this one inarguably absurd decision, and told at bedtime to frighten children into obedience. Don't you know better than to throw your life away on a lie, little one? Do you want to end up like Old Doran? A man who turned down the first role he'd been offered in four years to fly across the country to middle-of-nowhere North Carolina. A man who thought he could open a wound so recently closed, it still wept at the edges. A man who went looking for a monster.

Listen, they'd say. If you listen really closely, you can still hear his voice echoing through the mountains, calling out, *What am I doing here? What did I think I could change? Did I miss my turn?*

Julien glanced at the GPS on his phone, but it was still caught in an endless limbo of loading, the service having cut out about fifteen minutes ago.

"The town proper is on the other side of the mountain," the clerk at the last rest stop had told him. A woman with metallic-rose eyeshadow, a name tag that said Chloe and the unmoving smile of someone sick of delivering the same canned dialogue to every wide-eyed, monster-hunting tourist who passed through. "You'll see plenty of signs for Blue Tail Lodge as long as you stay on the main road. But whatever you do, don't get out of your car after dark. That's when Sweet Pea is his most dangerous."

Chloe had gestured with rote unenthusiasm to the huge display by the counter. A rack covered in souvenirs, and a six-foot-tall cardboard cutout of an ominous, pitch-black figure with glowing green eyes. It had hooves for feet, long, delicate claws instead of hands and the flat face of a primate, obscured by shadow. The figure was standing up on two legs but sort of stooped over, arms held awkwardly as if caught midway through dancing the monster mash.

"Mr. Pea, I presume," Julien had said, reaching out to touch one long, cardboard claw. Then pretended to shake its hand and added in a Muppet-voice, "Mr. Pea's my father. Please, call me Sweet." Chloe's smile hadn't flickered, which was very fair. Rocky would have known what to say. He would have known the right questions to ask, the right words to use, the best attitude to strike to get Chloe on his side, talking and spilling secrets that couldn't be sold on a souvenir rack. But then Rocky had always been the real actor between the two of them.

"Have you ever seen it?"

"Me? No." Chloe shook her head. "But my sister's ex was out hunting and swears it passed right through the campsite. Tore into his cooler and stole all his coyote traps."

"Wow. That's…" The way it always was. No, I've never seen anything. But my dentist's kid's teacher's nephew woke up in the woods with less beer than he'd remembered packing and a missing ham sandwich. Alert the media—They walk among us. "That's something."

"Are you in Maudit for—"

"The skiing," Julien cut her off quickly, and launched into his own canned dialogue, taking the opposite approach to Chloe, his voice a little *too* bright, smile *too* mobile, overselling his story. "I would never have thought of North Carolina for it, but a friend recommended the slopes here. He said it's 'Snow without having to freeze your, ah, nose off.'"

"We get our fair share. And plenty more than that up the mountain," she said, watching him closely, the beginnings of the same frustration in her eyes he'd seen in dozens of people trying to place the face behind the glasses, the fading stubble, the lines that grief and age had carved in unequal measure around his eyes like permanent tear tracks. "I'd pack an extra pair of thermals if you're skiing Blue Tail this weekend, though. For your, *ah, nose?* There's a cold front coming." She tapped the box of single-use heat packs by the register pointedly and Julien dutifully placed a handful on the counter. He attempted a casual nod at the looming cutout. "Why 'Sweet Pea'? Not exactly the most intimidating name."

"Well, he doesn't need it, does he? Anyone around here knows you don't want to be caught out at night with a monster like that, whatever you want to call it." She plucked a deck of novelty playing cards off the display and placed them on the counter next to the heat packs. "Everything you need to know about Maudit Falls and its most infamous residents is in here. Only $21.99. You know, something to do when you're not *skiing*." That's when her eyes had widened in genuine excitement. "Hey, aren't you…"

Of course, he'd bought them. How could he not? Sweet Pea wasn't the monster he was hunting. But it was why Rocky had first come to Maudit Falls and Julien was here because of him. Why else would he book a vacation in a town whose idea of a fun roadside souvenir was fifty-two fun facts about spooky local legends? Why else had he done anything at all this last waking-nightmare of a year?

Now, as he took a particularly sharp curve up the narrow mountain road, Julien wished he'd left the cards behind and bought a map instead. One a little easier to follow than what Rocky had left for him. This simply could not be the way into town. It wasn't even plowed for goodness' sake. Just sort of tamped down, which gave the road a colorless, unfinished look. Like nature itself had been peeled back to expose a slippery layer of quilt batting. On the other hand, it wasn't like he'd passed any paths more traveled. There'd been one unmarked turnoff that couldn't have been anything but a service road. That or the perfect set for the first ten minutes of a horror film, which might still be the case considering the seriously questionable choices that had led him to—

An animal leapt in front of the car. Julien had a split second to register the huge, dark shape darting out of the woods, the twin reflection of headlights bouncing off inhuman eyes, staring directly at him, before he jerked the wheel instinctively to the right at the same time a thud rang in his ears.

Weightless slipping. The feeling of suddenly being airborne

without getting out of your seat. And then the car dropped down with tooth-cracking finality, directly into the snowy ditch.

For a long moment the world felt impossibly still and silent. Empty. He couldn't hear himself breathing. He couldn't hear himself think. Julien lay against the steering wheel dazed, pain-free and peaceful for the first time in over a year. Then, like a lever giving way, his body sucked in an agonizing gasp of air. With it, the gears of his brain began to grind once more, and it all came flooding back.

"No, no, no," Julien whispered. He disentangled himself from the locked-up seat belt and opened the door, barely thinking, and then had to catch it when the gravity of the tilted car sent it hurtling back into his shin. Julien climbed quickly out of the ditch and stumbled down the road, unusually clumsy. "Please no. Please, please, please." His hands were shaking, a low, constant tremble, and his arms felt so light, so flimsy that he had the nonsensical urge to let them float above his head, like untying two trapped balloons.

Julien squeezed his fists tight at his sides. Enough. *Do something. No one else will.* He scanned the road, walking back to where he'd swerved, looking for the animal. Not wanting to see it—needing to find it.

But there was nothing there.

Julien found the gouged snow, dark with dirt where he'd first slammed on the brakes and skidded off the road, but that was the only sign of the violence he'd braced himself for. No body or blood. Fur or feathers. No sign that he'd hit anything at all. Except he had.

Hadn't he? That awful soft thud. Not soft in volume but in texture, if sound could have such a thing. Body-soft. Maybe it hadn't been hurt. He hadn't been going fast. Not at all. Even slower than the limit, with all this snow. Maybe the animal had been able to roll over the car and just keep running? Julien stalked from one side of the road to the other as if he'd find some clue as to what to do now. As if the animal might have left a note with a sad face and its insurance information. He'd never hit anything before in his life. If it had been there in the road, he could call…animal control? Some sort of wildlife rehab, maybe? But would they send someone to hike into the woods at nine p.m. at night to track down a wild animal that may be injured or may be fine?

Julien blew out a long breath that clouded in the air and reluctantly walked back to the car. With no cell service it was a moot point. He'd need to hike down the road until he could get bars, anyway. He'd need a tow truck, too. The very top of the windshield was shattered and long cracks ran like roots over the rest of the glass. The rental company wouldn't be pleased.

The right front corner of the car was flattened, as well. A pool of headlight glass was sprinkled like multicolored confetti in the snow. *Congratulations! You fucked up big-time!* Oddly, there wasn't any other sign of damage in the front. Not that Julien could tell. Nothing on the hood, either. Almost as if the only point of impact was the windshield. Was that even possible? If so, maybe the animal really was less injured than he'd feared.

Julien got closer to examine the roof. Even with the car at this awkward angle he was tall enough to see two distinct dents, right in the center. "What the hell?" Julien ran his hand over one. It was about the size of his palm but distinct. More than a mere ding. As if something heavy had…what? Landed on its feet, then launched itself into the air and kept running? The paint was scratched, too. Four short contrails behind each dent. Carefully he dragged his own four fingers down the white marks, and the back of his neck prickled as if someone was watching him.

Julien turned, scanning the road and the dark forest beyond. "Hello?" Barely more than a whisper, his voice still sounded disrespectfully loud. It was only then he realized just how quiet the surrounding woods were. *Unnaturally quiet.* Like every living thing was collectively holding its breath. Julien took a couple steps into the road, and his boots made a soft creaking sound on the tightly packed snow. "Hello? Is someone there?"

No one answered. Nothing made a sound. Well, of course not. What had he expected? Sweet Pea to waltz out of the trees doing his best Lurch impression? *You rang?*

Julien snorted at his own uneasiness. What did he know about the *natural* amount of noise wild animals were supposed to make, anyway? The closest he ever got to nature in LA was when his ex-wife Frankie sent weekly photos of Wilbur the mountain lion sneaking over her fence at night to drink out of the pool. He'd gotten one early that morning in the airport getting ready to board.

Call me back. I'm worried about you. And so is Wilbur!

He'd call her eventually. When he had good news. Or at least something better than this. And when he'd made it back to LA. If he told her he was in Maudit, he'd have to explain why, and right now he couldn't even explain it to himself. He couldn't even *think* it without wondering if the whispers were true. That maybe after years of being wound so tight, something in him really had just snapped.

Julien hauled his bag out of the car, ignoring the subsequent ache in his chest where the seat belt had bit into muscle and skin. There wasn't any sense second-guessing it now. He was either going to find what he was looking for in Maudit Falls or he wasn't. If the latter were true, he'd have proof that Rocky had been wrong, and there was nothing hidden on this mountain but superstition and perilous infrastructure. And if the former...

Either way, he wasn't going to find anything sitting around alone in the dark. He'd done plenty of that these last fourteen months already. Julien began the long trek back down the road, phone in hand.

Ten minutes later, the cold air killed his battery.

"Damnit," Julien whispered. Then, wondering why he was bothering to whisper, yelled it again as loud as he could, followed by a string of every curse he knew. Considering his upbringing on the back lots of Hollywood, that occupied a significant amount of walking time.

It took another fifteen minutes of swearing before Julien finally came across the lone turnoff he'd passed before. *Maudit Falls Retreat*, claimed a very discreet wooden sign tucked back into the woods. It wasn't abandoned or a service road at all—it was some sort of place of lodging. Julien felt a wave of relief. Here there'd be people, power, maybe even a bed for the night, if he couldn't get a ride on to Blue Tail Lodge. Julien took the turn.

Even less effort had been made to clear the snow, and soon the legs of his jeans were soaked with frigid water. He began to shiver and his fingers felt thick and clumsy with cold. Despite the urge to break into a jog and get the hell out of the dark already, Julien stuck his hands under his armpits and kept his steady, careful pace. He'd hardly be able to tell people he was here for the skiing with a broken ankle. When researching the area, there hadn't been anything online about a Maudit Falls Retreat. No mention of it in Rocky's notebook, either. Hopefully that meant it was a small, word-of-mouth bed-and-breakfast as opposed to shut down entirely. Five minutes later, he realized neither was true as the road spilled into a clearing in front of a large, gorgeous building.

"What are you doing hiding all the way out here," Julien murmured, impressed despite himself. Two stories, expansive and surrounded by a wraparound porch, the retreat was a mass of polished wood, stone and glass. Most of the front seemed to be windows, and past the reflected moonlight, Julien could make out a low light inside. He tried the heavy wooden double doors and to his relief they opened.

The lobby was even prettier than the outside—soothing in juxtaposition to the intimidating exterior. The back of the room was mostly taken up by a large wooden reception desk while to the side a couple of comfortable-looking chairs and a couch were centered around an enormous stone fireplace. Wide pine plank floors were polished to a soft gleam that reflected the light of the fire burning low. That and an old-fashioned green glass desk lamp were the only sources of light. The room was completely empty.

"Hello?" Julien called out. His voice echoed and seemed to get lost up in the high rafters. "Is anyone here?" Julien walked up to the desk. A large painting of a waterfall hung behind it. The titular Maudit Falls perhaps? The canvas was a violent mess of blues and purples and a lone figure stood on a cliff's edge with their arms extended, as if begging with the water, as if this very scene was where the falls had got its cursed name.

Vaguely unsettled, Julien called out again. "I've had some car trouble!" Silence. A bed was starting to look unlikely. He walked toward the open door at the back of the lobby and peered into the darkness. He opened his mouth to call out again, but something stopped him. Julien took a few steps into the hall, squinting into the gloom. There was an open door on the right and he peered around the corner. "Is someone there?"

A pair of reflective inhuman eyes stared back at him and Julien yelled out, stumbling backward. The eyes jumped to the ground with a soft thud and a cat darted between his ankles and scurried into the lobby.

"Fuck." Julien exhaled and laughed at himself. Thank goodness there really wasn't any such thing as monsters, if feline theatrics launched his heart into outer space. He felt ridiculous and frankly a little embarrassed, but also reluctant to wander farther into the building. Because it'd be rude, and not because his heart had thus far only sunk back down to the general vicinity of his throat, of course. All he needed was a working phone, anyway. Or power. Surely no one would mind that. Julien walked quickly back into the lobby and, with only a second's hesitation, helped himself behind the reception desk. The sooner he could make a call, the sooner he'd be out of here.

There was no landline. But crouching, he found the outlet the desk lamp was plugged into, deep at the back of a low shelf, and quickly got his charger out of his duffel and his cell hooked up. As he stood, the Sweet Pea card deck fell from his pocket and bounced under the bottom shelf. Julien knelt to retrieve it, gasping at the sudden pain that lanced through his chest when he stretched out his arm. Obviously, the adrenaline that had numbed the bumps and bruises was fading fast. He should—

"If you're down there looking for a bed that's just right, Goldilocks, mine's upstairs."

A man's voice. Behind him. Julien shot up to his knees so quickly he would have smashed his head into the desk's top ledge, if not for the warm, soft hand suddenly cupping his crown just long enough to act as a buffer between his skull and the wood, then gone. The only proof it had been there at all was a faint tingle where he'd been touched and the distinct absence of a painful head. "Thanks. Hell, you sca-scared me," Julien stuttered. For half a second it looked like the man standing over him had blank, colorless eyes, as flat as the cat's. But then he shifted his weight and Julien could see it was just a trick of the light. They were a perfectly conventional gray. Nice-looking, even, though perhaps a little washed-out in a pale face framed by black hair. Slightly less conventional was the dangerously short, peacock blue, silk dressing gown he wore over, Christ, nothing at all, if the cling of that fabric wasn't lying.

"My apologies." The man cleared his throat politely and Julien tore his gaze back up, embarrassed. "I'm not up to date on the proper etiquette for interrupting a thief. It seems an invitation to bed only terrifies one half to death. How disappointing for the ego." He squinted at Julien critically. "To be fair, a keen-eyed observer might argue you looked about three-quarters of the way there on your own. To death, that is, not to bed."

Julien gaped, unsure what to feel more offended by first. At least the critics had the heart to call him names behind his back. "I'm not a thief," he said finally, because it wasn't a crime to look old and worn-out quite yet.

"A housebreaker, then," the man said, inspecting one of his own fingernails with a bored expression. "An interloper. Persona non grata, though admittedly you look very *grata* indeed from this angle."

Julien felt warmth spread down his defrosting body and he quickly pulled himself to standing. The bruise across his chest throbbed and he had to bite back a grunt of pain—unsuccessfully it seemed, from the way the man's eyes narrowed with curiosity. "I'm sorry," Julien said, cutting off the potential for any more biting comments on his advancing proximity to death's door. "I didn't mean to trespass. I was under the impression that this was a hotel."

The man ran his hand over the wood of the desk with a thoughtful expression. "Is this the *impression* you were under? See, I would have called it a desk, myself, but then I'm a simple, straightforward sort of soul. What you see is what you get."

"Well, I can see quite a bit," Julien muttered under his

breath and to his surprise the man grinned and just leaned back against the wall, causing the robe to slip even higher up his legs.

"And what exactly were you hoping to get all the way down there?" He seemed totally untroubled to be practically naked in front of a stranger. Maybe soaking wet, half-frozen and *three-quarters of the way* to death, Julien didn't look very intimidating. Maybe the man felt physically secure with his younger body and thick, powerful-looking thighs.

The tingling on Julien's scalp where the man had touched him intensified and he dragged an impatient hand through his hair. "I was looking for an outlet to charge my phone."

"But of course you were. I've been known to get on my hands and knees for the sake of an outlet myself. Carry on, Raffles." The man tilted his head to the side, studying Julien in a lazy, knowing sort of way. "Unless you need someone to play Bunny?" It was the sort of over-the-top flirting men did when they were utterly certain it wouldn't go anywhere. Teasing and unserious with no genuine interest. Meant to fluster and nothing else.

"I said I'm not a thief," Julien said tightly, suddenly feeling as weary and washed-up as he apparently looked. The crash must be catching up with him. "I'm sorry; it's been a hell of a long day." He thrust his hand out, then quickly retreated when the man simply regarded it with a single raised eyebrow. Fair enough. "My name's Julien. I'm on my way to the ski lodge, but had an accident a little ways up the road. My phone's dead so I hiked down this way and saw the sign and, well, yes, I let myself in and helped myself to the power. I'm sorry if I surprised you or made you uncomfortable at all." He could hardly say it with a straight face. The man didn't look like he knew the meaning of the word *discomfort*. "Are you a, uh, guest here? Owner?"

"No." The man smiled sharply. He had a small heart-shaped mouth that gave his whole face a sort of pointy, foxy look. "I'm a thief." His gaze flickered toward the door with a distinct frown and Julien instinctively did, too, just as a loud banging sounded.

"What's that?"

"Some cultures call it knocking. You wouldn't be familiar," the man murmured, slipping past him with a sway in his hips that did interesting things to the silk.

Julien looked purposefully away and followed him into the lobby just as the man opened the door. On the stoop stood a woman, dripping with blood.

Julien swore and hurried closer. "What the hell!"

The woman took one wide-eyed look at him and sagged forward, forcing Julien to reach out and catch her. Her body felt cold and fragile against his and she let out a long shuddering sob and began murmuring something frantically into his chest. Julien looked over her head for help, but the man in the robe had backed away, expression closed, almost wary, and Julien felt a corresponding prickle of unease. "Are you hurt? What happened?" he asked.

"Sweet Pea," she cried. "I saw the monster!"

Don't miss Pack of Lies *by Charlie Adhara,*
from Carina Adores!

www.CarinaPress.com

Discover another romantic love story from Carina Adores

Werewolf meets human. Werewolf snubs human. Werewolf loves human?

Julien Doran arrived in sleepy Maudit Falls with a heart full of hurt and a head full of questions. The key to his brother's mysterious last days might be found in this tiny town, and now Julien's amateur investigation is starting to unearth things the locals would rather keep buried.

Eli Smith is a lot of things: thief, werewolf, glamour-puss, liar…and now the manager of a haven for rebel pack runaways. For the first time ever he's been entrusted with a real responsibility—and he plans to take that seriously.

Even if the handsome tourist who claims to be in town for some R & R is clearly on a hunt for all things paranormal. And hasn't taken his brooding gaze off Eli since he's arrived…

Don't miss *Pack of Lies* by Charlie Adhara.
Available wherever Carina Adores books are sold.

CarinaAdores.com

CARPOL0822TR

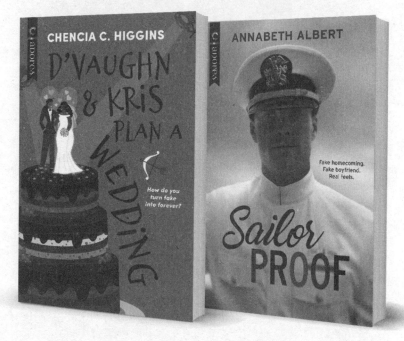